Love and Other Affairs in the Empire of Russia

Eva Martens

Copyright © 2016 M.M.Bruns
All Rights Reserved

Cover ***Portrait of Aleksandra Branicka***, 1781
Richard Brompton
(Public Domain, via Wikimedia Commons)

Cover design: www.wifo-digital.de

By the same author

A Princess at the Court of Russia
An Empress on the Throne of Russia

On her lips reposed an eternal smile ... but this studied calm hid the most violent passions and an inexorable will.

Prince Adam Czartoryski, 1795

Prologue

"You probably ate far too many peaches," General Grigory Potemkin said. "A basket of twenty, I wager. I know how partial you are to them, especially in the heat."

"It sounds like something you might do but I am known to practise more restraint," Catherine answered mildly.

"Actually, do you have any peaches?" Potemkin looked round. "Talking about them has really given me a craving for them. I shall ring for some."

"No, no, dearest Grigory," Catherine protested. "Come and sit by me a little. You will leave soon, I know, and then you can get your peaches."

Catherine lay in bed, her hair undone and tangled on the pillow, her face drawn and pale. She patted the silk covers. "Come, Grigory, please."

Potemkin sat gingerly on the edge of the bed. Catherine took his hand in hers.

"You have not asked me how I fare," she said.

"Ah, but you know I am no good as a sick nurse. I prefer you healthy. And I must say it really is most inconvenient, Catherine! I have arranged such festivities, such splendours and now you will miss them all." Potemkin's voice was peevish.

Catherine pulled herself into a more upright position. "Have the peace celebrations postponed for a day or two," she said brightly. "I will be up and about soon. In any case, they cannot proceed without the Empress."

"But you have spoiled all my planning, all my surprises, Catherine, Empress or no! You have worked too much and now you are ill. You only have numbers in your head! Why, even I am ill from them."

"It is true, dearest Grigory, that I have worked tirelessly these eight months since we came to Moscow. But you know how necessary it was. The Cossack Pugachev all but succeeded in taking over my Empire. And all because of the weakness and laziness, the corruption and injustice of local officials."

"Yes, and now you have divided your Empire neatly into columns of figures – provinces of 300,000 thousand inhabitants, subdivisions of 30,000 – but does that guarantee good local government? They will still be the same officials." Potemkin drummed his fingers impatiently on the night table, causing the carafes to shake.

"Oh, but you are in bad humour today! Let us not talk of it. It is my task as Empress," Catherine said sharply but then added more soothingly, "You must think of your celebrations. Leave the drier tasks to me."

"Yes, but they have made you ill." Potemkin's voice was now petulant. "And we can hardly say the Empress is ill from overwork. Rumour will immediately have you dead and buried!"

"Oh do not scold so! Where is your charm? It might have more effect on me than your reprimands," Catherine said reproachfully.

Potemkin stretched out on the bed. "Yes, I do have a way of charming women into happiness," he sighed contentedly.

"Grigory, I yearn for your affection. You know I do. But when I have to work, you scold me. When I am indisposed, you neglect me. I feel you have closed your heart against me. You even mention other women."

"Ah, now you are getting angry! But no need to upset yourself, my Empress. I hold you closely in my heart as always. And even on my heart. Look, there is the portrait you bestowed on me, worth more than all the other honours and rewards." Potemkin pointed to a miniature of Catherine framed in glittering diamonds pinned to his jacket. "I always wear it – and always will." He stroked her hand gently. "But," he continued, "I cannot be suffocated by love, Catherine. Love must give me air to breathe."

"Have we not been happy in our year together?" Catherine asked softly, clasping his hand. "You have been my love, my true husband, my fiery lover. All that a woman could desire. You have done much to help Russia. I am a better sovereign with you at my side."

"But not on your throne." Potemkin said curtly, removing his hand from hers.

"Ah, but we have agreed this would dilute our power. A married sovereign is open to more jealousies and attacks. An absolute sovereign can rule as she wishes," Catherine said firmly. "I am the Empress, Grigory. You must not forget that. I am so by the will of God, whether we like it or not."

"I will always be loyal to you," Potemkin said.

"But not faithful." It was almost a question.

"Fidelity is no more than loyalty's lesser cousin. I will do all in my power to keep you happy, to keep you firmly on your throne whoever is in your bed. Or mine." He took both her hands in is and kissed them fervently, murmuring, "My love."

Catherine seemed pleased. Freeing one of her hands, she ran her fingers through his hair. "Dearest Grigory," she whispered.

"My dearest Empress, I have a surprise for you," he said carefully.

"Ah, but Grigory, you know I do not like surprises. They do not always please. Remember when – "

"Ah, but you will like this one," he interrupted. "I have brought you a family!"

"What can you mean? I do not need a family! Families bring ... complications. I need only you." Catherine looked around in alarm.

"You know that my dearest sister Elena died some few months ago?" Potemkin resumed. "Her distraught husband has written to ask if I would take care of his five daughters. There are six but one is already married. I know how much educating young women means to you and so I have had them brought to us here in Moscow and they will be our family! And your ladies!" Potemkin declared triumphantly. "They are charming girls. The oldest is twenty-two and the youngest is but six years old. Is it not a wonderful idea? Are you not happy? "

"Of course, dear Grigory," Catherine said slowly. "Your family is my family. The girls are welcome. I will receive them in a few days when I am recovered from – this surfeit of peaches."

"Yes, and we will find some sons for you too. Children are so much more rewarding when they are grown. Nothing much can be done with them before that." He patted her hand. "Well, I must away. Postponing all the peace celebrations will require some work."

"But you are a magician, my love. You will make them even more magnificent."

"And they shall be enhanced by the Empress in all her splendour." Potemkin jumped up, snatched a handful of grapes from a bowl and asked, "Will a week be sufficient?"

"No, no," Catherine answered laughingly. "I shall be up in a day or two."

"But no more papers," Potemkin said. "We have over a thousand sheets already!"

PART ONE

Alexandra
August 1775

Dearest Anna,

How much we have to tell you! We have travelled only a few hundred versts from home but everything is so foreign here that it might be ten thousand!

Our uncle, who in his kindness has taken us under his wing, is as affectionate as you may remember him and has showered us with gifts of jewels and fine dresses. We must not let him down by appearing as the provincial gentry we are, for his position at Court is very elevated. (In public we even call him General Potemkin.) You cannot imagine how everyone runs to do his bidding, even, it is rumoured, the Empress.

The Empress Catherine has greeted us warmly and has already appointed me maid-of-honour. Her bearing is most elegant, most regal, and I have told my sisters we must emulate it. The Empress has a high forehead, large blue eyes and a well-curved mouth but her nose is a little long and her chin a little round. She has brownish hair. She is plump, with a very high bosom. Her complexion is not smooth and she wears dark rouge, perhaps a little too much. She appears healthy and has all her teeth, which are very white. My sisters, and perhaps myself, outdo her in beauty but her manner is graceful and kind. And she is said to be very educated – she conducts correspondence with the greatest philosophers in Europe. We, dear Anna, can make no claim to a good education but we have other talents which should secure us a permanent position at the Russian Court – and, of course, very advantageous marriages.

The Court is still in Moscow for the peace celebrations. I have had Uncle explain to me the significance of the treaty with the Ottomans since it seems to be a war which no one has won. "On the contrary," Uncle said, "while the Ottomans have not ceded the Crimea to us, they have been forced to recognise it as an independent khanate. And it is under our influence. We will make another attempt to annex it completely but for now we are content with what we have gained. War goes hand in hand with diplomacy." You will note, dear Anna, that I am anxious to learn and understand our new world.

There have been parades and processions of great splendour. Uncle took us to the main festivities outside the city. There were two pavilions which, he said, represented the Black Sea and all Russia's conquests. There were roads which stood for the rivers Don and Dnieper, the theatres and dining halls were named after Black Sea ports and there were many Turkish minarets. The coachmen and servants were dressed as Turks and Albanians and Circassians and there were even some black men in crimson turbans. I have never encountered a black person before.

There was a huge firework display such as you have never seen. The sky was filled as high and as far as one could see with huge bursts of bright colour. The Empress had gifted wine and roasted oxen to the people – Uncle said as many as 60,000 feasted on her beneficence. Can you imagine such a number?

We are overwhelmed by the magnificence of our new surroundings and while there are a few things one could grumble about, like the badly maintained water closets, I will not, for we are grateful to our Uncle for this chance to rise in the world – and to what heights! And I will do all in my power to ensure that our younger sisters make good marriages. As the eldest in your place, Anna, and as a substitute for our dear dead mother, I will put my own needs in second place to those of my sisters. Little Tatiana, with her mere six years, will need my guidance for some time to come.

I shall make myself indispensable to our Uncle and to the Empress, I will observe and learn. I will acquire, we all shall, the sophistication that we lack. The beauty of our sisters has often been remarked upon, especially that of Varvara with her golden hair, and that shall be our capital. Our sister Nadezhda has not been gifted with natural charm — where did she get that red hair and swarthy complexion from? She is but sixteen and good looks may still emerge. Although Katerina is younger, she already exemplifies a very fine beauty.

Yes, we must use our looks to gain what we can. I must harness Varvara a little — she flirts with everyone outrageously, including Uncle. I do not think the Empress will take kindly to that. On the other hand, it is better his attention is centred on one of our own, which I can control, than on an outsider, who may have another family to replace us. Listen to me! I who have been here but weeks talk of outsiders as if I am an insider! But yes, we are insiders because we are Uncle's family, and as such, the family of the Empress. I intend to keep it that way, no matter what it takes.

But enough of my responsibilities. I have instructed the girls to pen some lines to include in this letter and they will deliver some lighter reading, I am sure. Varvara will no doubt write to you of fashions (very French! very low cut at the bosom!), Nadezhda of food (have you ever seen an artichoke?), Katerina of the many compliments she receives (I think she keeps a note of them all) and Tatiana will no doubt tell you about her visit to an elephant, a gift to the Empress from an exotic Shah. I did not go, considering it more an outing for children, but now I wish I had since all the child can say about it is, "So huge, so huge!" I have tasked her with a small essay of description and perhaps you will be the beneficiary of that. Uncle says he will employ tutors for her as soon as we go to St Petersburg, where the Empress normally resides. It is almost at the end of the earth and I am somewhat uneasy at the prospect but I am told it is of great magnificence and that we will be well settled in Uncle's own palace there. Perhaps I can be mistress of his household.

We embrace you! Uncle says that since we are all truly one family now, he will secure a more elevated commission for your husband, to whom we also send warm greetings.

With affection,
Your sister Alexandra

Varvara
April 1776

We have been here in St Petersburg some four months now and it is indeed a very fine city, far from the muddle of Moscow. The streets are wide, like esplanades, and bordered with handsome stone houses built in classical style in pastel colours. The Palace is the largest one has ever seen – it would take days to walk through it all. It is situated along the banks of the mighty River Neva, which at the moment is still frozen, great chunks of waves jutting out, caught in ice. I feel like one of those waves, colder than I could ever imagine, condemned to inertia. Apart from some entertaining sleigh rides, we have kept to our furs and fires.

Alexandra is busy with her letters, Nadezhda is writing her diary, little Tatiana must learn her lessons and Katerina is stretched out lazily on the sofa, as always. During these enforced periods of quiet, I am bored and restless. Alexandra has suggested needlework but I have decided to write an account of my time at the Russian Court. It may serve as a ***roman*** later, although Alexandra says this is a low form of literature. I do not, however, recall her refusing to join in our readings of ***Pamela***, which she enjoyed as much as we all did. I do not intend to emulate Richardson's heroine but I relish a good story and I intend my life to be one.

It is the time of the Empress's rest after dinner when she may not be disturbed. Of course, everyone knows it is the time for her lovers. But should she have any when Uncle, the great General Potemkin, is her official favourite? If he falls from favour, we will be sent back to the dull provinces, which I could not bear. That would be the end of my story before it has properly begun. I have not even found a husband yet. Uncle says we must not hurry. He wishes to find the best for us and we must not take the first offer. I do not know if there have been any offers thus far.

Although I would like Uncle to come and visit us – he is such fun and can raise all our spirits, making us laugh with his wit and jokes – it would be better for us if he were with the Empress in her chambers. They are constantly quarrelling. I have to run backwards and forwards with their ***billets doux***. It is most tiring. There is a long and drafty corridor connecting the Empress's chambers to Uncle's which is meant to be a secret but everyone knows it exists. I am not supposed to use it but I do. I would be exhausted running downstairs and then up again.

I read their love notes. Uncle knows. "Take heed, Varvara," he says, "and learn how to treat your lovers, how to remain in favour and protect your power." The Empress might write chastising him for leaving her alone at some card party and he will reply ***My precious soul, you know that I am absolutely yours.*** Then she will write ***I know, I know*** and I have to run all the way to Uncle's chambers with such a meagre reply. And so it can go on for hours. The last note he wrote said ***I want to be in your heart alone and above everyone else.*** The Empress replied ***You are and will remain so***. So unromantic on her part. But Uncle always seems satisfied. We must keep the Empress happy, he says. It is our duty to Russia.

While he is thinking what to write in his notes, he has often invited me to sit beside him on his sofa, where he likes to lounge in his dressing gown until quite late in the day. On occasion, he has taken me onto his lap, which I like. When he visits us in our quarters, Tatiana is always allowed to crawl into his lap and snuggle up to him. Even Katerina is allowed to join them. I am considered too old for such childish behaviour but I am not, even if I am now twenty. I like to sit on his knee. He is large and strong and I pull his wild curls from under his bandana over his good eye so that he cannot see me. He has many different – and exciting – stories of how he lost his eye but we presume it was a Turkish sword. He is fond of singing, and has a very fine voice. He often croons into my hair as he rocks me backward and forwards. It is such a delicious time with him and I am sorry when he has penned his words and shoos me off like a kitten. That's what he calls me, his little kitten. I don't tell Alexandra about our little caresses. She is very strict. And she may even be jealous. We all love him and wish the Empress would love him more. But really, if she were to love him less, then it would be better for him to love one of us than any of those women who trail after him shamelessly like cats on heat. They are no kittens! And nor is the Empress. I am not to criticise the Empress, however. Uncle said it is treason. But it is only the truth, not criticism. She is nearing fifty.

The door to our chamber has suddenly burst open. It is Irina, the Grand Duchess's lady-in-waiting, of whom we are all fond. We are not fond of the Grand Duchess Natalya. As the wife of Catherine's son and heir, the Grand Duke Paul, Natalya will one day be Empress. She acts as if she already is. She is very beautiful but very scheming. It is said that she is more often in the bed of Paul's friend Andrei Razumovsky than in her husband's, which one can understand. Her husband, although unfailingly polite, is small and ugly. Razumovsky is all that a woman would wish for, and many women wish for him.

Irina is crying, the tears running down her face. "The Grand Duchess is very ill," she stutters. "The Empress thinks she will not survive." Natalya is with child and her labour started yesterday.

"Has a child been born?" Alexandra asks.

This is a silly question because we have been listening out for the cannon all day. 300 shots for a boy, 150 for a girl.

"It is dead," Irina sobs. "Dead inside her. The doctors say it probably died some days ago. She has been screaming in pain for hours. It is awful."

"Katerina, please take Tatiana to the next room," Alexandra says. Surprisingly unprotesting, Katerina unfolds herself from the sofa and takes Tatiana by the hand. Alexandra is right. The child's face is white and frightened. Once the door has closed behind them, Alexandra asks, "What does the Empress order?"

"The Empress has sat by the Grand Duchess's bedside for hours," Irina says, her tears still flowing. "She will allow the doctors to do nothing since the child is already dead. She says its mother will go the same way and there is nothing to be done. Oh, it seems so heartless! No one deserves to be abandoned like that. But I must return. I needed a few minutes respite. The ... smell is already overpowering."

We all embrace Irina, offering our lace handkerchiefs and pomade and some sweet syrup to drink. I fancy I do smell an unpleasant odour on her dress.

I do not ever wish to be with child. It is a dangerous undertaking. Can one have a husband without having children? I will ask Uncle.

Nadezhda
May 1776

There is much at the Russian Court which we do not understand, but Alexandra said we must observe and learn. I will record matters in this diary so that I will not forget anything while I am learning. Perhaps I will see patterns emerging, just as tea leaves arrange themselves when the water has gone.

Sometimes there is not much to write because from what I can see, it is a very lazy court. This suits Katerina, who likes nothing better than to lie around eating whatever titbits are brought. She has just finished all the dark grapes and I had not even tried them, which I am upset about because I have only ever had green grapes. Uncle said there will be more sent from the Crimea. I must make a list and drawing of all the exotic foods and fruit we have had here but for the moment I will record that the strangest and least agreeable looks like a large thistle and tastes bitter. It is called an artichoke. There is another prickly plant but it is a fruit of great sweetness. These pineapples, as they are called, have an ornamental green fringe on top and are kept on the table for decoration until they become brown but Uncle brings us fresh ones regularly.

Before we came to Court, we had heard that the Empress worked very hard and made many new laws but now she seems to do little, especially after we left Moscow. It is known that the Empress is not fond of Moscow and I cannot blame her. From what I saw of it, it is not elegant like St Petersburg. There the Court lodged in a hodge podge of houses put together, a veritable labyrinth of corridors and doors which led nowhere. Here the Palace – known as the Winter Palace because there are other palaces outside of the city, most notably the Summer Palace – is very grand and spacious. It has over a thousand rooms and twice as many windows and doors. There is much marble and gold and the public rooms are very grandiose. Otherwise, the palace seems to lack furniture and its empty spaces are not inviting, but the Empress's private chambers are well furnished and our own are comfortable enough.

I have not yet been appointed a lady to the Empress's chamber but Alexandra and Varvara have and they can tell us much of what goes on. One of those things is that our uncle, the great Potemkin, is falling out of favour. That is what they say – falling out of favour. What will become of us if this is true? Alexandra says the Empress spends much time with one of her new secretaries, Peter Zavadovsky, who is now in charge of petitions. I have often seen him at her side at the concerts and dinners we attend. But Uncle is usually on her other side. Zavadovsky looks the same age as Uncle but is not so ... dramatic in appearance. But he can be considered handsome all the same and he is very quiet and decorous, unlike Uncle who is prone to guffaws of laughter, even when it is inappropriate. Perhaps the Empress would like a quieter life?

Varvara, who spends a lot of time alone with Uncle, says he still loves the Empress but is bored with her and is happy she has Zavadovsky to entertain her. I think Varvara should be careful what she says. Or does. I am only fifteen but I see how Varvara's love of Uncle – we all love him but she is more affectionate in showing it – may make the Empress unhappy or even jealous.

But I must record facts rather than unordered thoughts. One fact is that the Grand Duchess Natalya is dead. It was a dreadful affair. The baby died inside her and then poisoned her and she died. Grand Duke Paul cried for days and would not come out of his chambers. He did not even attend the funeral. They dressed the Grand Duchess in beautiful white satin and she lay in state at the Alexander Nevsky Monastery, her dead child at her feet. I wondered how they got the baby out in the end.

The Empress ordered a post-mortem, which Uncle told me means 'after death' but I am still not sure what it is, and they found out that the Grand Duchess had a strange deformity in her spine which meant she would never have been able to give birth. And so it was for the better that she died, the Empress said, because Grand Duke Paul must have an heir as he will one day be Emperor. The Empress has apparently already chosen Natalya's successor as if, Alexandra says, she knew the Grand Duchess was going to die. Varvara says the Empress let the Grand Duchess die deliberately but I cannot believe such cruelty. I should not even write it.

The Grand Duke at first refused to even consider marrying again. He was inconsolable in his grief. However, once the Empress told him that his wife had been deceiving him with his best friend and showed him letters to prove it, he went off to Germany to fetch another princess. I hope he finds someone pretty and noble. At least, his friend has been sent off to serve in Crimea so he cannot steal another wife from Grand Duke Paul. Uncle says loyalty is more important than love and told me to write that as a fact in my book.

Alexandra
September 1776

Dear Anna,

I have much to tell you, not all of it happy. We are often dejected, for dear Uncle is frequently gone from Court and we miss his affectionate and cheerful presence. Perhaps the long summer nights when the sun does not set before it rises again have led to a certain restlessness at Court. No one sleeps and parties and revelries continue all though these white nights. The Empress complains of headaches and is not often in good spirits.

Peter Zavadovsky has been appointed personal adjutant to the Empress, which means he is now the official favourite in Uncle's place. Uncle says it is of no import. The Empress loves him and she is only playing with the meek Peterkin, as he calls him. And it certainly does not look as if Uncle is out of favour. He has been given command of the St Petersburg troops, he has received gifts of estates and many thousand serfs, and – most of all – he has been made a Prince of the Holy Roman Empire. He is to be called Serenissimus. The only other person in Russia with the title of Prince of the Holy Roman Empire is the Empress's former favourite Grigory Orlov. Orlov is also often by the Empress's side and it is whispered by some that he seeks to recapture his former position of favourite, but everyone knows he seeks imperial permission to marry his young niece.

The Empress gave Prince Potemkin, as he is now titled, the beautiful Anichkov Palace not too far from the Winter Palace, very prettily situated overlooking the Fontanka river. It was commissioned by the Empress Elizabeth for her favourite. Surely that is a sign that our Uncle is still in favour, is still the favourite? Zavadovsky has not been given a palace. In fact, he must work at papers all day and then entertain the Empress in the evening. I do not see much passion when they are together. I cannot imagine him being superior in any way to Uncle, certainly not in manliness.

Now that Uncle is not so often with the Empress, the ladies of the court, married or not, buzz around him like bees round a honeypot. I have instructed Varvara to take care of his needs. She is the most beautiful of us all. I know, as the eldest here, it is my duty to look after our interests and I would do so gladly, but it is Varvara that Uncle is most fond of. And after all, there are sufficient examples in good society of uncles and nieces being ... together. I approached the subject carefully with Uncle before talking to Varvara and he said, very cheerfully, "We are all one family. You are our daughters and the Empress's young men are our sons. We will have no secrets from one another. The Empress loves you and I care for any man she cares for." This may be true, for Uncle is invariably courteous to Zavadovsky and the Empress has shown nothing but kindness to us all.

The only times she is out of temper is when she and Uncle are alone. I hear their raised voices from the anteroom. She accuses him of thoughtlessness and extravagance. She reminds him that she is the Empress and he her subject. She says she does not hate him but nor does she love him as she used to when she gave him her heart, which he then cast aside when he bedded other women. The Prince accuses her of ignoring him, of forgetting that as her loyal subject, he risked his life in her service and won wars against the Turks and brought her Empire much new territory with thousands of subjects.

Their quarrels are often very loud but it is the Empress's voice which quietens to a conciliatory tone first. I once heard her say, "I think we quarrel about power not love." And this is true, for Uncle does not want to lose power, of which he has as much as the Empress as long as he remains in her favour. And we will help him do this. I would be mistress of the Anichkov Palace ... or something even grander. Uncle has asked the Empress for the Duchy of

Courland, which is under Russia's power even if the Baltic barons like to think they are independent. Uncle argues, quite wisely, I think, that he needs a guarantee if he is ever left to the mercies of the Grand Duke Paul. There is no love between Uncle and the Empress's son and heir. "He would send me to Siberia if he could," Uncle says. The Empress agrees but says she must first have the support of Prussia and Poland for a new Duke. This is excellent news. We will have our own Court, far enough from imperial considerations.

But there are happy times at Court too. The period of mourning for the Grand Duchess is over – it was only three months – and we can wear pretty summer dresses, which comes most fortuitously, for the Grand Duke has returned with a new wife and we are in the midst of great celebrations. We received the news of their coming some time in advance and the Empress designed the most charming chambers for the new bride. Her ladies were allowed to help and there was much excitement. The daily bedroom has blue glass columns – yes, glass! – and the walls are covered in white damask with pink wood trimmings and a bed to match. The state bedroom is decorated in blue velvet and gold brocade. The rooms rival the Empress's own.

The Princess of Württemberg is but sixteen years old and although she has brought her own entourage, we hope she may also appoint our Katerina, who is but a little younger, as a maid-of-honour. She is very pleasant in appearance, with a lovely complexion and a kind expression. Like the Empress, she is tall and carries herself well, towering over her new husband. The Empress has called her sweet and good and has described her complexion as "lilies and roses" which is unusually poetic for the Empress. The Princess has to be baptised before she can marry the Grand Duke so she must learn her vows in Russian, which she is doing most assiduously.

Best of all, dearest Uncle has returned from his travels – his enemies would say from his dismissal as official favourite – to take part in the celebrations. He will not yet live in the Anichkov Palace since there are many renovations to be done nor has he given up his apartments in the Winter Palace.

The Empress was playing cards one evening with Zavadovsky by her side when Uncle suddenly appeared. He looked so handsome! He had made an effort with his appearance – he often does not – his thick hair trimmed neatly over his collar, his uniform and medals gleaming. He bowed low to the Empress, gave her a most dazzling smile, inclined his head to Zavadovsky, who had half risen in alarm, and sat down calmly at the table! The Empress said nothing but dealt him a hand. This has put paid to all those who predicted he would be cast out. This is what the Orlovs want and they are tireless in their efforts to discredit Prince Potemkin. There is a rumour, well founded I am sure, that Alexei Orlov, the brother of Orlov whom they call Scarface, has offered to rid the Empress of Prince Potemkin once and for all. But I should take care what I write for although this letter will be brought to you by personal courier, interceptions are possible.

You will see, dearest Anna, that our life at court is not always frivolous. Yes, there are fine dresses and beautiful jewels to wear, we have concerts, plays and operas to entertain us, we dance for hours at feasts and banquets where an abundance of exotic food is served on golden plates but we must be constantly alert. Our future depends on it.

With affection,
Your sister Alexandra

Nadezhda
October 1776

The Grand Duke Paul and the Princess Sophia are married. The wedding took place on 26th September, a few days after the Grand Duke's 22nd birthday, and the celebrations lasted three weeks. I am happy to have such indisputable facts to record, for in this Court there seem to be few facts. Whispers and secrets lurk in every corridor. And there are many corridors.

Uncle is still out of favour, which appears to mean out of the Empress's bed because in all else, he seems in favour. He is still at Court, in his own chambers, and everyone still runs to do his bidding. It was very obvious that he was not chosen to hold the crown over the Grand Duke's head at his marriage ceremony. This honour fell to Count Grigory Orlov, the Empress's former favourite. "Ah there is no danger there," Uncle said. "The Empress will not take him back. Her affection for him stems from her gratitude for all the services he and his brothers have rendered her. And Grigory Orlov is loyal to the Empress. That is the only good thing I can say about him."

Portraits I have seen, and there are several in the palace, testify that Count Orlov was once very handsome but now he is over forty and rather fat. He walks with the aid of a cane for he cannot walk straight. Uncle says he suffers the disease that comes from too many delights but will not elaborate. In any case, Count Orlov is besotted with his niece Catherine, who is but sixteen years old, and he is constantly petitioning the Empress to allow them to marry. Uncles may apparently seduce their nieces but not marry them. Catherine is in attendance in the Empress's chambers. She is pleasant but plain. Uncle says the only danger from Orlov is the young men he can put in the Empress's bed. He thinks the Empress is tiring of Zavadovsky after only some months and so he must find an attractive alternative before Orlov does. So although these two former favourites do not have intimate access to the Empress, they choose who will share her bed. I record this for future reference – I wish to see if Uncle is right – not because it is fact.

The Court has quietened down after all the celebrations, which were very tiring in the end. Even Katerina complained and stopped writing down the compliments she received for they were too many. Varvara was the only one who rushed from one entertainment to the next.

Uncle has been in a rage. I don't know if it is a fact but he is said to have come across a note of the Empress to Zavadovsky, which read ***All will pass except my passion for you.*** I do not understand the need for notes. The Empress and Zavadovsky spend all day together, and all night. Uncle once remarked, "Time is not the Empress's to squander on lesser mortals. It belongs to the Empire."

In any case, Prince Potemkin charged into the Empress's chambers, shouting and throwing things, demanding that Zavadovsky be dismissed. It is said a candlestick narrowly missed the Empress's head. I wasn't there to witness this and therefore should not record it but Alexandra said there were broken vases and one dented candlestick to clear up.

Uncle has gone to a monastery. He bade us farewell fondly and said he would return soon, cleansed and calm.

Katerina
October 1776

I do wish Alexandra would not always tell us what to do. I am happy to do nothing. I like to lie on the sofa and dream. It is so much more pleasant and much less tiring to live in a make-believe world than in the real one. Alexandra has ordered me to write a journal. Every lady does so, she claims. If I do not, she will have me write letters to the family, to father and to grandmother. I said I would keep a journal but that she must not read it. "No lady would read another's private writings," she said. I will have nothing to hide from her but I do not wish her to see how little I might write.

Thanks to Alexandra's interference, I now have little time to myself. I must rise early, before dinner, complete my toilette, dress properly with my bodice tightened so that I can hardly breathe and my hair curled and pinned so that my head hurts. Alexandra says it is a great honour to attend the Princess Sophia – or Grand Duchess Maria as she is now known. I prefer her own name and I think she does too.

Alexandra says I must use my position in the Grand Duchess's entourage to our family's advantage. I know she really means that I should spy and report back to her and Uncle. I think I will tell Alexandra nothing but will report to Uncle when he is here, for his manner is so entertaining, much more pleasant than Alexandra's interrogations.

It is fortunate for me that the Grand Duchess is very kind. We have become quite firm friends and I may sit close to her and be privy to the conversations she has with her ladies she brought from home. It is good she has them for I imagine she would be homesick no matter how pretty the chambers that have been prepared for her.

The Grand Duchess has told me something of her past. It took me a little time to unravel this but she was betrothed to Prince Ludwig of Darmstadt, who serves at the Court in Prussia. The Empress asked King Frederick to persuade the Prince to relinquish Princess Sophia, as she was then, so that she could marry Grand Duke Paul. The Empress apparently pointed out that she had chosen Sophia for her son's wife some years ago but at eleven years old, the Princess was too young for marriage at that time. The Empress had, so to speak, declared her interest before Prince Ludwig. And so it was done. Princess Sophia – without being asked – was taken from Prince Ludwig and given to the Grand Duke. 10,000 roubles from the Empress may have helped.

"Was the Prince handsome?" I asked the Grand Duchess. "Did you love him?"

"I think I could have," she answered, "but I did not expect it. Marriage is arranged for us by our elders who know what is best for us. And I am determined to be happy with the Grand Duke. I will do my duty and be a good wife to him."

I am not sure that I could. He is definitely not handsome. The Grand Duchess read out to us his instructions on what kind of wife he expected her to be. She said it would be edifying for us to learn what to expect in marriage. The Grand Duke wrote that his wife must obey him and the Empress in all things. She must accept his criticism of her even if it were unjust, as it surely would be for he was, he wrote, impatient and at times volatile.

"You see how honest the Grand Duke is!" Maria exclaimed softly. "There will be no surprises. I know what to expect."

For my part, I think the Grand Duke is fortunate to have her as his wife. She is very pretty but very modest. She can read Latin and speaks French and Italian. She loves to draw and paint, can embroider beautifully, plays the harpsichord and sings like an angel and when she danced at her wedding celebrations, she was as light and graceful as a feather. She is very fond of reading and knows so much. I wish I and my sisters had had such an education but perhaps I may learn from the Grand Duchess. With her education and beauty, she is such a woman that could feed jealousies but everyone feels affection for her. Why, even the Empress has come to sit with us for an hour while Maria plays. The Empress is infatuated with her new daughter-in-law and showers her with affectionate compliments. I think that is because, as the Empress has pointed out, she herself came to Russia as a young German princess to marry the Grand Duke. And her name was also Sophia.

Will we have an Empress Maria one day? I asked Uncle this and he was most alarmed. "Katerina," he admonished me most severely, "we never ever talk about any sovereign of Russia except the Empress Catherine. She will rule us for decades." Well, I can count and I would say that one cannot add many more decades to the nearly five that the Empress has already lived. But I will not speak of it again. Uncle left us in such a sulk that day. Alexandra was very angry and reminded me that we live at Court at the beneficence of the Empress. I thought it was Uncle's.

The Grand Duchess will make a good Empress, I think. Unlike Catherine, who changes her richly brocaded and silk dresses several times a day, she is very moderate, even wearing her predecessor's clothes. I cannot imagine wearing a dead person's clothes. "Why," the Grand Duchess says sweetly, "they are much too fine to be discarded. We are all one family." And what she means by that is another bit of unravelling. Her former betrothed, Prince Ludwig, is the brother of Grand Duchess Natalya. I find it difficult to imagine that Maria has to share her bed with the husband of the dead sister of her own betrothed. It makes my head hurt to think of it. It is like mathematics, of which I know thankfully little.

Varvara
March 1777

My story takes a dramatic turn. I am called to the Empress. I am trembling with fear. I serve her in her chambers every day – mostly running backwards and forwards with notes – but she has never requested to speak to me alone. She has rarely spoken to me directly at all.

As soon as I receive the summons, I rush to Uncle, waking him from a deep slumber. He snores louder than a hunter's horn, which is one reason I would not spend the night in his bed. The other is that the Empress would find out. And now it seems she has.

Uncle is difficult to wake. When he does open his eyes, he growls, "Little kitten, this is no time to disturb a man!"

I shake him and only when I utter the Empress's name does he sit up startled.

"What shall I do? What shall I say? What will happen to us?" My voice comes in gasps.

Uncle takes a deep draught from the wine goblet on the stand beside his bed.

"Now, Varvara, be calm," he says. "The Empress knows I bed other women. It is our understanding, which does not lessen our bonds to each other."

"And does the Empress know about me?" I interrupt, shocked.

"Ah, little kitten, you are too young to understand men. But the Empress knows their nature well. She would wish, I think, that my affections should fall on someone without pretension to power or influence, someone loyal to her, just as I would wish someone loyal to me in **her** bed."

"But you are my uncle. Will she not object to that?" I ask, astonished at his calm.

"She knows it is but a game –"

"But not for me," I cannot help cry out. "I love you, you know I do."

"Yes, yes," he calms me, stroking my hair. "You must act towards the Empress as a loyal daughter. Wear something a little ... severe. Let her not see your charms or her jealousy will be roused. And as for uncles and nieces, we are all family. Why, she herself romped with her own uncle when she was but fourteen."

"Yes, but look at Prince Orlov," I remind him. "She will not allow him to marry his niece."

"But we do not wish to marry, child. That is the difference. We will find you an amenable and rich husband when the time is ripe," he says patting me on the head just as he comforts Tatiana when someone has scolded her. "And it looks as if it may be soon," he adds quietly, thinking I cannot hear him.

Alexandra helps to dress me in a sober fashion. My hair is pulled back and my only adornment is a pair of little pearl earrings. They are simple, but I like them. They are of an unusual pink colour. My dress also suits me. It too is pink, plain but smooth and silky.

"Remember," Alexandra says as we walk along the corridor to the Empress's chambers, "our futures depend on you. Be meek and obedient. Do not argue or answer back. You have already won. Prince Potemkin is in your bed, not hers. If you want to keep him there, and you must for all our sakes, then please the Empress by being ... compliant."

She gives me a little push towards the door and the guards move apart to allow me to enter. I do no expect to see the Empress in the ante-room but she is there, alone. Her toilette has been completed and she is radiant with diamonds. There is to be a ball this evening for her son and his wife. Our uncle indulges our taste for fine dresses and we have many in silks and brocades but none are as exquisite as the Empress's. At the wedding celebrations, she wore a dress which had nearly five thousand pearls sewn into it. But I have better hair, for which I receive many compliments. The Empress's is dull brown or powdered with grey. Alexandra was right to tie up my blonde curls.

I curtsey low and say "Your Majesty" trying not to make it sound like a question. My dress swishes slightly as I raise myself.

"Ah, Varvara," the Empress says warmly, "it is time, I think, we had a little talk together. After all, you are my family. You are like a daughter to me."

I bow again and quietly say, "Thank you, Your Majesty."

"And also to Prince Potemkin."

It sounds like a question and so I choose to answer. "To whom my sisters and I are most grateful."

"Yes, many are grateful to the General. But I do not wish it to be too many. People will take advantage of his kindness, of his generosity."

I do not know what to answer. Am I being accused of exploiting Uncle? I say nothing.

"Especially women," the Empress says, startling me. "Do you ... meet many women at your Uncle's?"

"No, Your Majesty. He is often gone."

"Ah yes, you are not always with him. But when he is here, I wish him to be in the ... right hands. I wish him to be cared for as he needs. There are enough women who would undermine my position and enough men who would send their wives to undermine it. I will not tolerate any favourites in the Prince's life who do not meet my approval."

The Empress's voice is becoming quite stern, almost angry. I remain silent.

"You meet my approval, Varvara. And I know you have already met the Prince's approval. Is my meaning clear?"

I think to myself, no, not really and so I ask carefully, "I am here to serve Your Majesty, who must only bid me do as she wishes, and it will be done."

"Oh, I think it is already done! But make sure you keep the Prince's bed warm enough that he has no other in it. Come to me if you have misgivings about − " she waves vaguely − " anything."

She is giving me permission to be Uncle's mistress, which I already am! What bliss! No more secrets.

"I will do all in my power to satisfy both you and the Prince," I say.

The Empress looks at me sharply. It was indeed an unfortunate choice of expression.

"But never forget, Varvara, that I am the Empress. Prince Potemkin's loyalty is first and foremost to me. In fact, that is his only loyalty. Do not overstep your boundaries, which are those of an obedient daughter and subject."

"I understand, Your Majesty," I say meekly. The Empress dismisses me with a curt nod of her head. I curtsey and as I stand and turn, I make my skirts swish. Deliberately.

There is no time to tell Alexandra everything for she must go in and attend to the Empress but I smile happily in answer to her questioning look. I make my way to Uncle's quarters. Openly. How liberated I feel.

As the messenger of ***billets doux*** between the Empress and the Prince, I had used the secret corridor furtively. I continued to use it for my own means all winter when I could not keep away from Uncle's caresses. I loved being his little kitten. He was especially attentive when he returned from his stay in the monastery, pure and cleansed, as he said. How he cherished me, how he kissed me, gently at first but later more passionately. I remember the first time he carefully undid the hooks on my dress. I wanted to tear all my clothes off and lie in his arms. And I did one day while he remained fully dressed.

"I love your beauty," he murmured in my hair, "and your innocence."

The loss of my innocence was inevitable ... and exciting. I am not so innocent now and I know what I like. I like making love to my Uncle.

He is dressing for the ball when I rush in. He dismisses his chamberlains and I tell him my good news.

"You clever little kitten," he says touching my lips with a light kiss. "Come to me tonight and you shall have your reward."

I look forward to the ball. I am Prince Potemkin's official mistress under the Empress's protection. If any other woman comes too near, I shall report her to the Empress.

This has been an excellent chapter. My story develops well.

Nadezhda
May 1777

It is a fact that Varvara has the Empress's permission to be in our Uncle's bed and so, Alexandra says, our futures are secured. For the time being. Prince Potemkin will never marry her, not just because she is his niece, but because the Empress does not wish him to marry. Alexandra says the Empress and Uncle were once married in secret but this is a rumour not a fact. It is better for us if Prince Potemkin remains unmarried. We are his family and his heirs. Were he to have his own children, his own legitimate children – as he may well do since at 37 he is not yet old – then we will be dispossessed. I think we must find husbands quickly.

Uncle has given Varvara a truly magnificent necklace of diamonds – that is a very visible fact and one I do not think the Empress approves of. He likes to have all of us around him when he dines and we are often at the Empress's for card parties. The Prince is gallant and pays many compliments to the ladies in attendance. The Empress laughs but Varvara sulks. Alexandra scolds her later but it does no good. She says she is in love with the Prince. She adds, dramatically in my opinion, that he is her life and she cannot live without him. But we all love Uncle. She cannot have him to herself. She has his bed and surely that is enough. He turns to Alexandra for advice for she is very clever. He gathers facts for me because he knows I like them. Katerina and Tatiana can sit on his knee or at his feet while he strokes their heads. We are a happy family and Varvara will only spoil it all with her wish to have Uncle all to herself. Even the Empress remarked on it the other day as we sat together listening to the Grand Duchess Maria playing the harpsichord. "My dear Prince," she said, "you look so contented sitting there in your garden of flowers." She meant us!

Katerina
July 1777

The Grand Duchess Maria is with child. The midwives say it will come at the end of the year. I shudder to think what she went through with the unhandsome Grand Duke to be in this state. Varvara has enlightened us as to how one may get a child should one wish to. She asked Uncle. I can hardly look at the Grand Duke without feeling embarrassed on the Grand Duchess's behalf. But she seems more than content. And − best of all for me − happy to stay in her chambers. This means my duties are much reduced and I am free to "go out and enjoy some fresh air in the gardens" as the Grand Duchess kindly exhorts me. "You must not be confined just because I am," she says. She is not in official confinement yet. That will come later when she must lie in the dark for some six weeks before the child is born. I shudder again when I think what might happen to her. The Grand Duke's first wife died in such agonies in childbirth. And a child was not even born.

I distract myself from such thoughts by lying on the couch in my chambers. I loosen my tight corsets and unpin my hair and have the maids bring me cooled apple juice, for the summer heat lies heavily even within our stone palace. I have opened all the windows in the hope of a breeze from the Neva. The Empress will soon order the Court to move to her summer residence. In the meantime, I read or dream and relish the bliss of doing nothing.

Occasionally, Tatiana comes to play. She is a dear child. Although not quite eight, she is a keen and quiet observer and can imitate to perfection. I have to guess who she is acting and she is so good that I rarely err. For example, she walks up and down with small quick steps, wiping her brow, pulling out an imaginary watch to check the time, sits at a desk, writes feverishly, then jumps up and goes down on one knee to kiss an imaginary hand, losing her balance as she does so. I know immediately it is

Zavadovsky. The poor man is tense with overwork and with pleasing the Empress. He will indeed fall over soon.

Varvara had to take a note to him recently from the Empress. In it the Empress exhorted her tired lover to replace his hypochondriac thoughts with amusing ones. Love, she wrote, needed amusement. Varvara says Uncle Potemkin will provide that. Oh, not he himself but one of his entourage. The ladies at court all know who it will be. He has been singled out but not yet officially chosen. He is a major of hussars, a few years younger than Zavadovsky, about thirty years old. He is Serbian and a favourite of Uncle. He is very handsome. We ladies at court call him Adonis. Uncle says he is ***un vrai sauvage*** and thus will please the Empress. Already there are romantic stories about him. It is said that he fought valiantly against the Turks but was captured. About to be beheaded – the normal fate for ordinary soldiers – he quickly declared himself to be a Count and was imprisoned for ransom instead. No doubt he will be made a real Count soon if the Empress likes him.

Varvara is flirting with every man at court, including this new candidate for the Empress's favourite. She is such a beauty and with a toss of her blonde curls, she can turn any man's head. But Alexandra is very strict with her. She admonishes her to look after Uncle despite his many admirers and his many absences. The Empress wishes it so. But Uncle says he also wishes to find good husbands for us and that Varvara must select a gentleman of nobility that pleases her and Uncle will arrange the rest. I find a lover or a husband a tiring prospect. Would I be able to relax on the sofa in a state of déshabillé?

Alexandra
August 1777

Dear Anna,

This Court tries my patience. My sisters try my patience. They think life is about fine clothes, entertainment and admirers. And in that, they are certainly creatures of this Court. The Empress sets the example. Where is the Prussian princess who became sovereign and laboured twenty hours a day to make of Russia an enlightened empire? There is little devotion to work but much to the selection of favourites. Zavadovsky has been dismissed with a pension of 30,000 roubles a year, much less than other favourites received, and the usual silver service, but only for sixteen places. It is said that he received a mere three or four thousand serfs. It has been quite a drama. Zavadovsky was heartbroken and even came to me to intercede on his behalf. "My hopes, my passions, my fortunate lot have all gone, like the wind that one cannot halt. Her love for me has vanished," he said most piteously. Uncle chortled when he told us how Catherine had advised Zavadovsky to translate Tacitus to calm his spirits.

His replacement, the Serbian hussar Semyon Zorich, proud of his sobriquet Adonis, struts around like a peacock in his fine new clothes. Uncle Potemkin even gifted him a spray of diamonds for his hat and a jewel-encrusted cane. The Empress is besotted. It is not elegant to see an elderly lady, Empress or not, fawning over a young upstart like Zorich, handsome or not. But Uncle would have the Empress kept happy. And in this I agree with him. Just as I must continually exhort Varvara to do her duty to us all by keeping Uncle happy. But she acts like a spoiled child. "He doesn't love me," she cries petulantly. "He has other women." What has love to do with it? I admonish her. I remind her that the bedchamber is a political arena and she must learn to use it to our advantage. Love!

Otherwise, I keep my own counsel while working assiduously but quietly to secure our position at Court and the Empress's trust.

The vagaries of fate can often be tempered if one has wealth but, as you know, we came here with little but Uncle's favour. He is generous and we lack for nothing but if anything were to befall him – and he talks of returning to quell the Turks, who are not adhering to the peace treaty – then to whom should we turn while my sisters remain husbandless? Your husband cannot provide for us all, dear Anna. Uncle may also lose the Empress's favour, as many have done. Why, even the great Grigory Orlov, who once had as much power and influence as Uncle has now, must find ways to keep the Empress's good will towards him. They say he is happy with his child bride, by the way. The Empress finally gave her consent for the marriage. Many wonder what changed her mind but one need not look too far. She is now in possession of a legendary diamond, which she had apparently tried to purchase some years before but considered the price too high. When she spoke of this diamond, which was quite often as she compared all her other diamonds to it, she did so with great longing.

On his visit to Europe last year, Prince Orlov apparently went to Amsterdam and bought the stone for nearly half a million roubles. While it cannot be said that the diamond bought the Empress's permission to marry his niece, it is noteworthy that approval came soon after the diamond came into the Empress's possession. She has shown it to everyone and even the foreign envoys have been invited to view "the Orlov diamond".

It is, in truth, quite an ugly thing. It is shaped like, and as large as, half a pigeon's egg. It has many facets and its saving grace is its very fine blue-green colour. The Empress says it had once been the eye of a god in an Indian temple, which gives one the feeling of the eye watching you. I wonder if the god sits there one-eyed now. I could not imagine how the Empress would wear such a clumsy diamond and apparently neither could she for she consulted with the Court jeweller several times. She has now decided to have the diamond set in the imperial sceptre where all can see it. I nearly added, "And where it can see everyone."

Uncle is furious that Orlov has not only secured the Empress's gratitude but also a permanent place in the sceptre of Russia. The Empress said quite pointedly to him, "My dear Prince, you now see the true measure of love, which I once had but never lost."

I cannot see the excitement about diamonds as such but I do admit that it is indeed a measure of Prince Orlov's love to have given up such a valuable treasure for his niece. I cannot imagine many men doing it or indeed many women being worth it. It is said Orlov danced for joy at his wedding although he can hardly walk without a cane.

I am befriended by some of the foreign dignitaries, mainly because I have shown an interest in, and perhaps a talent for, matters political. An Empire cannot exist surrounded by enemies. Alliances must be made. Sir James Harris, the new British envoy and already a firm friend of Uncle, has taught me much. Britain would be our ally but the Empress demands that in return they would support our fight against the Ottoman Empire. This, Sir James says, is unacceptable in London. But he is tireless in his efforts to effect an alliance between Britain and Russia. France has always been hostile to England and is now joining the side of the rebels in the new British colonies in America. Prussia is Russia's ally, even if a lukewarm one, but Uncle says our interests should lie with Austria, who would help in quelling the Ottomans. "It is time," he says, "to look southwards and forget the north." Meanwhile, the British – and everyone else – run about looking for allies. You can see that the political board is a complex one, more so than chess, and much is paid by foreign governments for reliable information or influence in the constant search for political friends. Sir James, in particular, has been most generous and I have accumulated quite a little fortune, which I have wisely invested with good returns.

An advantage of Russia's late emergence as a powerful state is that much of our country is still in a pristine state. The British have plundered their forests for some centuries to supply their formidable navy and are now running out of oak. The French too need good timber for their ships, especially tall masts. And so, with Uncle's help, I have invested in timber forests and the export of wood through our Baltic ports. This I consider a better investment than diamond necklaces. The world will always need timber for its ships and although diamonds sparkle most gloriously in candlelight, they are not forever.

In return for the gifts I receive from Sir James, I give him good advice on how to proceed at Court. I tell him when the Empress is in good spirits; I present him well to the Empress in that I pass on his compliments, most of which I have to invent myself for the English do not seem to have that talent while the French excel at it The best advice I have given Sir James is to do everything to please the Empress. She must never be contradicted. More than that, she must be praised. Uncle once said to him at dinner, "Flatter the Empress as much as you can, you cannot use too much unction. But flatter her for what she ought to be not for what she is." I thought that very wise.

You will see, Anna, that I am very busy at Court and while I have secured a place of trust with the Empress and my Uncle, I am not complacent and look to our future.

This letter will be delivered to you by personal messenger and is for your eyes only. I think I may have to turn to encryption if I am to continue to correspond with you in a frank manner. But know that my loyalty lies unshakably with the Empress and with our family.

With affection,
Your sister Alexandra

P.S. I can furnish you with contacts in the timber trade should you and your husband wish. Trade can bring the wealth that one was not fortunate enough to be born or married into.

Nadezhda
October 1777

At last I have a dramatic event to describe. It happened just after our return from Tsarskoye Selo, where the Empress and the Court spend the summer. Tsarskoye Selo is about 30 versts from St Petersburg. I like the palace there. The exteriors are turquoise and white with many golden figures. The roof is said to be solid gold and shines most brilliantly in the sunshine. The rooms are large and airy. The Grand Hall runs the whole width of the building – and that is very wide because it is more than one verst to walk around the whole outside of the palace – and has huge windows on either side where one can linger to enjoy the views.

There is a most fascinating room made entirely of amber. It has no windows and is lit by candlelight and the amber gives off a resin scent in the heat. The Empress says many thousands of pounds of amber were used and that amber is ten times more valuable than gold. The Empress likes to linger in the amber room. She says she can meditate peacefully. I find it too hot. I prefer to be outside and that is why I am happy when the Court moves to Tsarskoye Selo. The grounds are extensive and designed to surprise at every turn, of which there are many. There is a Chinese village, a ruined Gothic castle, an Egyptian pyramid where the Empress's favourites dogs are buried, many monuments to military victories, a lake, surprising bridges ... it is a true delight to wander.

But I digress too much. The day after our return to St Petersburg, the sky darkened with storm clouds and I thought it was such a pity if winter were to begin so soon when the sun had just been shining so warmly. A ten o'clock that evening, a window in our chamber burst open and the wind blew in great gusts of rain. The men servants ran to and fro trying to secure windows, of which there are thousands in the palace, but many panes were ripped from their frames — and sometimes the frames too. We cowered under the table, not daring to brave the corridor again where we had encountered all sorts of things flying about: tiles, iron sheets, windowpanes, flowerpots, cups and plates. And with the water came hail and snow. The courtyard was quickly turned into a raging lake, threatening to swallow the palace. Tatiana said we would have to build an ark just as Noah had done. "But for what are we being punished?" she asked. Katerina answered in a tone unusually sharp for her. "This Court does not live as Christians should! We shall all die because of it!"

We did not die although we got very wet and cold. The storm left about five in the morning as suddenly as it had come. When we ventured to open the windows, we could not see the banks of the Neva. Indeed it looked as if the palace was now in the middle of the great river. The merchant ships had been pushed by the torrent on to what was once the quay and lay there on their sides, their tall masts broken. I counted one hundred of them before I gave up. All sorts of objects floated on the churning waves — baskets, chairs, even a carriage — but we did not look too closely after Tatiana shouted, "I see a dead body!"

Now two weeks later the waters have receded although the footmen who stand at the back of carriages have their feet in water. The Empress complains about her wine cellar being flooded. "We will just have to have our wine mixed with water," she said. I think that was meant to be a humorous remark.

The Summer Garden is completely destroyed: the aviary with all the pretty little birds, the orangerie, the gazebo, where we often sit on summer evenings to enjoy a cool breeze, and the beautiful fountains which function from a steam engine built by Peter the Great himself. And all the marble statues in the garden have also been swept away. Maybe it was a statue that Tatiana saw that day but there are whispers of over a hundred people having perished in the flood. The Empress will not have anyone speak of deaths. She says the people have been eating well of fish. I am not sure whether that is another humorous remark.

The Empress was taken ill with a stomach colic, as were many others at Court. Dr Rogerson said the flood has brought disease with it and we must avoid drinking the water or anything which has come in contact with it. Perhaps it has seeped into the Empress's wine after all.

I have not many other facts to report. Varvara is constantly in a bad mood because of Uncle and we have all lost patience with her. Uncle remains kind and patient when he is here and we all love him. Why can't she? She used to, I am sure of it, but she wants him all for herself. Alexandra says he is not a man to be possessed by one woman. Why, even the Empress shares him. Uncle said he will find Varvara her very own husband.

Alexandra continues as bossy as ever. She would make a good Empress. Katerina asked Uncle why Alexandra should not have her own husband before Varvara because she is older. Varvara may be very pretty, and she is aware of it, but Alexandra is very beautiful in a regal way. She is tall and slim, her auburn hair is always glossy, and she has fine features with high cheekbones, bright blue eyes and a perfectly shaped mouth, which admittedly could use more exercise in smiling. I wish I had her perfect skin – it is as smooth and pale as alabaster.

I will have difficulty finding a husband. I have none of the attractions of my sisters. Even Uncle says it may be hopeless. I know he was joking but there is always truth in a joke. Although a year younger, Katerina will find a husband before me if she can force herself from the sofa. She is like a beautiful but lazy cat, one of those Persian types that the Empress keeps in her Hermitage. The other day I came across her lying wrapped in not much more than that huge black fur Uncle had given her. I was shocked and remonstrated with her. "It is so soothing," she said, almost purring, "and warm."

Varvara
November 1777

My story threatens to end just as it has started. I am at my wits' end. I decide to go to the Empress. I fall at her feet weeping. I tell her I cannot bear it anymore. When she asks me what I cannot bear, I want to cry out, "Where is the passion of our first weeks together? Those days when he contrived to be alone with me as often as possible, when he smothered me with kisses and ripped the clothes from my willing body, when he called me his angel, his love, his life. I lived only for him, to be with him." I want to say, "You allowed Orlov to marry his young niece Why cannot we marry?" But Uncle had made it very clear. "We will not marry," he said. "I will never marry for my life lies with the Empress, forever."

Well, I must not mind the Empress for she is the Empress. But in his rooms I found letters from other women and I take some of them to show the Empress. She takes one of them reluctantly, holding it at arm's length. She reads it aloud.

I hope to see you at the ball tomorrow. I hope you will kiss me. I hope you will carry me away for an hour of pleasure that I can experience only with you –

The Empress stops reading and says calmly, "But, Varvara, these are but the hopeless pinings of a lovesick woman, probably trapped in an unhappy marriage. *I hope, I hope, I hope* – they have no foundation in fact."

I offer her another letter.

Tell me that you love me. Your kisses said so and I return them a million times. Your caresses said so and I return them ten million times. Our ecstasy said so and this I would have thirty million times. Tell me that you love me and I will leave everything to come to you. We shall leave court and live in love forever.

The Empress raises her eyebrows but returns the letter to me, again calmly.

"He has not declared his love," she says. "Another infatuation, more wishful thinking. She, who has not dared to sign her outpourings, is no more than a distraction for the Prince. He is a man and needs ... distractions."

"But what about me?" I say before I can stop myself. "Am I too just a distraction?"

"No, you are family," the Empress says, "my family. You were right to come to me with your worries. I will speak to the Prince."

I leave the Empress meekly with my thanks but on the way to my chambers, I give rein to my anger. I will not suffer through any more long, lonely cold winter nights. I will write to Uncle, absent once more in the south. I will tell him I do not love him, that I am tired of his caresses, or lack of them. I will tell him I will find another to love, someone younger, more handsome and with two eyes. And who will want to marry me. I will begin my search this very evening. I will make the great Serenissimus suffer. I will reject him as no other has. Oh yes, this is the stuff of novels but this is my life and I wish for a happier turn of events.

Nadezhda
January 1778

I have a pleasant fact to record. The Grand Duchess Maria gave birth to a son on 12th December 1777. He is the heir to the throne of Russia, after his father the Grand Duke Paul. Uncle hosted a most magnificent dinner, which cost 50,000 roubles but it was outshone by the Empress's celebrations. The Empress invited high-ranking nobles and some foreign dignitaries to attend an opera by her favourite composer Paisiello. She says it is the only music she can understand and it is indeed very light and comic.

After the musical entertainment, the guests were conducted to a room where tables were set up for cards, but only for the game of Macao, where the aim is to hold cards totalling nine points. On each of the velvet-covered tables a little dish of diamonds with a golden spoon had been set. Each guest who made a hand of nine points received a diamond. The Empress said one only sees devotion to cards, of which she is very fond, when the stakes are worth it, otherwise no one concentrates. And it is true that there was very little conversation and very little wine drunk during the games. A group of musicians played quietly in the background, disguising the silence. We ladies did not even dare to whisper such was the atmosphere of concentration. In the hour and a half allocated to this part of the evening, perhaps twice as many rounds had been played as would normally have been in that time. The Empress, seemingly well satisfied, ordered the remaining diamonds to be distributed amongst all the players. All in all, 150 diamonds were given away that evening. We did not receive any, nor had we played, since we had been invited, along with several other ladies of the court, "to form a fitting background for the beauty of the diamonds" as the Empress said, which was indeed a very generous compliment.

Afterwards, we proceeded to the Dining Room, where we gasped in amazement. All the walls – and even the ceiling - had been lined with sheets of mirrors. They reflected the tables in dizzying number. All kinds of jewels sparkled in the table centrepieces – and in their reflections on the ceiling. (Sir James Harris told Alexandra later that he estimated the worth of the jewels used for the ornaments at some two million sterling. I think this can be taken as a fact.) Twenty pages dressed in gold with blue sashes waited to serve the guests, who sat along one side of the tables so that they faced their own reflections. I am sure that pleased Varvara. She and Alexandra were permitted to attend the banquet. Katerina and I left with the other ladies once the food was served. Before that, we had to stand in groups in the background behind the seated guests while an artist sketched. The Empress wishes to have an engraving to record and commemorate the event for posterity. "They should know," she declared, "the magnificence of their ancestors."

The tables were set with the much talked about Sèvres porcelain dinner service, a gift from the Empress to Uncle. Catherine had received permission from King Louis XVI of France for the Sèvres manufactory to make copies of the antique cameos in his collection. It was an expensive and unique undertaking and because I like facts and figures, I shall record here that 3000 pieces were fired to achieve 800 of satisfactory quality. It is truly beautiful, a startling turquoise colour, with rosettes of gold, the cameos taken from Greek and Roman history and mythology. The centrepiece is some three feet tall and features Catherine herself as Minerva, the goddess of wisdom, at the top of a fluted column. Uncle said the table service cost some 350,000 French livres. When I asked him how much that was in roubles, he replied, "Too much, but the Empress has apparently not calculated the exact amount since she has not yet paid the bill and it has now been sent to me." He laughed when he said it.

And now we have begun a new year and my diary awaits new happenings. We have been in Russia for two and a half years now, but none of us has found a husband yet. I have turned eighteen and will be an old maid if Alexandra and Varvara do not marry soon.

Katerina
March 1778

I feel sorry for the Grand Duchess. She bears a healthy child and may not be its mother. That role has been taken over by the Empress. The Empress even chose its name – Alexander. This should connote both Alexander of Macedonia, who, Uncle said, conquered the whole known world before Christ was even born, and St Alexander Nevsky. The baby was one week old when he was baptised on the 20th December. The Empress held him in her arms and said, "St Alexander Nevsky was respected by the Tatars, the republic of Novgorod submitted out of respect for his virtues, he gave the Swedes a good thrashing, and the title of grand duke was conferred upon him thanks to his reputation." Alexandra whispered, "Well, that describes Russian foreign policy quite well." Nadezhda said she had read in the Book of Saints that Alexander Nevsky's great deeds took place long ago in the 13th century. In the chronicles of the time, Alexander is described as taller than others with a voice as loud as a trumpet, with the power of Samson and the wisdom of Solomon. It says he used to defeat but was never defeated. This is what the Empress would wish for a future ruler of her Empire.

After the baptism, the Empress took the tiny child from his mother's chambers. The Grand Duchess wept for days. "I only had him for one week," she said between sobs. The Empress allows her to see her child but she may not pick him up. A wet nurse has been engaged and she must feed him to a very strict schedule, whether he cries or not. And she may not caress him in any way or indeed even speak to him. It is cruel. I remember in our household how much joy we had with Tatiana when she was born. We hugged her and kissed her and we still do. Our poor dead mother used to say, "A child cannot have too much love." Perhaps that is the way of the provinces, it is certainly the way of the serfs, but in the city, amongst the nobility, children are raised differently, although Alexandra says the Empress is being extreme. She wishes to raise a strong heir. One wonders why she did not do that with her son Paul. Perhaps that is why she is doing so now – because she failed so badly with her own son.

I accompanied the Grand Duchess on one of her visits to her baby son. She may not go when she wishes. It must be arranged with the Empress first. The child has his own room and it is very chilly. There are instruments called thermometers in golden stands which measure the temperature so that it may be kept cool at all times.

The child does not sleep in a cradle, for he is not to be rocked, but on an iron bed on a leather mattress. He has a pillow and instead of furs, he has a light cover in the English style. He has not been swaddled and his limbs jerk around most alarmingly. There are no curtains round his bed. It is set on a raised platform, surrounded by a balustrade so that people cannot come too near him. The windows were open on my visit and I very nearly fell over with shock at the great booms from the Admiralty cannons across the way. The child opened his eyes wide but did not otherwise stir. "You see," the Empress declared proudly, "he is afraid of nothing." The baby is bathed every day in lukewarm water. I shudder at the thought. Once the warm weather comes in, he will bathe daily in cold water, just as the Empress does. A future Emperor must not be cosseted.

As we were leaving, the Empress picked him up from his bed. "You see, my dear Grand Duchess, he likes me. You need not worry about him."

Poor Maria fled to the corridor where the tears coursed down her cheeks. "My son will be a stranger to me!" She has been inconsolable and will not be distracted by any entertainment we devise. It is very tiring and I am more often in attendance than I wish to be. I have advised her to have another son, whom she can keep for herself.

Alexandra continues with her ambassadors and her business interests. I fear her acquisition of political and commercial skills will reduce her chances of finding a husband. They are not attractive womanly traits. And she is already 24. But she is right when she says that if she did not look after our interests, no one would. I am, by my own admission, too fond of doing nothing, Varvara is too impulsive and is constantly sulking about Uncle, who is often absent from Court but when he is here, he is as grumpy as a bear. He is no longer polite to the hussar Zorich and this upsets the Empress. Nadezhda has little interest outside her books and dear Tatiana is too young. She is now nearly nine and can speak French most tolerably and has learned to dance well. Her skills with a needle leave something to be desired but she sings most pleasantly and the Empress often calls on her to perform.

While there has been much glitter and luxury in our lives since we came to Court, I wonder if it is so much different from our quiet life in the provinces. There at least I could lie under the apple blossoms while my sisters laughed and played nearby.

Alexandra
July 1778

Dear Anna,

I write this less for you in faraway Astrakhan than for myself. I must order my thoughts after a tumble of events, which followed a quiet spring. Ripples began with the Empress's headaches and Zorich's sulks, then swelled with Uncle's disappearances and Varvara's tantrums. The Empress moved the Court between St Petersburg and Tsarskoye Selo every two to three weeks. She did not seem to know where she wanted to be. Uncle has had many loud quarrels with her and her headaches have increased. Zorich is of no help to her. He likes his position and the wealth it brings but he does not seem to like the Empress. Uncle said he must go and a new adjutant must be found for the Empress if she is to regain her vitality. I tried to tell Uncle that it is normal for a woman of fifty to lose her vitality but he will hear no word against the Empress – unless he is the one to utter it.

In May Uncle appointed a new adjutant in his own retinue. He is tall and very fine looking – and very young, being the same age as myself. On our way to the theatre one evening with the Empress, Uncle stood in the corridor with his new protégé. They both looked very handsome with their hair well dressed, the jewelled buttons and medals of their uniforms sparkling in the candlelight. The Empress stopped and conferred with them for several minutes. The young man said little but gazed in open admiration, or perhaps awe, at the Empress. We moved on and I fancy the Empress's step was a little lighter. Zorich excused himself and turned back. We heard later that he had attacked Uncle most violently, demanding satisfaction. Uncle remained calm and said, "We must all move on, Zorich."

A week or two later, Uncle arranged a house party at one of his estates I had never been to, near the border to

Finland. Varvara and I were invited. It is truly beautifully situated with wide views of mountains, lakes and forests but the house is not spacious and the Empress had only ten rooms for her entourage. I, as one of the Empress's main ladies, had to share with Countess Bruce, who describes herself as a long-time confidante of the Empress but in whom, as everyone knows, the Empress no longer confides. The Countess is known for her fondness for the company of men and it is rumoured that she used to check candidates for the Empress's favourites, what the French might call an *éprouveuse*. Uncle said it was once true but that her services were no longer needed now that he chooses the young men. He says he knows better than the Countess what the young men need to know to please the Empress and also how to make sure they are healthy and carry no disease, which is the Empress's main concern.

On the evening of our arrival, the Countess fell into lavish praise for Major Ivan Rimsky-Korsakov, for such is the name of the charming young man whom Uncle had brought to the Empress's attention. "Prince Potemkin is such a good friend," the Countess said, "I know he will help me to what I desire." I was alarmed since I knew of the Empress's interest. She had already dismissed Zorich. "I was fond of him yesterday and today I am not," she said in explanation although an Empress need not explain herself to anyone. "He only speaks Russian and now must go to France and England to learn foreign languages," she added. "His ignorance makes me blush." For a woman of education, a year is a long time to find that out. But perhaps his talents lay elsewhere.

Uncle had arranged the house party as a means for the Empress to acquaint herself with Rimsky-Korsakov in a discreet setting. At dinner that evening, both the Empress and the Countess bestowed much attention on the young man. I felt sorry for him. Two ladies, older than his mother, one the Empress, vying for his attention. He smiled and did not say much but he was flushed. I warned

Uncle of the Countess's interest, although it was perfectly obvious, and he called her away on some pretext. When they returned, she sat at another table and scowled. She left the next day.

The Empress is enamoured of her new adjutant, for such he is since we returned to Court. She praises him constantly in our presence. "He is of such classical beauty," she says, "and must be the failure of painters and the despair of sculptors." She calls him ***Pyrrhus, King of Epirus***. I asked Nadezhda who this person was and what did it mean, for she is very well read, but she could only tell me he was a Greek general who fought against Rome before Christ. She advised me to look among the classical statutory the Empress has collected and there is perhaps a statue of Pyrrhus, likely unclothed. I have not had time. I am often busy delivering confidential notes between the Empress and Rimsky-Korsakov or between the Empress and Prince Potemkin. The Empress does not trust the servants. I read the notes, of course, since they are rarely sealed but I do not divulge their contents to any but Uncle. To Uncle she writes that she is now ***as happy as a lark*** and thanks him for her King Epirus. ***He is***, she writes, ***never ignoble, always graceful. He shines like the sun and spreads brilliance where he goes. Yet, although artistic, he is all you would wish a man to be. He is nature in all its beauty***. Her notes to the 'King' himself are less poetic. ***I am impatient to see you***, she writes. ***Where are you? I shall come to find you. Thank you for loving me. Do not stop***. If I were Empress, I wouldn't write such things. One cannot deliver oneself into a man's power. She sounds like a lovesick girl, worse than Varvara.

Rimsky-Korsakov is pleasant but empty-headed. He has one saving grace – he sings like a nightingale and is otherwise very musical. The Empress has arranged music lessons for him and showers him with gifts after almost every song. "Even the birds flock to listen when he sings," she enthuses. Uncle estimates that Korsakov has amassed half a million roubles worth of 'singing awards' in this short time. And land with many serfs. But Uncle is content that the Empress is happy.

The Empress's infatuation with her new favourite has helped her to bear the news of the death of the great philosopher Voltaire. "I never met him," she said, "but I loved him and he esteemed me. No one can replace him." She is horrified at the refusal of the Roman Catholic Church to bury her friend in consecrated ground in Paris. "He shall have a sacred memory here in Russia," she declared, "for this is a country he helped, through me, to shape." The Empress wishes to buy his library of 7000 books and all her own letters to him. She plans to re-create his house here. She has two busts of the great philosopher on display and prefers the one without a wig. (In general, she has an aversion to wigs, saying they can often cause her to burst out laughing). She has had a new burst of energy and is copying all the letters she has received from Voltaire. "I want my subjects to study and learn Voltaire's work by heart, their minds to be nourished by it. It will form citizens, geniuses, heroes and authors. It will banish the darkness of ignorance." It will certainly banish my ignorance for I have never read anything of Voltaire. I am not sure he concerned himself with commerce. In any case, we are all happy to see the Empress at work, For weeks, she would not touch pen or paper.

With affection,
Your sister Alexandra

Varvara
September 1778

It is finished now. Months of uncertainty are over and I feel relief. I need no longer wonder whether he will write, whether he will call on me, whether he is with other women, whether he loves me. But I must catch up with my story in the right order. Last winter I wrote to Uncle: ***I wish you to be loved by another, as you yourself wish, but no-one will love you as I have loved you. The loss is yours.*** I think that was clear and generous. He wrote back at once calling me an ungrateful fool. He said he would box my ears when he returned but when he did return, we had the sweetest reunion. My hopes were rekindled. Not even a letter from grandmother could spoil our idyll. She wrote that we were creating a scandal, and worse, that it was against the laws of God and the church and she ordered my obedience to her in stopping the affair with her son forthwith. She also wrote to Uncle at the same time. He laughed angrily and threw the letter in the fire, "Since when do I allow my mother to interfere in my life?"

I was his little kitten again.

Despite my happiness, I began to feel unwell in the summer heat. I could not bring myself to eat, I was tense and anxious. I took no pleasure in Uncle's caresses. It was the Grand Duchess Maria that identified the source of my unease. I had been sitting with her and a few other ladies as she dined. The smell of the meat was rich and cloying in the heavy summer air and suddenly I found myself rushing to the nearest plant pot to void my stomach. I was very embarrassed. "Come with me," the Duchess said kindly, indicating that her ladies should remain at table. She took me to her own chamber, where she gave me cloths and scented water.

I apologised most abjectly. "Dear Varvara," she said, "I think you may be with child."

I was shocked. This was not something I had wanted. I had watched the Grand Duchess swell and had been glad my figure retained its slimness. I had helped care for her after her confinement and wrinkled my nose at the seepings of blood and milk.

The Duchess excused me from my duties for the rest of the day and I stayed in my chambers, agitated, pacing and pondering. And then I saw the light. Uncle's child would bind him to me. We could marry and be a family. The Empress would give her permission for she was well disposed to me and would no doubt be glad if Uncle settled down. His mother, my grandmother, would wish her grandchild – at the same time her great grandchild – to be born legitimate and inherit the Potemkin name and fortune. Yes, I thought in relief. It was really a blessing.

I told Uncle the same night. "Ah, Varvara," he said sadly, "I love you but this is our end. We cannot marry. I am bound to the Empress. But you shall marry and the child will have a father and a family. If that is what you would wish."

I berated him, shouted at him that he was the father, beat him with my fists as we lay there but he remained immovable.

"I will go to the Empress," I threatened. "She will make you marry me."

"Do so, my little kitten," he said as he caressed me soothingly, trying to quieten my sobs.

I did go to the Empress. It did not go well.

I told her of my condition. She glanced at my figure quickly and said, "Good that you come to me early enough. I presume the father is Prince Potemkin."

I assured her that I had been with no other man, that I loved my Uncle with my whole heart. The Empress frowned at my words.

"Ah, love," she said. "It comes in many forms."

I took a deep breath and pleaded, "Perhaps we might marry?" I had meant to present my case in a more

54

persuasive way, using reason rather than emotion, for the Empress, it is known, can often be convinced by good argument, but I was overcome by my feelings and tears came unbidden to my eyes.

The Empress gave a startled look and did not speak for a few moments. I was afraid to interrupt her thoughts. When she resumed speaking, her voice was cold. "Many love the Prince, including, as you know, myself. But can he marry us all? And can he serve his Empress loyally if he is married to one? Would not another woman then stand higher than his Empress?"

Anger was creeping into her voice but I blurted out, "But the child?"

"It is not his first," she said. "All children in my Empire and especially at my Court are taken care of regardless of who fathered them. Or indeed, who their mothers are."

The tears coursed down my cheeks. I knew now my dream was a hopeless one.

"But," the Empress continued more briskly, "if you wish a family for your child, we shall find you one. You may marry someone of your choosing. Prince Potemkin will help. You may then stay at Court. But if you wish, you may return to your father in – Smolensk?"

"Chizova, Your Majesty, some hours from Smolensk." Its name conjured up the provincial boredom I had escaped.

"Ah yes, quite ... remote. Well then, you may return there or marry here. That is all I have to say on the matter. And it is a sign of my affection for you that I have given you a choice."

I curtseyed, knowing I had been dismissed.

As I reached the door, the Empress called my name.

I turned back and she said, in the voice of a strict governess, "And I do not wish Prince Potemkin to be troubled by this matter. I ordered you to keep him happy and this is still your duty. Do not burden him. Do I make myself clear?"

"Yes, Your Majesty," I whispered.

My initial shock has been replaced by relief. I think Uncle will always be fond of me, and I of him, but I need a calmer love, a safer one. As the Empress suggested, I have been looking for a suitable husband. I must not delay for obvious reasons. There are many men who have paid me court but there is one who is handsome, rich and belongs to a very influential family. If it had not been for Uncle, I would have fallen in love with him. Perhaps I will now. I will ask Uncle.

Alexandra
October 1778

Dear Anna,

I sometimes envy you your married idyll, removed from the responsibilities which normally befall the eldest of six sisters. I have taken your place and it is not easy. I navigate the intricacies of this Court, which revolves around the Empress's favour, trying to sail my sisters into safe waters. Varvara has demanded much of my attention recently. First, she is petulant about our Uncle, demanding his undivided attention, then she declares herself with child by him and tells the Empress she is going to marry him. Ah, she is fortunate not to have been sent off to Siberia! But it would have cooled her hot head.

The Empress was generous and allowed her to seek a husband at Court. She has many admirers and chose one of the most sought after young men in the Empire, Prince Sergei of the famous Golitsyn family. He is cultivated and rich, handsome and impeccably mannered. He is a most excellent match. Our Uncle arranged the betrothal and it took place with great pomp at the palace on a warm autumn afternoon. I admit that they seemed a happy couple, even if Varvara lacked the normal rosiness in her cheeks. Prince Golitsyn brought her fine gifts of jewels and silks and even diamond necklets for her four sisters.

On the evening of the betrothal, Varvara woke screaming with pain from stomach colic. Dr Rogerson came and administered a tincture of opium, which calmed her. He opined that she was not with child and therefore had no child to lose – and indeed her stomach was very flat, almost concave for she had eaten little for weeks, and her breasts, as Dr Rogerson politely pointed out, were not swollen or tender. He said she was suffering from a digestive disorder and prescribed that the next morning she take a purging liquid, which he brought in a lidded metal cup. But when she woke, her courses came. This is what happens when one is as impulsive as Varvara. She catapults from one drama to the next, most of them of her own making. Still, she has got herself a most suitable husband and professes even to have fallen in love with him.

This leaves our Uncle unattended and vulnerable to all kinds of ambitious women. This is the Empress's opinion. She invited me, or rather summoned me, to a tête-à-tête. The conversation required all my skills of diplomacy. The Empress did not sit but paced up and down restlessly. While this is not conducive to a calm exchange of ideas, it did have the advantage of the Empress not being able to see my face when it showed shock or surprise despite my best efforts to hide my personal feelings, which should never receive consideration in imperial matters.

The Empress fears that Prince Potemkin will now be used by ruthless and ambitious women to gain power for themselves and their families. "But Prince Potemkin's loyalty and affections lie with you, Your Majesty," I say quietly. I do not add that the young men she has shared her bed with may also be hungry for power.

As if reading my thoughts, the Empress says, "The Prince and I have the highest regard for one another but we cannot live together. Our flames are too bright and burn the other. But there is nothing I would not do for him, or he for me."

I murmur my agreement.

"The danger, Alexandra," she continues, "is that one of these women may persuade him to take the throne himself."

It is a dreadful thought and I let out a gasp. "He would never —"

"Ah," she interrupts, "men in the throes of passion will promise anything. And the Prince is very fond of power, perhaps more fond of power than of me."

It is a terrible admission and I suddenly see the woman in the Empress. I think of Uncle and I see that there is some truth in what the Empress says. He is always at great pains to please the Empress but not because he loves her, as he may very well do, but in order to keep his own station in life, which is akin to being Emperor of all Russia. The lot of my sisters and myself relies on his station in life and so I must do everything to please the Empress too.

"If I or my sisters can be of any help, Your Majesty ... ," I say softly.

The Empress turns and looks at me sharply. "Yes, precisely. That is our solution. One of you must take Varvara's place!"

I think rapidly and know where the choice will fall.

"It must be you, Alexandra. Nadezhda will not ... attract the Prince and Katerina is too young. You have a level head and possess physical attributes that can be much enhanced with − " she waved her hand vaguely, " − well, we shall come to that. But most of all, you are loyal to me. You are like a daughter. I have taken you and your sisters not only into my Court but into my heart."

I am touched and pledge our eternal gratitude. But I have my doubts about the plan.

"Our Uncle, the Prince, may not ... desire me," I say hesitantly.

"Alexandra, you are said to be an astute businesswoman. I think you can apply the same principles to achieving success in this field too. Do what it takes. I rely upon you to protect Prince Potemkin for me."

I wonder whether she should have said "to protect me from Prince Potemkin".

And so I have a new task, dear Anna, and one I would rather not undertake. But the Empress is right − we cannot risk anyone usurping the affections of our Uncle, the great Prince Potemkin, Serenissimus, to their own ends and to our detriment. There is too much at stake and he is, as the Empress indicates, volatile and passionate in his affections. I will do my duty.

By the time this letter reaches you, you will be leaving for your husband's new post in Astrakhan. You will be the

Governor's wife! How good of Uncle to arrange it. But it removes you over 4000 versts from us! A letter cannot now be sent by personal courier – it would take him half a year there and half a year back! I will continue to write and save the letters for your return, which should be in two to three years, Uncle says. Where shall we all be then?

    With affection,
    Your sister Alexandra

PART TWO

Tatiana
February 1779

The Empress has advised me to keep a diary. She herself does and has done since she was younger than me, when she was still a German princess. The Empress says it teaches discipline and a tidy mind and will form my handwriting. I should start by writing about the good things that happen every day. And that is easy. My favourite time of the day is when I am with the Empress and her grandson.

I don't know why I used to be afraid of her. Perhaps she always seemed so strict and sad. But now she is really very gay and bright. She works very hard, always writing and thinking. "I cannot neglect my Empire any longer," she says. "I must leave it in good order for Alexander." I thought her son, the Grand Duke Paul, would be the next Emperor but we are not allowed to speak of any ruler except Empress Catherine herself so I am afraid to ask.

The Empress works all morning on new laws for Russia but in the afternoons her grandson Alexander is allowed to come to her. He is such a charming child, always smiling. He can walk very well now although he is just over a year old. I am permitted to keep him company and it is a great pleasure. The Empress thinks up all sorts of little games for him to play. "He thinks he is playing," she says, "but he is also learning." She laughs and claps her hands when he does something clever. I have never seen her so happy.

After Alexander, I think she loves her dogs best. They sit on her lap and knock over her ink and she just laughs. She gives them titbits to nibble. Alexander and I are allowed to play with them. They chase us and we chase them. The Empress can recognise each of her greyhounds by its bark. She covers her eyes and we tickle each in turn till they yelp. The Empress guesses and is never wrong.

She says one day her dogs will talk. It is very merry to be with the Empress. Today she had the court orchestra play some tunes for us. There was one piece that was made to sound like coughs and then we all tried to cough in a musical manner. Such music lessons are so much more fun than my singing lessons with Monsieur Chabot, who makes me sing scales till my head is throbbing. But I must only write about good things and my time with the Empress and Prince Alexander is a very good thing.

Varvara
April 1779

It is already the middle of April and the Grand Duchess Maria's second child has still not come. The Empress is impatient and berates the doctors, who said the child would arrive with the spring in March. "If the child does not come soon," the Empress says, "I will declare that the entire faculty of medicine doesn't know what it's talking about when it insists that women are pregnant for nine months. In future they must always add **but Mother Nature knows best."** I think the Empress remembers how the Grand Duke's first wife's child died within her, thus causing its own mother's death. The Empress is very fond of the Grand Duchess Maria and would not wish anything untoward to happen to her. The Grand Duchess assures the Empress that she can still feel the child moving within her.

I have already felt the quickening of my own child. I am content with my life. I miss Uncle but my husband is kind and affectionate. He is also very handsome and it is said we make the finest looking couple at Court. My very own Prince is also very rich and I want for nothing. I could not have chosen better. Our wedding in January was as sumptuous as I could have wished and even the Empress praised the celebrations. Uncle was present too and whispered his congratulations with a suggestion that brides were always welcome in his chambers. But I love my husband who is as passionate as Uncle. I would not betray him – at least, not without his permission. And in any case, Alexandra stands guard at Uncle's door.

The Empress is very happy these days and much as she was in the years before we met her, everyone says. If she knew what was going on behind her back, however, she would not be so happy. Her favourite Rimsky-Korsakov is deceiving the Empress in front of her very eyes. Everyone knows he is Countess Bruce's lover. But no one will dare to tell the Empress. Uncle is the one who recommended Rimsky-Korsakov and he should be the one to tell her but he is rarely at Court and when he is, he says we should not destroy the Empress's happy state – a state which has little to do with Rimsky-Korsakov. She is infatuated with her grandson and spends hours with him. When my child comes, I will not be so besotted that I do not see what my husband is doing. I will also continue to take care of my appearance. The Empress has taken to wearing a more Russian style of dress, which falls loosely and unattractively from her shoulders, perhaps to hide her growing plumpness. No amount of diamonds – and she wears many – can bring back the brilliance of youth. And she should wear less rouge.

Countess Bruce, on the other hand, although the same age as the Empress, masks her five decades with fine French fashions and a slim enough figure. Thankfully, I do not have to think about such things for several decades. My beauty is often praised, especially by my dear husband. My story is now our story.

Nadezhda
July 1779

I do not have many facts to record since life at Court has become peaceful and regular. The Empress is happy. She celebrated her 50th birthday on 21st April and her second grandson was born on 27th April. He is to be named Constantine because he will be heir to the Byzantine Empire of the Greeks. Uncle says that once Russia has defeated the Ottoman Empire, Constantinople will return to Russia. The child is to have a Greek nurse and learn to speak and read Greek in preparation for his great future. But this great future is not being prepared as Alexander's is. Constantine cries a lot and the Empress says he may stay with his mother. The Russian Empire seems more important to her than the Greek one but Uncle says the Greek Empire is part of Russia's future and he will work towards achieving this great goal.

The Empress has a new project, which has caught my interest. She wishes to add ten new rooms to the palace at Tsarskoye Selo inspired by designs in a book of architecture she received from Naples. I find architecture so satisfying. One deals with indisputable figures, lines and angles. The result is a pleasing tangible whole.

I am allowed to be present when the Empress consults with different architects. She is not so fond of the French ones because, she says, "they know too much and therefore they put too much into their buildings." The Empress declares she is addicted to building. Once you start, she says, you cannot stop. But she is not easy to please and is dissatisfied with most of her architects. "They are," she complains, "too old, or too blind, or too slow, or too lazy, or too young, or too idle, or too much the grand seigneur, or too rich, or too respectable, or too stale ... " One might wonder who is left.

However, the plans of a Scottish architect, Charles Cameron, have at last caught her attention. I find him very grumpy and cannot imagine him designing harmonious buildings but his drawings are meticulous and pleasing in their pure, classic lines. I do not think this style will suit the exuberance of the palace but the Empress has said Mr Cameron may begin by adding something to the gardens. She wishes a design which would "summarize the age of the Caesars, the Augustuses, the Ciceros and such patrons as Maecenas and to create a building where it would be possible to find all these people in one." The Empress aspires to the purity of the classical. Varvara, who has a sharp tongue, says that would be the only purity in her life.

Alexandra
August 1779

Dear Anna,

Oh, I am tired of all the talk of births and babies, of clever children and dogs! That is all this Court is engrossed with. One can add balls and masquerades, music and art, but is that how to rule an Empire? What energy the Empress does not use in educating her grandson and dogs, she invests in projects which will bring Russia no power or territory. She is determined to have copies of the Raphael murals from Rome and has promised to reconstruct a part of the Vatican Palace here in St Petersburg to house them – and she declares she will have neither peace nor repose until they are with her. She underwent the same fever of acquisition with Voltaire's library, which she has now bought for 30,000 roubles in addition to "gifts" of many diamonds and furs. Would that not be enough? No, she must also have the late Sir Robert Walpole's collection of paintings. Sir James Harris says the price agreed on was 40,000 sterling pounds and a frigate has just left for England to collect the 204 paintings, which include works by Titian, Rubens, van Dyck, Murillo, Holbein, Rembrandt, Velazquez and Raphael. I cannot think why King George did not wish to rescue this national treasure but apparently he has been too embroiled in war with the colonies to think about or fund art. Sir Walpole's son is said to be beside himself with rage, his dislike for our Empress well known. He has called her the Crocodile and other such terrible epithets. The Empress is positively gleeful. "Horace Walpole should know that crocodiles sneak up and snatch their prey with no mercy," she said.

I think the only serious political thinkers at the Russian Court are Uncle and myself. The foreign envoys approach us for they know the Empress is preoccupied with matters domestic and artistic. She will not make any decision. She is polite and friendly and accepts all gifts graciously – the

French are particularly extravagant – but will not be drawn out of her neutrality in Europe. Sir James Harris is downcast. He complains that diplomacy costs too much, most of it from his own pocket.

"Then your government must pay more for what it values," I tell him gently.

"We do not have the funds to influence those who have influence," he complains politely. "They are too rich already."

In this he is right. The Empress rewards her courtiers well and ensures their loyalty. But in truth, most of them are interested only in their own lives of ease and would not put themselves out.

"And even if one does present gifts," Harris continues, "no matter who it is – the French, the Austrians, the Prussians, myself – I cannot recollect that the donors did not think they had given too much and the receivers that they had got too little. In this we envoys all agree."

I assure him that I am always grateful for any gift, however small. I have expanded my timber business and have now added hemp. The British have been importing it from us since the time of Peter the Great for sailcloth for their ships, and their needs have not decreased. The British may boast of their navy but without our raw materials, they would not have one. I have also heard that iron is much sought after and we have started mining that in the Urals. In truth, I will soon be in a wealthy enough position not to take gifts for my influences, but what is given for free is never valued and thus I will continue to act as an ally where I can. Political knowledge, I have learned, is invaluable capital with good interests.

The British become more desperate in their overtures. They have offered the Empress the island of Minorca in exchange for Russian help to rid the American colonies of the French but the Empress does not want to enter war, especially not in Europe, if she were to receive no help against the Ottoman Empire in return.

Harris asked the Empress, "Since you will not support our sovereign claim over our American colonies, Your Majesty, can I assume you would give them their independence?"

"I'd rather lose my head," she retorted.

Minorca, Uncle points out, would draw Russia into war, for the French and Spanish have wrested it from the British several times and will try to do so again. "We must save our resources and ships for further seas." By this, he means the Black Sea.

The Tartar Khanate is now ruled independently from the Ottoman Empire but under Russian guarantee. Those were the terms of the peace. The Khan is Shagin Giray, whom Catherine invited to Court some years ago. He seems to have made a most favourable impression on her. "He speaks Italian and Greek, having been educated in Venice," she says, almost wistfully. "He is a most gentle Tatar, very talented, bronze-coloured, good-looking, circumcised and writes poetry. He wanted to see and learn everything." It would have been better had she not mentioned the circumcision.

Her gentle Khan, however, rules most despotically and his infidel ways have roused the ire of the Sultan, who is still the religious head of the Crimea. Although the peace treaty forced the Sultan to relinquish the Crimea, the Ottoman Empire has clung to strategic forts. It is a tense situation and must be resolved. It has cost the Empress seven million roubles to keep Shagin Giray on the Crimean throne these last five years and Uncle rightly says it is time for action. The Crimea must be annexed and become a part of the Russian Empire before the Sultan claims it back for the Ottoman Empire.

But how do we claim the attention of the Empress from her children, dogs and art? She rises early and professes to work on legislation in the morning hours but she seems to spend more time on her Russian primer to teach children to read, which she plans to follow with Russian stories for children. Russian? On would think an educated child must first read French.

Uncle assures me, however, that she is still working on her great Provincial Reform. She has already structured the justice system with new courts and the financial administration and is now working, he says, on ideas for the welfare of her subjects. "No subject is too small for her," he adds. "She directs schools to be set up and what should be taught but also how long the windows should remain open – in summer and in winter. She rules who should lie where in hospitals and for how long. She lists punishments for the new correction houses, food plans for the workhouses for the poor – there is no detail which escapes her attention." Perhaps that is the problem.

You will be more interested, dear Anna, in my personal life which in truth is inseparable from the political. I have fulfilled my duty to the Empress and our family by taking Varvara's place at Uncle's side – but not in his bed, although we do not dispel those rumours that say I am his mistress. I am his closest confidante after the Empress, which is a position of more substance and durability than that of a lover. I think he treats me much as one would a wife. I host his dinners and parties, I organise his household and I act as a deterrent to the droves of women who would seduce him away from me – and the Empress. He listens to my advice on all matters and helps me with my business ventures. We have an amicable and productive partnership. The Empress is pleased. There are occasional dramas of a minor nature due to Uncle's passionate nature but I have a reliable system of well-paid informants amongst the servants and am normally apprised of any dangerous liaison before it happens.

We have just had the infamous Count di Cagliostro in St Petersburg. I do not know whether his notoriety as an alchemist and necromancer of the Egyptian Masonic rite has reached you in Astrakhan. He claims to be able to make gold out of base metals, even out of urine, if you will forgive my lack of delicacy – although I do not know whether animal or human.

He also claims he can provide eternal life or eternal youth – his own master, he says, has lived for 2000 years and witnessed the Crucifixion of Christ. What blasphemy!

But many fools believe him – and are easily parted from their money. The Empress does not. Uncle professes not to but has been to several séances. The Count is an ugly little man but his wife, or she who he says is his wife, is young and ... exotic. I learned from my informants that Uncle's visits were not to the Count but to the so-called Countess and that he was in thrall to her charms.

The Empress was not pleased when she found out. Until then she had joked about the gullibility of her courtiers who fell for Cagliostro's tricks, as she called them, but now she says, "I tolerate the Freemasons – many of my most loyal officers are members – but I remain vigilant. Their secrecy is an unknown weapon, and I do not like that women are excluded from membership. Who knows? They may be plotting to get rid of me and put Prince Potemkin on my throne. Or even my son. Both are vulnerable, the Prince for his passion and my son through his naiveté. We must save the Prince from the sinuous Countess and the greedy clutches of the Count."

I suggested the Empress just banish the charlatans from Russia but she said that would be seen as banishment of the Masons, which would incur great opposition not only in Russia but in all Europe. She would bide her time for such a move.

In the meantime we hatched a plan. I, veiled and incognito, arranged to meet the Countess. Oh, she was such a courtesan! She had little finesse but much of what men like, which was very evident since her dress was scanty and gaudy. I offered to pay her to leave the Prince, arguing that it was more than she received from staying with him. She knew how to bargain but was also greedy for money and we agreed on 30,000 roubles (the Empress had said I may go to 50,000).

Uncle found out about our ploy, I do not know how, but he too has well-paid informants and I think that although we are both on the same side, several of our informants take money from more than one party. Uncle thought it was all very amusing and laughed quite heartily. "I am especially pleased that the Empress looks to my welfare. Perhaps there was a touch of jealousy?"

Indeed Uncle is in very good spirits, as is everyone at Court, but I fear the peace will not last long. The Empress's favourite becomes bolder in his liaison with Countess Bruce and it cannot escape the Empress's attention for much longer. I hope the storm that is brewing passes without causing too much damage.

With affection,
Your sister Alexandra

Katerina
October 1779

Oh, the last weeks have been dreadful. The Empress has been betrayed most cruelly, her happiness in shards like a broken mirror. When I said this to Alexandra, she remarked, "Well, the mirror was badly cracked and needed replacing." Alexandra can be very harsh and only someone of her character could have done what was done. Everyone knew that the Empress's favourite was spending all his time with Countess Bruce, who was besotted with him. One would come across the Empress in the corridors asking, "Has anyone seen Rimsky-Korsakov? Where is he?" It was indeed pitiful but no one would have told her what was going on.

Countess Bruce became arrogant, behaving as if she were the Empress herself. Uncle no longer had any influence on her. She refused to give Rimsky-Korsakov up. "Bring the Empress to me and let him decide between the two of us!" she declared. Meanwhile, the Orlovs were said to have found a new favourite and were preparing to expose Rimsky-Korsakov. Only Prince Orlov's deep affection for the Empress made him hesitate to make her unhappy and so the matter was delayed, giving Uncle and Alexandra time to make their own move.

When the Empress was next found in the corridor asking for her favourite, Alexandra appeared and offered to take her to him. They walked into Countess Bruce's chambers without being announced – the Empress need never be announced – and witnessed the couple in a very compromising situation. I myself fail to see the attraction and do not wish to imagine what the Empress actually witnessed. The Countess is as old as the Empress, and Rimsky-Korsakov, although young, is empty-headed and bad-mannered. How awful it must have been. Alexandra said the Empress turned pale but kept calm and said, "You are occupied. Forgive my intrusion." But when she reached her own chambers, she wept bitterly. "Who can I trust? I am betrayed on all sides." Uncle came and took her in his arms, most tenderly, Alexandra said, and they both stayed with her for several hours.

Rimsky-Korsakov was dismissed from Court – with a generous allowance from the Empress, which shows such nobility and magnanimity. That should have been the end of the story but he immediately fell in love with Countess Katerina Stroganova, a great beauty at Court, and she left her husband and child for him. The Empress was very angry. She dispatched Rimsky-Korsakov to Moscow and ordered Stroganova to return to her husband. The rejected Countess Bruce, however, seized her chance and followed her lover to Moscow.

She has now returned, much chastened, since Rimsky-Korsakov will not have her. Twice spurned, she is now much disillusioned. And so she should be. He is apparently making a name for himself at dinners recounting his sexual exploits with both the Empress and Countess Bruce, at times together he says, in lurid and untrue detail. Such a monster! Countess Bruce would now seek reconciliation with the Empress, who has refused, ordering the Countess to return and serve her long-suffering husband in atonement.

I sit embroidering with the Grand Duchess Maria. It is peaceful here, a place of goodness. When she listens to the unfolding drama, which I recount in lighter strokes for she is a pure soul, the Grand Duchess sighs. "If these are Russian ways," she says, "I do not wish to learn them."

Tatiana
November 1779

Varvara has had her child. She has called him Grigory after Uncle. We call him Little Grigory. He is still swaddled tightly so there is not much to see of him but he seems content and does not cry as much as Constantine. As a mother, Varvara is not like the Grand Duchess. She leaves Little Grigory to his nurses, visiting him briefly once a day. But so it is with many of the ladies at Court. They return to the balls and masquerades as if nothing has happened. "There will be time enough to form him when he is out of babyhood," Varvara says. "There is not much one can do beforehand."

The Empress would not agree. She has had Alexander with her for hours every day since he was a few weeks old. She talks to him in an adult way, discussing topics even I do not understand. He can hardly talk but she is teaching him his letters and he can recognise A. He is dressed in a little chemise with a loose knitted jacket. "A child must have freedom of movement," the Empress says. In summer, he toddled around barefooted and without a bonnet. The Empress says she will teach him to swim next summer.

Although it is now winter and I wear my little fur cape even indoors, little Alexander still wears much the same clothes as in the warmer months and must still have his cold bath every day. But he is a very happy child and is never sick. His brother Constantine, on the other hand, is always poorly. The Empress says she will be surprised if he survives. Still, he has been given a Greek nurse, who is to speak only Greek to him. Her name is Helen and she is very beautiful and kind.

Uncle says that the only language of civilisation is Greek, which he reads well. "We cannot rely on incompetent translators," he says. "We must get to the origins ourselves." The Empress has agreed to add Greek to the Princes' education but she is more interested in writing Russian books for children. She has finished the reading primer and is now composing Russian tales for young people, which are to be edifying as well as entertaining. The Empress will try them out on me and I look forward to it.

Alexandra
January 1780

Dear Anna,

The New Year has brought fresh winds! The Empress has declared her intention to rid the Court of lazeabouts. "Everyone must have something useful to do," she says, "and I shall set an example. As I used to. I have been distracted and betrayed by love and I shall now devote my whole attention to my loyal subjects."

There has been a great flurry of papers. Her Provincial Reform has been brought from the Academy and Zavadovsky has been recalled to help. She has made it clear that his position will be one of able – and well-paid – secretary and administrator for he excels in these functions. The Empress says she trusts him and that since he had transcribed the reforms for her, he knows where everything is.

She explained all this when she was at dinner with us recently, ***en famille*** with Uncle and my sisters and Prince Golitsyn. The Empress intends to undertake a tour of her Empire to inspect how her reforms are being implemented. "It has been almost five years and I would hope to see a leap from paper to practice," she declared.

"It would be an excellent opportunity to visit your new territories gained from Poland," Uncle suggested. "The Pskov and Mogilev Governorates. It would be encouraging for your new subjects to see their sovereign."

"Yes, it shall be a Grand Tour," the Empress said enthusiastically. "We shall set off as soon as the snows have melted." She then turned to Nadezhda. "You may come and record as much as you can in your diary. You are an alert observer."

"And may I come too, Your Majesty?" Tatiana asked.

"Ah, but little Alexander must not miss both of us," the Empress answered gently. "I confess I am reluctant to leave him and you must keep him cheerful in my absence."

The Empress drank a second glass of wine, which was unusual. She had also eaten well.

"Perhaps Your Majesty would care to meet Count Falkenstein on your travels?" Uncle asked.

The Empress looked up sharply. "Who?"

Uncle then turned to Prince Golitsyn, "My dear Prince, perhaps you would accompany the ladies to tonight's musical entertainment. The Empress and I shall join you forthwith."

As I rose to go with the others, Uncle asked me to stay should the Empress require anything. I knew what the subject of the conversation would be. Uncle had informed me and I had given what advice I could. The English would not like it. And it would make of Prussia an enemy.

As soon as the door had closed, the Empress asked, "And who is Count Falkenstein?"

"Ah, that is the incognito the Emperor of Austria has decided upon," Uncle said. "He apparently always uses it when he travels."

"But I have not agreed to meet him!" Catherine said, almost angrily, I thought.

"Emperor Joseph goes against his mother in seeking a meeting with Your Majesty," Uncle said carefully. "The Empress Maria Teresa has not been a friend of Russia."

"She rules too long," Catherine said dismissively. "Some forty years. Why, she must be very old." In truth, the Empress of Austria is not much more than ten years older than Catherine herself.

"It is said she is indeed not in good health," Uncle said.

"Which is why her son has the courage at last to do something on his own initiative," Catherine retorted.

It is true that the Emperor Joseph had sought a meeting with the Empress. Uncle had shown me the letter from Vienna.

"This is the opportunity we have dreamed of, Catherine!" Uncle took the Empress's hands in his own. "An renewal of our alliance with Austria will pave our way south, to the Empire of the Greeks. We will civilise the world! With Austria on our side, the Ottoman Empire is no threat!"

"Prussia will not like it," Catherine said hesitantly. "I do not wish to turn an ally into an enemy."

"Prussia will not seek war," Uncle said firmly. "At least, not with us."

"I will not be drawn into Austria's squabbles with Prussia," Catherine said. "Austria has been an unreliable ally, courting the French to stave off Prussia."

"But it has been at times a most worth ally, fighting at our side, especially against the Ottoman Empire," Uncle said. "We would not want the Austrians on the other side. An alliance between Austria and France would destroy our dreams of a great Empire in the East. You must rule this new Empire, no other. No other can bring enlightenment. And civilisation. The French would try once they are free of their feuds in the American colonies. Joseph is Holy Roman Emperor and does not seek another Empire but he would see you as his partner – Empress of the Holy Russian and Greek Empires, perhaps?"

I could see that Uncle's words had roused the Empress's interest. Her face was slightly flushed and she smiled.

"Yes, we could bequeath such a legacy to my grandsons. Alexander as Emperor over Russia and Constantine as Emperor in the East. We could establish court in Constantinople. Or even Athens."

"Then you will meet with Emperor Joseph?" Uncle could not disguise his eagerness.

"Yes," the Empress agreed, "it is my duty to rescue those peoples who have lived too long under the yoke of the infidel. We must salvage what vestiges of Greek civilisation remain and rekindle its flame! Arrange a meeting with ... Count Falkenstein when I am inspecting Mogilev. It is indeed a good opportunity, dear Grigory."

Sir James Harris will not like this new turn of events. He knows of the Empress's Greek passion – why, they sometimes even converse in Greek together. But the British do not want Russia to turn southwards. They would have us as an ally in the north, particularly against France. But in truth, their main interest is to protect their trade routes. In my opinion, the British excel more in commerce than in empire building. They were careless enough to lose their colonies. Empress Catherine would never have allowed that.

Your affectionate sister,
Alexandra

Katerina
April 1780

The Empress's new lover is younger than Alexandra and Varvara. He is but 22, scarcely older than me, not just young enough to be her son but even her grandson. Countess Vorontsova is the same age as the Empress and her grandson is eighteen. I know because he seems to have been paying me particular court and I made it my business to find out as much as I could about him. He is too young for me. I would like someone older, like Uncle.

The Empress, however, likes her favourites young. The older she becomes, the younger her adjutants. Varvara says she looks at them as she would fine horses, for which she has a very good eye. They must show good pedigree, strong muscles, particularly in the leg, have a certain gloss and symmetrical features. This Varvara has from Uncle. "I once possessed such attributes," he said, "but now I must content myself with affection and loyalty. I will not be usurped by one of these young colts. All I can do is make sure they come from my own stable and answer to my commands."

But Uncle did not choose Alexander Lanskoy. The Empress did. He had been one of Uncle's aides-de-camp for a few months, a Horseman Guard with a very fine figure. Uncle actually had another Guardsman in mind for the Empress – and the Orlovs were also busy selecting their own candidate.

Whenever we attended Church, the way was lined with handsome young men, standing upright, perfectly groomed, hoping to catch the Empress's attention. And one of them did. Uncle was taken unawares when Catherine demanded that he bring Lanskoy to her. Although he was not able to dissuade the Empress in her choice, Uncle's acquiescence did not go unrewarded. He has added another estate to his possessions as well as several thousand serfs. He must own half of Russia by now,

I joked. "Ah," he said, "I think you will find that Count Orlov and his brothers own more."

I do not understand Uncle's concerns about Lanskoy. He is affable and, like Rimsky-Korsakov before him, loves to strut around bedecked in jewels. He wears a cluster of diamonds on his shoulder, rather like an epaulette but in the form of a large brooch, and this is now much imitated at Court. The Empress is happy with his companionship. She has gifted him a library of some 10,000 volumes. Alexandra declares, in her waspish way, that he will never read any of them. "Fortunately," she adds. "For we do not need an educated favourite. He should concentrate on the Empress's pleasure while Uncle and I take care of her power and politics."

The Empress's plans to inspect her Empire are near completion. The entourage will leave in some few weeks. I am not to be of the party and I am glad. Alexandra and Uncle will go and Nadezhda too. She is very excited but the travails of travel hold no attraction for me. I will stay with the Grand Duchess Maria and savour the quiet such an enterprise will bring to the Court.

Nadezhda
May 1780

I am so glad the Empress allowed me to come on the inspection of her Empire. She was right – it provides ample opportunity to fill my diary with matters of substance.

We left from Tsarskoye Selo on 9th May. It was a fine day as we set off and the ways were crowded with people watching our procession pass. With nearly a hundred carriages we must have made quite a sight. At every stage, 450 horses are needed.

As chief lady-in-waiting, Alexandra travels in the Empress's carriage and I am often invited to join them. Uncle has travelled ahead to make sure all arrangements are as they should be for the Empress, and we all miss his company. Alexander Lanskoy, the Empress's new favourite, sometimes rides on horseback but the Empress likes to have him near her and often bids him join her in the carriage. "I like to ride," she says, "and I am a very able horsewoman, but I would rather not risk my bones when I have so much work to accomplish." Alexandra says she is much too heavy for a horse.

Our first stop was Narva, a distance of some 120 versts. We did not reach it till late the next day due to several stops for the Empress to receive courtesies from the local nobility on the way. Narva is protected by a huge bastion, built by the Swedes, which faces an equally imposing fortress across the river, built by the Russians two centuries ago. "Thus you see," the Empress said, "the confrontation of empires so much more vividly than on the pages of a history book. Narva has swung from being Swedish to Russian and back several times but it is now in my hands and I do not intend to allow the Swedes to regain it. The people are my subjects and are no doubt content to be so."

The old city is built in what I must suppose is the Swedish style, with fine stone houses and narrow streets. But the Empress was anxious to travel on so we did not linger although I would like to have seen the sea, but a few versts from the city. Our itinerary, however, as I could see from the map the Empress took from the large roll she had with her, led us south away from the coast.

On 13th May, we were already in Pskov, the way there dotted with small villages. The city is one of Russia's oldest and it too is a living history lesson. It is surrounded by stout walls – at one time five rings of them, witness to the many sieges it suffered as the Polish, the Livonians, the Swedes and many more tried to take it throughout the centuries. Alexander Nevsky reconquered it from the Teutonic Knights in the thirteenth century, and the Empress ordered wooden models of the fortress and walls for little Alexander.

The Empress writes notes constantly, mostly with a frown. She does not seem to be pleased with the government of her provinces. She has begun a list of Urgent Matters to Attend To.

There was an amusing incident during our stay in Pskov. I was helping Alexandra make the Empress's room comfortable and warm for the night. The Empress had been dining with a local princess and came into the chamber, licking her lips in distaste. "My lips seems saturated with salt " she said, "and it is very unpleasant." Alexandra rushed to her and said, "But Your Majesty, your lips are quite white." Alexandra spent some time rubbing the Empress's lips gently to remove the strange oily substance. "Why, Your Majesty," she said, "I do believe it is Venetian ceruse!" The Empress laughed. "Ah yes, the princess's face which I kissed in friendship as I left was indeed very white! If her husband makes a habit of kissing her, he must get very thirsty!" I was happy to see the Empress in such good humour. Alexandra explained to me later that ceruse was made of white lead and used by ladies to whiten their skins, which was considered a sign of nobility. "It is very old-fashioned but we must keep a flask

84

of water at hand at all times for no doubt the Empress will have to embrace many more provincial whitened ladies."

We continued south, about fifty or sixty versts each day. The hilly landscape south of Pskov was gentle and well cultivated, vividly green in the May sunshine. In Ostrov, we attended church before travelling on to Opochka, the capital of one of the new governorates created by the Empress's Provincial Reform. On 19th May, we arrived in Polotsk, which had, until recently, belonged to Poland.

The Empress once more pointed out the lessons of history to me. "You will note, Nadezhda, that there is no unity of inhabitant here. All are mixed: Russians, Polish, Finns, Germans, Courlanders, Orthodox, Catholics, Jews ... There are no two people dressed in the same costumes who speak the same language correctly or accurately. It is a mixture of people and languages as at the building of the Tower of Babel." Indeed, I had noted the lack of common dress and language and found it more intimidating than fascinating. Everyone seems to be a stranger and one cannot tell friend from foe. "My task," the Empress continued, "is to bring unity and conformity to my subjects. They must know they are Russian and act like Russians and follow Russian laws. It is a tremendous task and I have much more work to do but people will obey what they see as fair. And I am a just and fair sovereign."

This is why her Provincial Reform is so important, she said. Her laws must be administered by loyal governors. There must be systems and procedures and all must be the same throughout the Empire. Her list of Urgent Matters to Attend To is already very long.

In Polotsk, the Empress visited the Jesuit colleges and was impressed by their schools. Still, she said they must follow her own school reforms, which would be put in place the following year.

We have almost reached Mogilev, where the meeting between the Empress and the Holy Roman Emperor, Joseph II, will take place. We are to refer to him as Count

Falkenstein but everyone knows who he really is. We stop at the estate of Semyon Zorich, one of the Empress's former favourites. It is still light when we arrive and the Empress praises Zorich's vast gardens. The landscape is indeed green and pleasant but I see no gardens. "That is the point of the English style," the Empress says. "Nature should be seen in her own glory rather than that of the gardener." We pass through a great triumphal arch. "For me or for him?" the Empress asks, but she greets Zorich most cordially. He has arranged lavish celebrations for the Empress's visit – theatre, a banquet (served on a dinner service said to have cost 50,000 roubles), a ball, fireworks ... but we do not stay for all the entertainment. The Empress pleads fatigue during the banquet but as we reach her chambers, she says scornfully, "What low company Zorich invites to his tables – Frenchmen, Italians, Germans, Serbs, Greeks, Moldavians – I don't think there was one Russian apart from my entourage. And the music was agony to my ears but what can one expect from a Jewish band dressed in Turkish costumes?" I agree with the Empress – such a mélange of people is confusing. Alexandra whispers later, "Why, the Empress herself is not even Russian!" This is treason and I immediately put my hands over my ears.

Tomorrow the great meeting will take place. I wish I could be there but it is a secret meeting (which the whole of Europe knows about) and only a very few will be with the Empress, including Uncle and Alexandra. I will occupy myself by finishing my copies of the Empress's maps. I have marked our passage and note that although we have travelled much in fifteen days, it seems we have not travelled very far. We are just over 500 versts from St Petersburg, which is a hundred versts less than the distance one would travel directly to Moscow, which now lies east of us, about equidistant to St Petersburg. If we return to St Petersburg via Moscow, we will have completed a fairly neat triangle, which is evidence of good planning. I also see that Smolensk lies on the way to Moscow, but I doubt the Empress will wish to visit our home village of Chizova.

Alexandra
May 1780

Dear Anna,

There has not been much time for correspondence on our tour but it is of little consequence since I do not send my letters to you in Astrakhan but write them to remind me what to tell you when we do meet again. And to remind myself of events as they happen. I suppose in a way I am now keeping a diary, although Nadezhda is our diarist. Still, although observant and conscientious, there is much she does not know.

We have had to cancel many parts of our tour in the last few days due to some sense of competition in the Empress. She suddenly wanted to reach Mogilev before the Emperor (whom I refuse to call Count Falkenstein since it is all a meaningless charade) and so ordered the tour to be cut by four days. The Emperor heard of this and raced day and night to get there before her, which he has done by two days. So childish.

Our entrance into Mogilev was impressive and ceremonial, most fitting for an Empress of Russia. Her carriage, in which I also sat, was preceded by a procession of Polish nobility on horseback and enough hussars, cuirassiers and generals to impress a Holy Roman Emperor. Cannons boomed and church bells rang. But etiquette soon trapped us in an anti-climax. The Emperor insisted on his incognito and would only meet the Empress with no others present. "That is well nigh impossible," the Empress said. "When I get back from mass, people will be milling around me. To postpone it till dinner would be discourteous." Eventually, she suggested the Emperor come to her ante-chamber while she was at mass, and she would make her way directly there.

Fortunately, everything worked out well and our week here has been most successful. The two great rulers liked each other instantly. Even although the Empress knew she had to like the Emperor if she wanted him as her ally, she was almost light-hearted with relief that she genuinely liked him. "The Emperor likes to talk," she observed happily, "and he is brimful of ideas for reform. He has much learning but wears it lightly. We are very comfortable with each other." This was most noticeable when they were both chatting and laughing most irreverently during a Roman Catholic mass. The Emperor has also attended Orthodox services.

Uncle had arranged lighter entertainment – some theatre, a comic opera and fireworks. The Emperor, however, is of a very abstemious nature, going to bed early, rising early, eating only once every 24 hours and drinking nothing but water. Our week, therefore, has been very modest.

What the Emperor does like is inspections and parades – as if, Uncle says disparagingly, it would turn him into a Frederick the Great. But we comply and a tent is built for the monarchs to view displays of horsemanship, in which Uncle also took part. His regiment charged from some distance, Uncle at the head, and one felt the earth tremble as the hooves thundered towards us, stopping suddenly in perfect formation just as we gasped with fear. Uncle grumbles about having to accompany the Emperor on his early morning rounds of troop inspection, using predicted bad weather as an excuse to postpone, but the Empress says he must do what Joseph wishes even if the heavens themselves were to open.

And so, Empress Catherine has now secured Austria as her ally. Uncle would wish that she address the Greek Project more but the Empress has reassured him. "Both the Emperor and I have Byzantine in our very souls," she declared. With this we must be content and trust that the souls communicate with political realities.

The weather has been very hot and the Empress suffers her habitual excess of sweating. She confides that she is embarrassed when conversing so enthusiastically with

Emperor Joseph and so wears more wraps to mask her condition, which only serves to make it worse. She does not like to use a fan, although I have laid out her largest one with the ivory mounts and the rich painting of classical gods and goddesses, which I thought most appropriate. "It would seem as if I were rebutting the words of the Emperor," she said, "if I wave a fan between us." I have had the maids place a large tub of water in her chambers and they are instructed to keep the water cool by changing it regularly.

We leave for Smolensk tomorrow, 30th May. The Empress and the Emperor will travel in one carriage together. They are inseparable. I do not know why she brought Alexander Lanskoy with her. He has been most neglected but bears it patiently, as he must. If two great monarchs are pleasing to each other, there is nothing he, or any of us, can do. The Emperor, at least a decade younger than the Empress, is not unattractive, and is said to be inordinately fond of women. Word has seeped out from his retinue that when he feels that he might fall in love, he goes to a woman of pleasure to rid himself of the desire. He does not wish to be tied to a woman, nor does he wish to lose another. His first wife was the beautiful Isabella of Parma, whom he married when he was but twenty years old. It is said he loved her dearly but she loved his sister the Archduchess Maria Christina more. Still, Isabella bore Joseph a daughter before she herself died of smallpox after only three years of marriage. Joseph was distraught but worse was to come when his only child died of pleurisy when she was seven years old. Joseph took a second wife in order to lay claim to Bavaria but he did not love her and she too died of smallpox. The Empress said, "None of this would have happened to him had the Austrians had their people inoculated against smallpox as I have done. There is no fear of my dying of the disease."

While Uncle is very pleased that the alliance will now take place, he is concerned about the growing intimacy between the sovereigns. "I will not be usurped or have my dreams destroyed, even by an Emperor," he said to me on the eve of our departure from Mogilev. To remind the Empress of her true loyalties, he has arranged that she visit our home village of Chizova, where Uncle was also born.

I have no great longing to see our old home, which we left five years ago. I am a different person now, someone of note, and if I have not acquired the veneer of sophistication that I first aimed for at the Russian Court, I have acquired power and influence as Uncle's mistress and the Empress's trusted confidante.

    Your affectionate sister,
    Alexandra

Nadezhda
June 1780

The journey back to St Petersburg was uneventful but very hot and dusty. We came straight from Smolensk where Uncle left us to travel to Moscow with Count Falkenstein. Uncle was in very bad humour about this but the Empress insisted the Count must see the "other capital" but she herself had no wish to return to a city she did not trust or like. Besides which, she added, Uncle was more in tune with the traditional Russia, of which Moscow was the capital. She, the Empress, was sovereign of a new Russia, an enlightened one.

Our visit to our birthplace Chizova, just a few hours detour from our route through Smolensk, proved how right the Empress is. It is a world apart from St Petersburg but not as Russian as the Empress thinks. Smolensk has defended the road to Moscow for centuries. Lithuania, Poland and Russia all fought for it, with terrible sieges and slaughters. It has been part of Russia for over a hundred years now but its Polish past has not been completely eradicated. Many still wear the long tunic of the Polish nobility – I remember Grandfather did – and Uncle does when he is at home. "But we are not Polish, Nadezhda," he tells me. "When you write in your diary, say that we are descended from Italian and Dalmatian nobility."

Father greeted us at the gates of the village, of which he is now sole head. It had been Uncle's inheritance but he relinquished it to his eldest sister, our mother, when he left to make his way in the world. Father was pleased to see us but his full attention had to be given to the Empress during our visit, which was too short to allow for any private family time together. And after all, we are now the Empress's family. Father looked well and hardly a year older. He has not taken a new wife but the peasant women assured us that he was well looked after by his house serfs.

The Empress admired the green and fertile plains, the tidy peasant houses, and the new wooden manor house which Father had had built. The old banya, where we were all born, even Uncle, still stands, and Father ordered the spring nearby to be renamed the Catherine Well in the Empress's honour, which was done with a splash of holy water. The peasants served us spicy cabbage soup, which we all ate with relish, especially the Empress. Oh, how much better it tasted than the finest dishes in St Petersburg! How I have missed our simple food from home! Afterwards, berry wine was offered to the ladies while the men drank vodka. The Empress also drank one or two glasses of vodka, saying it aided digestion. She is often troubled by stomach ailments.

The village musicians took out their instruments after we had eaten and the peasants whirled and twirled in their lively dances. I remembered the steps and danced happily with my childhood friend Sonya, a serf from the village as all our childhood playmates were. We used to spend all day running through the fields with them until Mama considered us too old and restricted us to our house to learn housekeeping and sewing. Poor Mama! What would she think of our life now?

As I looked up at the sky filling with stars, the strings of the balalaika tugging at my heart, I thought perhaps I would indeed be happier in the village than at the Russian Court, where nothing was as it seemed. Here in the village, life was simple and although harder, it seemed more honest. The summer evening air was fresh and clean, the heat of the day blown away by the winds as they crossed the plains.

We all travelled back to Smolensk together in one carriage by the light of the full moon. The Emperor awaited us there. And poor Lanskoy. Was the Empress thinking of replacing her favourite? It was not only I who raised this question. The Empress is very fond of Lanskoy but has spent little time with him. Emperor Joseph received much of her attention but an Emperor was not a candidate for a favourite. A political alliance founded on affection, however, would be a lasting one, Alexandra said. Perhaps the Empress was thinking of reinstating Uncle as favourite? They were both being unusually kind to one another. As we left Chizova, the Empress took Uncle's hands in hers. "Thank you, dear Grigory," she said, "for showing me more of who you are. I see the wide plains in your nature, I hear the music in your voice, I feel your yearning for that which is free."

I think the Empress forgets that only the landowners are free in the countryside. My father owns some 500 serfs, a very small holding. He is a just man and treats his serfs well. But many do not. One of our neighbours kept a young female serf in a cage in her chamber. It was her duty to dress the old lady's hair but she was not allowed to leave the room because the lady did not want anyone to know she wore a wig. This may be a rumour but the point is that it could very well be fact.

I think of Sonya, who can never leave Chizova, unless she is sold to another landowner. Runaway serfs are hunted and severely punished – but in any case, there is nowhere to run to. If I returned to Chizova, I would ask Father to give me Sonya and she could live with me as my friend.

I have read this over and note that I have strayed from my rule of recording only facts. The visit to our home village has left me unsettled. The Empress may declare herself to be Russian but we never have spicy cabbage soup and the music we listen to is Italian or French.

Varvara
September 1780

The summer has been hot and I am with child again. But life at Court has been quite eventful and I am content when there are entertainments to enjoy, of which there have been many since the Empress's return from her tour of inspection.

At first, the Empress closeted herself away in her study, working on improvements which have to be implemented as soon as possible. Nadezhda says her list of Urgent Matters to Attend To runs for several pages. The maids complain that they cannot remove the ink splatters from her dresses.

However, once Uncle returned from Moscow with the Emperor Joseph, whom we must call Count Falkenstein, the Empress emerged in her most beautiful brocades and diamonds. The Emperor, in contrast, plays his incognito with gusto. He wears a plain grey uniform with no orders and insists on sleeping on a military mattress in simple taverns or a tent. We all laughed when Uncle told us that on their travels, he had manor houses made to look like inns. The best fancy of all was Uncle's idea to have the Empress's English gardener at Tsarskoye Selo make a special tavern for the Emperor. They even hung a sign on it: ***The Count Falkenstein Arms***. We were all invited to dress as simple peasants and come to supper there. What fun we had! I was able to disguise my condition with an apron but I left my kerchief off so that my bosom rose gently but fully above my bodice. My husband was enchanted, as were several of the men, including the charming Prince de Ligne, who many say may be the Empress's new favourite. But he is Austrian although he declares he likes to be a foreigner everywhere. "One loses respect for a country if one spends too much time there." He is very witty and full of ***bons mots***. The Prince is about fifty but has attractive boyish looks, always smiling with a glint in his eye. He talks very freely, telling the company at the "tavern" that he himself had benefited from the more natural ways of the serfs in bringing up children. He said he was raised by a peasant nurse who slept naked with him. She was also a good dancer, he added. The ladies at table all blushed but I looked him straight in the eye.

The Empress intervened smoothly, "Ah, my dear Prince, you are then a disciple of Monsieur Rousseau?"

"Why, my dear Empress," the Prince answered, "did he sleep naked with his nurse too?" There was relieved laughter which turned riotous as more vodka was consumed to enhance the tastelessness of our boiled beef supper. There was also that spicy cabbage soup, which I have never liked.

It was a most entertaining evening and the Emperor seemed pleased but I do not think he noticed it was a masque specially prepared for him. The Prince de Ligne paid all the women many compliments although I like to think I received the most. I doubt whether he can be part of my own story, however, since the Empress gives him much attention. Lanskoy was placed several seats away from the Empress and seemed pale and listless. Still, he is well rewarded for his patient loyalty. The Empress is having a grand palace built for him and there is hardly a week goes by but he has a new trinket to flaunt: a jewelled sword case, diamond buttons and most recently a fine hat bordered with rubies and sapphires. He also has a numerous family and since the Empress allows him a table of thirty, they can all dine and wine at her expense.

Definitely not part of my own story is the dreadfully boring Prince Frederick William, Frederick of Prussia's nephew and heir. Alexandra said in her clever way that he has been sent to counteract the Austrian influence on the Empress. Well, he has already lost for he is no match for the charming Prince de Ligne. The Prussian Prince is of huge girth and slow movement. His speech is ponderous and unmannered. No one wishes to sit beside him and there is a scuffling and shuffling of chairs at concerts and card parties. Only the Grand Duke Paul, who reveres all things Prussian, is willing to offer him company. The other evening, the Empress suddenly rose from table where the Prince was seated beside her, and left the room with uncharacteristic haste. The footmen barely had time to open the doors. I followed her swiftly and she was muttering, "God save me from bores and boors!" She spent the rest of the evening playing billiards with Uncle and the Prince de Ligne.

Prince Frederick William has divorced a first wife, married a second, and keeps a mistress. It is hard to imagine him – and really one should not – summoning the energy to father the brood of children he has. The only thing one can say in his favour is that he plays the violoncello well.

Alexandra
December 1780

Dear Anna,

The year draws to a close with many events to relate. I must write them down or else lose them in the onslaught of more.

The Empress and Uncle still strive for the Austrian alliance. It must be done in secret for the British still hope to sway the Empress to their side. They dangle the island of Minorca as bait and even Uncle now says it would make a good base for Russian ships in the Mediterranean Sea. Sir James Harris has promised that the British would leave supplies worth some two million sterling. But the Empress says, "The bride is too beautiful and the British are trying to trick me." I agree with her. We have as yet no navy to base there and it is too far away for us to hold without British support. Uncle, however, is determined to lead Russia southwards.

The Emperor Joseph is now sole Emperor of the Holy Roman Empire. His mother Maria Teresa died in November. "While she may be respected as having been a conscientious ruler for over four decades," Empress Catherine said, "one cannot divide a throne as she did. Now her son can rule freely, unhampered by maternal reins." The way to an Austrian alliance with Russia might be unhindered but it must be kept secret until everything is signed. I do not like to deceive Sir James Harris, who has spent large amounts of money, much of it his own, on furthering the case of Britain, but my first loyalty is to my own country. He has asked London to recall him but his government insists he stay. His career here will end in failure, and for that I am sorry.

Winter quiet has descended on the Court after the departure of our visitors and their retinues. Emperor Joseph left first, with many affectionate farewells. We had all grown fond of him. Despite his devotion to discipline and correctness, he was a well-informed and stimulating conversationalist. The tedious Prince Frederick William left us in October and there were many sighs of relief, the loudest perhaps from the Empress. Prince de Ligne lingered longer at the Empress's request but he did not wish to brave the Russian winter and departed with many gifts just as the autumn leaves fell: horses, serfs, diamonds, chests full of paintings. Prince Frederick William's parting gifts from the Empress, however, were four pieces of silver brocade, forty pounds of rhubarb and forty of tea. I estimate that to be about 8000 roubles worth. The gifts for Prince de Ligne amounted to more than 80,000 roubles, which clearly indicates the tendency of our foreign policy.

Just as the Court was taking up its old rhythms, news reached us of our grandmother's death. Uncle was much grieved although in truth they had been estranged for several years. "But to allow one's mother to die without being reconciled to her is a hard burden to bear," he said as he wept. The Empress consoled him and I comforted him by listening to the stories of his childhood which were released with his tears. Many of them I did not know but his history is also ours. I did not know that Grandmama Daria was the second wife of my paternal grandfather, Alexander Potemkin, Uncle's father. She was twenty years old, beautiful and already a widow when Grandfather, advanced in years, saw her. He married her at once although he had a wife. The whole village knew but Daria only found out after her first child, our mother, was born. Having two wives was against the laws of both church and state but many of the gentry did it and a blind eye was turned as long as the first wife entered a convent. Tales of first wives being tortured to comply are not uncommon. Daria went to her husband's first wife and begged her to go to a convent so that her own marriage would be legitimate. "It would have been better had she been the one to go to a convent," Uncle remarked morosely. "But then I would not have been born and what would my poor Empress have done without me? She is my destiny, my fate, my very soul. Just before I was born, my mother had a dream that the sun fell from the sky onto her swollen belly. What clearer augur is there than that?"

Grandmama Daria suffered from her husband's terrible jealousy. Uncle says he remembers when his sisters married, their husbands were forbidden to kiss their mother-in-law's hand since such a kiss could lead to temptation and sin. But Uncle, as the only son in the family, was spoiled. When he was six, his father died, leaving him heir to the village and his mother widowed at age forty-two with six children to care for. Uncle was the only way out of this genteel poverty so Grandmama Daria sent him to Moscow to make his way. And you know the rest: how he excelled at all he did, brilliant with languages: Greek, Latin, Russian, German, French, Polish, Italian and English, how he rose in the ranks to become a military hero, how he made his way at Court.

I do not know why I bring this all up. Perhaps it is the need to spin a thread to where we came from and who we are. The Empress seems to have no such need. She neither talks about her family past nor pays attention to any of the children she has borne, the only official one being the Grand Duke Paul and the only openly acknowledged one her son by Grigory Orlov. When I bring this up with Uncle, he says, "Ah, but we are all her children, She is the Mother of all Russians. She cannot limit herself to being the parent of any one child." I was just about to ask how many children she might have when Uncle added, "And nor can I."

Forgive my ponderings. I look forward to your return from Astrakhan, dear Anna!

With affection,

Your sister Alexandra

Tatiana
March 1781

Prince Alexander is three and his brother Constantine will soon be two. And my little nephew Grigory can toddle quite well now. And so we are a merry group. They all have their own nurses but I am in charge when we visit the Empress, which is often. The Empress says I have developed a fine sense of responsibility for my age, which is twelve. She thinks I will make a good teacher and has embarked on a small course of instruction for me. She says I may attend classes at the Smolny Institute, which she herself founded for the Education of Young Ladies.

Sometimes we have to cut our afternoons short if the Empress's arm troubles her. She has something called rheumatism and when the weather is cold and windy as it has been, it is worse. The doctors dress it with Spanish fly, which makes the skin blister badly. "Ah," the Empress sighs, "I exchange one pain for another."

"Are they really flies? " I ask.

"They are dried beetles," the Empress explains, "and are useful for particular treatments, not just rheumatism." Then she adds with another sigh, "One of them you will not need to know about for many years." I do not know what the Empress refers to but I will ask Varvara.

But I am to learn about education not medicine. The Empress says the basis of a good education is a free and willing mind. Alexander is never forced to do what he does not want but there are so many things he does want to do. He can spell and write, he draws well, he can fence and ride and he loves to talk and ask questions. The more he asks, the more the Empress is pleased. He is very intelligent. The Empress commissioned a famous English artist to paint his portrait. Alexander sat so very still for such a long time. Later, the Empress asked him to show her how he had sat for the portrait. "I do not know, Grandmama. I cannot see myself. You must ask Tatiana."

Alexander's little brother Constantine is no longer sickly and is much livelier than his older brother. But he amuses the Empress and she is very fond of him. "He does not concentrate," she says, "but he has very intelligent eyes." The boys look very funny in their little dresses designed by the Empress herself. They are all sewn in one with hooks at the back and the boys just push their arms and legs in and they are dressed. The Empress is very proud of this design and the King of Sweden has asked for a copy. "My grandsons will be living testimony to the success of my methods of education," she says. She calls Alexander her Cupid and Constantine her little Bacchus.

Her next project for the boys is their inoculation against smallpox. The Empress will bring Dr Dimsdale from England to do it. He inoculated the Empress and her son many years ago. I think it sounds dangerous. They put smallpox under the skin and I cannot think how that does not make the patient get the disease. But, as I said, I am to learn about education not medicine. And the Empress is kind and always right.

Alexandra
June 1781

Dear Anna,

I still write to you but I know my letters have taken on a form very unlike correspondence with a dear sister. Perhaps at the age of twenty-seven, one does not usually have much to write about – household, children, entertainments, what one has read, who one has met - but there is much in my life that I am witness to that affects the whole world. I write for my future memoirs. Memory is notably unreliable in old age.

Uncle is not convinced the alliance with Austria will go beyond a mutual admiration between Empress Catherine and Emperor Joseph and so he has turned his attention once more to a secret policy in Persia. You, dear Anna, may already know about this through your husband but I have only learned of it from Uncle. I now see the true purpose of sending your husband to Astrakhan. It is from there that Uncle intended to launch an invasion on the Persian Empire and the ships that have been built these last two years at Kazan on the Volga had already moved south for this purpose. The Persian Empire is a large one and encompasses Armenia and much of Georgia, where our fellow Christians live. It is Uncle's wish to free our brethren from the Persian yoke.

I urged patience on Uncle. The Austrian alliance seems so near and we cannot attack two empires at once. The Ottoman Empire or the Persian Empire – in truth it is all the same to him as long as he has his own empire to govern – he would never say 'rule' for that is the privilege of a sovereign. Still, he sent – as you may very well know as your husband must have been part of the planning on Uncle's behalf – a small force of three frigates with some 600 men across the Caspian Sea to Persia to establish a trading post, which would open up a valuable commercial route, as it would be only five weeks to India. In this venture, Uncle said he could rely on the co-operation of Aga Mohammed Khan, satrap of the Ashkhabad province, who hopes to become shah and take revenge on his father's enemies who castrated him as a child.

Our Russian force built a small fort and entertained the Persians. Word has now reached us that the leaders of the expedition were captured by Aga Khan and given the choice of losing their heads or sailing away at once. And that was the inglorious end of the Persian Project. "One must never treat the infidel as a Christian," Uncle said gloomily. "He has no word to give and lives by caprice. His cruelty is unmatched. Did you know that the Aga Khan once blinded 20,000 men in a village that opposed him?"

Sir James Harris still pleads Britain's cause although he knows the Empress will commit no troops to the American venture. French and American forces are amassing under a General George Washington to retake New York from the British. At least, no one will be blinded or have their heads chopped off. There is more honour, I would think, when Christian fights Christian.

We must devote all our efforts to the Austria alliance now. The Empress still corresponds with the Emperor – frequently. His letters give her great pleasure. I once saw her blush as she read one. It lay unfolded on her desk, perhaps deliberately, and I glimpsed the lines which the Emperor had written. ***As the proverb says, what Woman wants, God gives, and once in their hands, one always goes further than one wants.*** There is still hope.

With affection,
Your sister Alexandra

Nadezhda
July 1781

I may record the niceties of a recent diplomatic setback, Uncle said, as a lesson in finding solutions.

Russia and Austria have agreed on a treaty of defence in the first step to a full alliance. But the treaty cannot be signed. It is customary, I have learned, for monarchs to put their signature first on one copy and second on another so that neither has precedence. The Holy Roman Emperor, however, always puts his signature first on all copies of treaties. Our Empress will not accept this as she argues that Russia does not belong to the Holy Roman Empire and therefore will not be second to Rome. Emperor Joseph refuses to sign any document in second place. Uncle has tried to persuade the Empress that the treaty is more important than where the signature is but she will not yield. "Then so be it," she says, "no treaty." Uncle has been rushing backwards and forwards to the Austrian envoy but the Austrians are equally adamant. It is what in chess they call a stalemate – although I do not see what political advantage calling a draw would bring.

It is the sign of a great statesman, Uncle says, to find a solution without yielding any ground, rather like the military. And such a solution has been found. Instead of signing a treaty with each other, Catherine and Joseph will now exchange secret letters and they shall be as binding as a treaty. Since they are "personal" letters, however, no diplomats need be informed and thus the matter will remain secret until the time is right. I am not sure why the treaty has to remain secret, nor am I sure what secret means since there are so many secrets which everyone knows.

The Empress has just celebrated her accession to the throne nineteen years ago. She has had her secretary compile a list of the achievements of her reign for the foreign envoys. In all, there are 492 achievements: 29 local governments have been set up according to the new system of administration as well as 144 towns; there have been 30 conventions and treaties (I cannot ascertain whether this figure includes the letter treaty with Austria), 78 military victories, 88 important edicts of law and 123 edicts for the relief of the people of the Empire. This does not include all her contributions in music, art and architecture, which are considered too numerous to even count. I consider this an impressive list, which can surely not be matched by any other sovereign.

Katerina
July 1781

Alexandra has chided me for not writing my journal. I do not know why I must obey her. She and Uncle act like my parents and the Empress is generally in agreement with them. There is always activity of some manner whether dressing for a ball, being polite at gatherings, playing cards – I would shun all society but I am not permitted. I plead my duties with the Grand Duchess Maria, who may keep to her chambers as she wishes, but Alexandra says I must be seen in society in order to attract a suitable husband. And now I have the added duty of my Uncle to attend to, but that I do willingly. At first I thought it was selfish of Alexandra to wriggle out of her duties.

"I was never his bedmate," she said, too proudly I think, "but he needs one of us to be ... affectionate to him. His eye wanders and there are too many young ladies who would take advantage of him. The Empress wishes him to be ... looked after by us. I will continue to be at his side for all social occasions. You need only ... welcome him when he visits you." It is not like Alexandra to be hesitant with her words. What she meant was I must become Uncle's mistress. I did not dare tell the Grand Duchess. The ways of the Russian Court shock her. She whispered once confidentially that the Empress did not set a good example.

Uncle came to me as I was resting on the sofa one hot afternoon. He brought an exquisite white silk **robe de chambre** which fastened at the front. It was so fine that it was transparent. "This will keep you cool," he said. "Let me help you put it on." And so I let him undress me, just as one would a child, and it pleased me to have someone look after me in this way. It was always I who had to dress and undress the Grand Duchess. The robe felt smooth against my skin, fluttering slightly in the movement of air. Uncle made me stand in front of him. "You are the most beautiful of your sisters," he said, "and you remind me so much of my dear sister, your mother." He loosened the fastenings of the robe and gazed long at me. I did not mind. "So young," he murmured, "so perfect." I was glad that I pleased him. "Turn," he said. I did so and felt his fingers slip the robe from my shoulders. "Venus," he murmured. I let him turn me round again and he gently held my shoulders, moving his hands down my arms, over my hips and down my legs. He rose abruptly and said, "I must go!" He did but I wish he hadn't. I wanted him to stroke me more. So this was love, I thought. This was the feeling everyone talked of.

Uncle came again and showed me how to reach such effortless pleasure that I was impatient for his visits. Then he showed me how he liked to reach his pleasure and since then we are often together on the sofa and it is relaxing and dreamlike. I let him do what he wishes and it is always what I wish too. I think I would call it an ecstasy of pleasure. The best part is that I need only lie there and do nothing.

Alexandra is pleased with me and the Empress often has me sit beside her and thanks me for being kind to Uncle. I look at Lanskoy and wonder whether he gives the Empress what Uncle gives me. I cannot imagine the Empress lying as I do, naked and relaxed. I cannot imagine Lanskoy, so pale and slender, being so kindly vigorous as Uncle. But the Empress is very fond of Lanskoy. She is always explaining things to him and stroking his hair.

News has reached Court of the sudden death of Count Orlov's young wife. She was never very healthy and has died of consumption in Switzerland, where the Count had taken her for a cure. Count Orlov's two brothers have gone to fetch him since he is apparently mad with grief and unable to do anything for himself. "Poor Orlov!" the Empress says. "To lose a love is a terrible thing. I should know but I hope I may never ever need to know again." She then took Lanskoy's hands in hers. "You will be with me forever," she said most tenderly. Uncle looked a bit surprised. I wonder if he would go mad with grief if something happened to me.

Alexandra
September 1781

Dear Anna,

The Grand Duke Paul and his wife have now left and what a commotion they caused. It had been arranged that the Emperor Joseph would invite them to Vienna and greet them with a magnificent welcome. It was the Empress's hope that this would make her pro-Prussian son more favourable to her pro-Austrian policy. The Grand Duke was at first taken with the idea and set about planning a Grand Tour, which would take in Versailles, Berlin, Venice and many more cities. But poisoned whispers spoke to him of a ruse to remove him from the succession, that his sons would be taken from him, that he would never be allowed to return to Russia, that he might even be assassinated. The Grand Duke voiced these fears openly, almost hysterically. They were obviously instigated by Uncle's enemies at Court as well as those envoys who stood against an Austrian alliance.

On the day of departure, the Grand Duke refused to get in the carriage while the Grand Duchess Maria wept quietly saying she would not travel without her sons. The Empress had said the children should not travel so soon after their smallpox inoculation, which Tatiana tells us caused Alexander some days of fever and pustules, and Dr Dimsdale, who was still at Court, confirmed that such a tour would be strenuous for the little Princes. "Then we shall stay with the children," the Grand Duchess said and walked back to her chambers.

For three days, messages and tears went back and forth. Dr Dimsdale tried to reassure the Grand Duchess that the children would be perfectly healthy in her absence. "If that is the case," she said quietly, "then they are healthy enough to travel with us. I will not travel without them."

The Empress was at first patient but the foreign envoys remarked – quite rightly, I think – that it was a weak sovereign who could not keep even her own family in order. Even Sir James Harris was perturbed. "The Empress should not tolerate defiance or disobedience." Harris would far rather Russia had Austria as an ally than Prussia.

In the end, the unhappy couple were forced to go. The Grand Duchess wept all day and clung to her children until the Empress removed them saying that such emotional upheaval was detrimental to their healthy development. While I am of the opinion that we are all called on to do our duty and none more so than the heir to the Russian throne, I did feel sorry for the Grand Duchess. She had to be half carried to the carriage and before her attendants could settle her, she fainted. The Grand Duke ordered the doors of the carriage to be closed and the curtains drawn and shouted to the coachman to drive on.

Katerina was crying as she waved goodbye to them. "It's as if they are being banished to Siberia," she said. Katerina, although one of the Grand Duchess's ladies, will not be part of the entourage of some sixty people. Uncle says he cannot do without her for so long. I was a little startled when he said this. "Why, how long is so long?" I asked. "Oh, the best part of a year," he said. I felt uneasy and wondered if there were any truth in the rumours which had frightened the young couple. The Empress is very fond of her nephews, particularly Alexander, whom she often refers to as her heir.

With affection,
Your sister Alexandra

PART THREE

Alexandra
December 1781

Dear Anna,

Another year draws to a close and our situation could not be more different from when we first left our home village six years ago. Imagine, all your sisters, apart from little Tatiana, are now married! Yes, it has all happened so quickly. Let me begin at the beginning.

The Empress, as you know, has trusted us to look after Uncle. Katerina, however, has done this too well, it seems. As I attended the Empress one evening, she suddenly said, with an emotion she does not often show, "The Prince is in thrall to your sister. He neglects me. She must be married!"

Uncle does spend much time with Katerina – too much. There are rumours in Court that they may marry, rumours which have obviously reached the Empress and incensed her.

I had already confronted Uncle with his infatuation with Katerina. "She is so undemanding," he said. "She is my angel of sensual delights." I do not wish to know the intimate details of their time together but I do know that it is time for Katerina to take on some duties now that the Grand Duchess is absent from Court. She cannot lie around ***déshabillée*** on her sofa all day distracting Uncle from ***his*** duties. I agreed with the Empress and she determined to speak to Uncle the very next day in my presence.

The Empress was peremptory with Uncle, and he was circumspect enough not to mention the "sensual delights" to the Empress. "I am grateful to you, my dear Empress," he said, "that you have taken such an interest in my motherless nieces. Their own mother could not have done more for them. I, on the other hand, have neglected their futures."

"Yes, you have monopolised them too long. It is time to find them husbands," the Empress said curtly. Her words shook my complacency. ***Them?*** I thought. ***Surely we are only talking of Katerina!***

"But the matter has been on my mind," Uncle continued unperturbed, "and I have suitable candidates for all three, Alexandra, Katerina and Nadezhda. Tatiana is still too young." The Empress listened to Uncle's proposals while I sat in shock.

I tasked him later about arranging matters without consulting me as if I were some witless girl. "No, no," he said. "I had to come up with some ideas to avert the Empress's displeasure. She may have had you all sent back to Chizova – and that I could not have borne." Well, a choice between Chizova and St Petersburg did put a different light on matters. "Your proposed marriage is a stroke of genius on my part," he said with a laugh. "I should have thought of it earlier. It will be of great political advantage and should ensure our future should ever we fall out of favour." I knew he still feared being usurped by one of Catherine's many favourites, that indeed she might even marry one of them. The shadow of Paul on the throne also loomed as a real enough danger. The Grand Duke disliked Uncle intensely.

The husband Uncle chose for me is his loyal Polish ally, Count Francis Branicki, who, disillusioned with the Polish King, seeks support in Russia. He and Uncle are firm friends and I had met him several times. He used to say laughingly when he was visiting Court, "Give me one of your nieces, Potemkin!" My sisters and I took it to be gallantry on his part and smiled modestly.

It was the Count who was responsible for Uncle's matriculation in the Polish nobility. Without such status, Uncle could never become Duke of Courland, which the Empress has promised him, or even King of Poland, an idea which Uncle once had but has now replaced with his Greek Project, which will give him an empire rather than just a country to govern. Still, I do agree with him that one cannot have too many sureties for the future.

Count Branicki is nearly fifty but his vitality and health belie his years. He is somewhat lacking in sophistication but is very good-natured. His past has been colourful – he was once called out by the adventurer Giacomo Casanova for insulting his mistress and both were badly injured in the duel. "But it was worth the time I had with La Binetti," Branicki guffawed. As I said, he is lacking in the manners we are used to.

The Empress was very kind to me, supervising all the wedding arrangements. She helped to dress me in her own chambers in a gown of lightest pale blue silk and lent me some of her own jewels for the day. "Russia must outshine Poland," she said. My sisters declared, perhaps with a little too much surprise, that I looked beautiful. My husband seemed satisfied and we agree to be a contented couple despite our differences.

Nadezhda was married a few days later to Uncle's friend Senator Shepilev, in a simple ceremony. He is a quiet, serious man of some forty years and has ownership shares in metal works, making him a good commercial contact for me. I think he will be kind to Nadezhda. He has a fine library and Nadezhda seems content.

Katerina's wedding followed closely. She was married in the Palace Chapel with most of the Court in attendance. She looked very beautiful, quite ethereal, in an almost transparent dress of silvery material and flowers in her hair. I am sure we could hear the sighs of regret from her many admirers. Katerina's husband, Pavel Skravonsky, is a descendant of Peter the Great's first wife, Catherine Skravonskaya, whom no one talks about except as "the Livonian washerwoman". Still, she did reign as Catherine I after Peter's death and so Pavel belongs to the imperial family. He is affable and very rich, but most eccentric and slightly comical as well as clumsy. Even the Empress expressed her doubts about his ability to please a woman.

But I think Uncle has chosen him deliberately. Pavel Skravonsky was brought up in Italy and talks of nothing else but returning there. I am sure Uncle will enable this for him. And Katerina will stay here. With Uncle. The Empress will not be pleased.

I must be careful myself not to displease the Empress. We all must. Varvara was overheard criticising her in a loud voice at a recent card party. I was there but fortunately the Empress was not. "She has Prince Potemkin," Varvara said, "she has Lanskoy, she takes any man she likes, and out of jealousy she orders my sisters to be married! This is no way for a sovereign to gain respect!" Those present tried to change the subject while I rushed over and asked her quietly to leave the room with me. "What?" she said arrogantly. "Shall I be knouted? Shall I be exiled for speaking my mind?" Her husband, Prince Golitsyn, normally so quietly charming, stood up and said, "Enough, Varvara! Leave the room with your sister!" She was shocked into compliance.

Uncle was furious when he found out and has ordered Prince Golitsyn to take his wife to his estates for a few months. We miss Varvara but she seeks drama, as if she lives in a ***roman***. She has taken her two children with her and perhaps a little quiet family life will be good for her.

Since I am still a lady of the Court, I must attend the Empress and am not bound to my husband's household, which in any case is still only temporary in St Petersburg. Count Branicki has estates in Ruthenia, which I intend to visit early next year. Katerina has removed to her husband's house since she has few duties at Court until the Grand Duchess returns. It is better that she is not in proximity to the Empress for the time being. Nadezhda too has gone to her husband's house but when he is absent in Moscow or at his works in the Urals (which I must find out more about), she attends at Court.

Life, as you see, dear Anna, has changed for us. I guard our futures vigilantly but am relieved that my welfare does not now depend solely on the favour of the Empress, which can change as fast as the clouds which cover the sun on a windy spring day. Marriage also holds more attractions than I had thought and I am glad my husband is an experienced and kind man.

With affection,
Your sister Alexandra,

Katerina
December 1781

Although Alexandra is not here to supervise me, I will write a few lines in my journal to escape the constant unrest in my husband's house. When he sees me with pen and paper, he will leave me in peace. Or he will suggest that we transcribe my journal into musical notes. And therein lies the problem – music. Count Skravonsky is obsessed with music. He has even forgotten how to speak. Everything must be sung, his orders to the servants, his conversations at dinner. The servants must deliver their messages in a sort of church chant. The dinner guests must sing too with the Count encouraging them and conducting them with his spoon. He does not notice that they make fun of him. He gives concerts and we must all sit and listen to his quavering out-of-tune voice.

I tell him I cannot and will not sing. I plead for quietness. I long for it. I long for Uncle, for my life at Court. I only married the Count to please Uncle. He begged me to and promised he would always love me and that we would be together. My husband's friends bring the latest gossip to our table. Prince Potemkin, they sing, has a new mistress here, a conquest there. It is very hurtful. I do not really mind that he has other women to comfort him but I do mind that he has abandoned me to this madhouse, full of false notes.

My husband does not importune me. He is, by his own admission, sickly. He has nothing against me finding comfort elsewhere, he sings, but all I need is some peace. And Uncle. I hope he sends for me soon.

The outside world comes to me in the form of letters from the Grand Duchess Maria. I miss her calmness. She and her husband have been in Vienna for six weeks, where they have been very well entertained by Emperor Joseph. Maria writes of many lavish Court balls, of which she wearies. But she enthuses about a certain Wolfgang

Amadeus Mozart, ***the best keyboard player in all Europe***, she writes. ***He has even played variations on Russian folk tunes for us***. I cannot bear the thought of any more music.

The Grand Duke Paul, however, has not won Emperor Joseph's trust because he tries to discredit Prince Potemkin and swears he will break any Austrian alliance when he is Emperor. It is no secret here in St Petersburg that Paul works against the Austrian alliance and his mother's plan to refound the empire of Constantinople at the expense of the Turks. My husband's guests sing of Potemkin's intrigues to discredit and banish Paul's allies at Court so that when the Grand Duke returns, he will have no supporters. If he returns. The Grand Duchess writes that they now move on to Tuscany to visit the Emperor's brother.

One must observe that I am so bored that I even take note of political matters now. Alexandra would be pleased.

Tatiana
March 1782

Winter does not wish to leave. Snow still lies and the Neva is frozen. It has been bitterly cold for months so that we have spent most of the time indoors. The little Princes are not allowed to play outside if it is too cold. They may go out in a sleigh if the temperature is no lower than seven degrees below zero and in a carriage if it is down to ten below zero. If it is any colder, they must stay in the palace, which is what we are forced to do now, for although it is March, it is minus fifteen degrees with no sign of the thaw. Still, we are as happy as any family can be. That is what we are now, the Empress says, a family. The Grand Duke and Duchess have been on their European tour for almost half a year now and the little Princes have become the Empress's children. I am always present as the Empress's "assistant" when the children are with her, which is twice a day. Alexander Lanskoy, the Empress's particular friend, joins us in the evenings. The Empress is in good humour and we play games, make music, listen to stories.

The Empress says that the day is successful if one has a plan. This is her own plan, which she has given me as an example.

6 a.m. to 9a.m	Legislation
9 a.m. to 11 a.m.	Business of the day
11 a.m. to 12 noon	The Princes
12 noon to 2p.m.	Dinner
2 p.m. to 4p.m.	Uninterrupted rest
4 p.m. to 6p.m	Letter writing; reading
6 p.m. to 8p.m.	The Princes
8 p.m. to 10 p.m.	Friends, entertainment etc

I too have my own plan but I do not rise as early as the Empress. My main task at Court is to be with the Princes, which I do happily and I learn a lot as they learn. The Empress likes me to report on what they do when they are not with her. Alexander can now count up to 1000 in Russian and French. "But," he told the Empress, "how can I know it is a thousand when I cannot see it?" The next day, the Empress had a leather bag of polushkas. "There, Monsieur Alexander," she said laughingly, "count your thousand now!" And he did. He also learned, as I did, that there are four polushkas in a kopeck and 100 kopecks in a rouble. The Empress told Alexander to count out 400 coins. "There," she said, "that is one rouble!" That seemed a large amount of money to me. I do not possess any money and would not know what to do with it.

Alexander must write letters to his parents. He dictates what he wants to say and the Empress transcribes it in pencil. He then follows the letters in ink. Sometimes I am allowed to take his dictation and I am very careful to form my letters well.

The Empress has a huge map of her Empire in her study and Alexander and Constantine can now point to any governorate that the Empress calls out. There are about thirty and the Empress says there will be more for she has not quite finished with her reform or indeed with gaining more territory. The children are allowed to colour them in on the map. We are going to do cities next but we already know St Petersburg and Moscow. And after that rivers and mountains. The Empress says Alexander must know the Empire he is going to rule. Constantine is going to rule the new Byzantine Empire when it is finished and the Empress will get a map for him.

We are learning to dance. That is, the little Princes are for I already know many dances. Alexander and his brother are allowed to come to the balls in the evening and they dance with all the ladies to practise their steps. Everyone laughs but the boys are very serious. The Empress does not tolerate silliness. They are to learn the polonaise for the Empress's birthday ball next month.

While my days are busy and I am very fond of the little Princes, I miss my sisters. Alexandra is the only one at

Court and she is always very occupied. Varvara is still at Prince Golitsyn's estates and may not return until the Empress is better pleased with her. Katerina only comes to Court for official dinners. I wish the Grand Duchess would return, for then Katerina could take up her duties with her once more. Nadezhda comes to Court more often and I am always happy to sit with her and listen to all the things she knows. She knows a lot. But I too now know a lot, thanks to the Empress.

Nadezhda
April 1782

I have neglected my diary due to my new responsibilities. I was married on 18th November 1781. It was a cold grey day, the clouds hanging low and heavy in the sky. But such was not my mood. Uncle and Alexandra had made a suitable, if rather sudden, choice for me. Senator Shepilev is a gentleman with good manners. He is forty years of age, just two years younger than Uncle, who is his good friend. I am glad I have an older husband. Young men are so restless. While the Senator may not be as dashing as Uncle, he is pleasant and his quietness suits my own. He allows me much freedom and is pleased I enjoy his library. I am happy to be a married woman, in charge of my own household, and I do not miss the bustle of Court life. I do try to see little Tatiana, who is so much a part of the Empress's close circle now.

As soon as the snows melted, which was late this year, the Empress set out for Tsarskoye Selo to plan the next extensions to the palace and, knowing my great interest in architecture, invited me to be part of her retinue. I packed my ink and sketch pads and looked forward to the fresh air of the countryside after a long winter wrapped in furs with my feet on the stove in the library. We do not have a fireplace there for fear of the books catching fire.

The Empress first inspected her hothouses, anxious to see if the plants had survived the winter. Last summer they were flourishing with all kinds of fruit: sweet melons, water melons, peaches, nectarines and even China oranges. The head gardener, Mr Bush, showed us the complicated system of heating ranging from hot bricks to flues fed with hot air from wooden fires. He explained how difficult it was to keep the temperature regular in the large building, some 800 feet long, but he seems to have succeeded since there was much greenery and even signs of blooming in the many exotic plants from all over the world. The Empress was pleased and handed Mr Bush a leather purse as we were leaving.

The carriage then drove us through the gardens to view the Lebanese cedars and the Siberian pines, which had all thrived in the cold. The Chinese pavilion, with the bridge Charles Cameron had added in the autumn, looked very picturesque in the snow which still lies at the foot of the trees.

The new rooms of the palace are delightful. The Empress, as I noted in my diary at the time, had asked Mr Cameron for "peaceful rooms where the spirit could be refreshed" and he has succeeded in this with a clever use of light and symmetry and fine materials. The Empress's study is lined with solid silver striped with red leaf foil. There is a sofa the colour of green in spring with sprigs of silver. Four slender pillars, with the same striped pattern as the walls, hold up a canopy of mirrored glass over it. A balcony overlooks the garden and its door is made of double mirrors so that it looks open even when it is closed. There is another smaller study in white and blue glass with bronze arabesques, which the Empress declares perfect for card parties.

Every room – and there are eight new ones so far – is different. They should "surprise, refine and refresh their dwellers" the Empress said. Some should also "broaden the horizon of our view" like the Chinese room which is lined with silk of the most startling turquoise blue painted with delicate scenes of daily life in China.

The Lyons room is perhaps the most impressive and the Empress's favourite. According to Mr Cameron's drawings, which I copied, it measures 36 feet by 32 feet and it is 28 feet high. There are twelve long mirrors, 13 feet long and 4 feet wide. The dimensions are pleasingly proportionate and symmetrical but are fully brought to effect by the fine French silks hanging as light as air between the mirrors. The walls are lined in bright yellow silk form Lyons in France and are embroidered with peacocks, pheasants and swans. The parquet floor is intricate in pattern and the fifty types of wood used are inlaid with mother-of-pearl. The room is said to have cost over 200,000 roubles, excluding the lapis lazuli brought from Lake Baikal to decorate the doors and cornices.

The Empress would now like Cameron to design a classical bathhouse with pillars and promenades. It should be Roman in style but open and light, using materials from Italy where possible. There must be a banya and a pool, for the Empress goes to the banya very often, but also rooms for rest. Cameron showed us drawings and diagrams of Roman baths and the Empress made many suggestions. I liked her idea of an open terrace overlooking the gardens, sheltered from the weather, with niches for busts of philosophers and poets. Cameron intends to decorate the rooms in jasper, agate and marble if the Empress condones the expense. She does.

Cameron showed much enthusiasm – he is generally a rather morose character – when the Empress described her new project. She wishes him to design a new town, a model town, to form part of the view from the new bathhouse terrace. It will represent Constantinople and will be named Sophia. The Cathedral of the new town must be a replica of Hagia Sophia in Constantinople. "Thus we will accustom ourselves to the view of what will once be ours with little Constantine on the new throne," the Empress said.

Alexander Lanskoy will have a house of his own built there and may choose its design. He discussed with Cameron ways of including jewel-encrusted panels which would catch the light. Lanskoy is very fond of jewels and the Empress indulges him.

When the Empress had concluded her discussions with Cameron, she sent for the children to come from Moscow. They were happy to be running about outside throwing snowballs at one another. Perhaps I will also have a child one day soon. I think I might like that. I have checked in the library for anatomy books to make sure that what my husband does is the correct way to have children. So many children are born that it must be a straightforward procedure. Varvara writes that she is expecting her third child.

The celebrations for the Empress's birthday were quiet, just as she wanted them. She is now fifty-three years old, but she does not like to be reminded. "I am grateful for what God has given me," she said, "but I still have much to do and cannot stop to think that most people do not reach five decades."

She looked most regal on the day, with perhaps a little too much rouge. There was a Te Deum sung first in the chapel and then we all processed to the mirrored hall for a musical concert. The Empress wore a beautiful gown of rich purple studded with diamonds. She often wears the loose Russian sarafan and has now ordered the ladies of Court to do the same except on the occasion of major feasts and festivals. The ladies complain bitterly since the loose robe falling widely from the shoulders is anything but flattering, covering breasts, waist and hips. Alexandra says we must all comply since the Empress does not boast a slender figure and would not have attention drawn to figures better than hers.

In any case, all the ladies were happy to don their fine robes and jewels for the Empress's birthday. We had a modest banquet of sterlet in aspic, chicken, duck, lamb and seven desserts. The Empress had her favourite dish of boiled beef with pickled cucumbers.

At the ball in the evening, Tatiana and I partnered the Princes Alexander and Constantine in the polonaise, which they danced most perfectly, pleasing the Empress greatly. She smiled and clapped her hands and kissed them both. The Empress danced with Lanskoy and then with Uncle. She retired early as she often does now, which can be forgiven in someone her age.

I have enjoyed my days at Tsarskoye Selo and the Empress has been very kind. But I look forward to returning to my own house tomorrow, where I am less restricted by Court etiquette. And dress. Although I admit that the sarafan is comfortable, I do not think my husband finds it attractive.

Alexandra
November 1782

Dear Anna,

The summer at Tsarskoye Selo was peaceful. The Empress was relaxed and the Court was released from most formalities. She was content working with Mr Bush in the gardens, overseeing all the new constructions – there is to be a new palace built for the Grand Duke and his wife in nearby Pavlovsk. The Empress herself inspected the delivery of three and a half million bricks. If you saw her for the first time, you would take her for a peasant woman in her sarafan and leather shoes. But she is happy and spends most of her leisure time with the little Princes and with Lanskoy, who must practise patience for he has become one of her educational experiments. The Empress has devised a curriculum of poetry, philosophy, history and geography for him but he takes it with good humour especially as he is richly rewarded in jewelled trinkets if he performs his lessons well.

Uncle left at the beginning of July but no one knew for where. He said he had private business to attend to. I tried not to see a coincidence in Katerina's absence with her husband in Italy.

Perhaps Uncle's travels accounted for the peaceful interlude at Court. There were no sulks or arguments between the Empress and Uncle. Or perhaps he just needed a change. He did mutter the day before he left, "I am not made for domestic life and gardens and I prefer women not to be swathed in shapeless sarafans!"

In August we donned our normal court attire and processed to St Petersburg for the inauguration of the great monument to Peter the Great, which Monsieur Falconet started as long ago as 1768. It is indeed a colossal work. The inscription reads ***To Peter the First from Catherine the Second*** thus cleverly establishing a hereditary link which does not actually exist.

The Empress was very moved as she gazed up at the figure on the bronze horse. "He looks so alive, so majestic, so powerful," she said with tears in her eyes, "and although I think he is well pleased with me, I will try better." The young Princes were very excited. "Can I have one too, Grandmama?" Constantine asked. "You shall have yours in Constantinople," she answered, "as your name predicts. And perhaps Alexander can have one made for me when he is Emperor and write on it ***To Catherine the Second from Alexander the First***." One wonders that her son Paul is not mentioned.

We stayed only a few days in St Petersburg, which was unbearably hot, before returning to the quiet and coolness of Tsarskoye Selo, where life continued peacefully until the outside world intruded. Word reached us that Khan Shagin Giray had once more been driven out by a rebellion initiated and backed by the Turks. The Empress was overwrought. "This is a declaration of war! I need Prince Potemkin! Where is he? He and I could decide the matter in half an hour but nothing scares me more than to miss something or be wrong! He must be found and return at once." The Empress wrote to Uncle, as I did, and gave instructions that couriers were to be sent to find him.

Uncle turned up dusty from his rushed ride back to the Empress. "I did not even stop to sleep," he said. No time was wasted on pleasantries. Uncle hardly had time to change out of his riding clothes before the Empress called us to her study. "Russia must reinstate the Khan!" she declared. "But," Uncle said patiently, "this will be the third time. We cannot keep allowing him to be deposed by any rebels who see fit to do so. We must annex the Crimea once and for all."

"But that will cause war," the Empress said.

She was less decisive than she used to be. I thought her anxious and timid. Uncle seemed to think so too. "It is time for decisive action," he said. "Nothing has been gained in history without bold moves. War may ensue but it may not.

The timing is perfect. France is still occupied with Britain in the Americas but negotiations for a peace treaty have begun so we do not have much time. Austria has pledged its support in case of war with Turkey and we must take advantage of that promise while it is still warm. The Emperor is fond of you, Your Majesty. I do not think he will refuse."

The Emperor's answer to the Empress a few days later did indeed show enthusiasm, at least in its opening: *My dear Empress, my friend, my ally, my heroine.* In principle, the Emperor wrote, Catherine's grand vision of a new Greek monarchy wrested from barbaric Turkish rule was dazzling – yes, that is the word he used – but there were practicalities to consider. His missive outlined plans to cede territories to Austria including Belgrade, to give Cyprus and Crete to Venice in return for Istria and Dalmatia, to ask for French help in return for Egypt. The letter contained an abundance of place names which I could not place geographically. I was glad when the Empress called for a map to be brought. But Uncle interrupted and said decisively, "We will take the Crimea. This can be done. All else is theory."

"No," the Empress said, "first, go and reinstate the Khan and then we will see."

Uncle became irate and accused the Empress of indecision. Their voices rose and I left the room, not knowing who was right. But sometimes I think matters of war should be left to men who have fought in the field rather than to an Empress who is more interested in gardening and marble baths.

Uncle left on 1st September to quell the rebellion in the Crimea. He wrote proudly that he had covered the 3000 versts in 16 days. It took him just four weeks to defeat the rebels, killing 400 of them, and reinstate Shagin Giray as Khan under Russian protection. The Sultan has not reacted, which proves Uncle's belief that a show of strength intimidates. Uncle has stayed on to supervise shipbuilding and other enterprises at the Black Sea. He writes to me of excellent commercial opportunities, which I intend to take advantage of. I have to invest safely, for my husband has the weakness of gambling and while he has considerable wealth, I do not wish my money to be recklessly squandered.

On 22nd September, the Empress celebrated twenty years on the throne. It was a quiet celebration and the list of her achievements was not read out this year. She founded a new order of St Vladimir, named after the Grand Prince of Kiev who converted to Christianity in the year 988. This, she said, was to honour Russia's forthcoming victory over the Turks and the foundation of a new Greek Empire under Russia. She named the new Black Sea port which Uncle is building "Kherson" after the ancient Chersoneses, which Prince Vladimir captured after he was baptised a Christian. And while I am not sure of the relevance of all these references to old history, Russia seems committed to expanding into the Turkish Empire. It is a bold undertaking.

Sir James does not seem unduly perturbed and has said England will not interfere if Turkey is to lose territory or power. However, it will not make an enemy of the Turks by actively helping the Empress since commerce is so important to the British. Uncle has promised to guarantee trade routes for the British once the Crimea is in Russian hands. Sir James takes this on trust. For myself, it is indeed a grand plan but it will remain no more than that unless the Empress concedes that military action is called for.

Domestic events now eclipse the drama of the clash of empires. A great sadness has fallen over the Empress. Grigory Orlov, whose young wife's death caused him to fall into madness, turned up at the palace accosting the Empress as we sat in the garden on a fine autumn day. He fell at her feet, weeping most piteously, crying out, "Please help me! Don't send me away!" Close on his heels were two of his brothers, who apologised most profusely. "Our brother is ill," Alexey Orlov said, "he has lost his reason and has been confined for his own good."

But the Count had somehow escaped his brothers, who then pursued him all the way from Moscow. They tried to persuade him to leave with them, quite forcefully, but the Count clung to the Empress. "Leave him," she said gently. "I will look after him. Perhaps he will come to his senses when he feels safe."

The Count has been with us since then and he is no better. The Empress allows him to come to her whenever he pleases and is very patient with him. She is the only one he seems to recognise. He is incoherent and sometimes wild but the Empress will not have him restrained or disciplined. She says it pains her to see the handsome, courageous man she once loved reduced to madness. If I were in her place, I would not wish to see my former lover in such circumstances. I would prefer to remember him as he was. Often, after she has tried to calm the Count, the Empress weeps and can devote herself to neither business nor pleasure for the rest of the day. The Count has now had an apoplectic stroke and is confined to bed, which at least spares the Empress his sudden interruptions.

All in all, the Empress is in a very low mood (worsened by the death of one of her favourite greyhounds). She has sent Lanskoy to St Petersburg and the little Princes with their English nannies and Tatiana to Pavlovsk for a few days. I ask what might cheer her and she replies, "When Prince Potemkin returns, he will remind me that I am an Empress – and how to be one."

I must write to Uncle to return at once. I do not know what will happen if the Empress falls ill. The Grand Duke does not return for a few weeks and in any case I doubt he could rule in her place.

My husband grows impatient to leave for his estates. We expect our first child and he is sure it will be a boy. He wishes his son to be born at Bila Tserkva and while I can understand this wish, I cannot leave the Empress until Uncle's return.

With affection,
Your sister Alexandra

Katerina
December 1782

I am so happy to be back at Court. I could not have borne another week in my husband's madhouse. Wrapped in fur, I take up my old place on the sofa in the afternoon and dream peacefully. I have been here since October, summoned to supervise preparations for the Grand Duchess's return. She has been absent for over a year and her chambers have to be redecorated and the tapestries and linens freshened.

Uncle arrived shortly after I did and it has been such bliss to be with him again. Our snatched hours in Italy at the beginning of the summer were too fleeting – and there were too many distractions for him, too many women falling at his feet. He is more handsome than ever, leaner since he returned from the Crimea – due to riding and battling, he said. His complexion has been pleasantly darkened by the sun and his thick hair is shot through with light. He does not laze around in his dressing gown as he used to but rises early to attend to business. He has started to sell many of his possessions: horses, estates, jewels. He has even paid all his debts, he said.

One afternoon as we lay together, I asked him about this sudden flurry of gathering money. "Why, I am planning for a new future," he said as he kissed me.

"But where?" I asked. "What about us? You are not going to leave me again?"

"Let us just say I am planning to retire to Italy," he said and kissed me again. "I will make your husband ambassador in Naples and we can see each other whenever we wish without the eyes of the Court on us." He meant the Empress's eyes. I cannot envisage Uncle in Italy. He enthuses so much about the Crimea and I suspect that is where he is going. But I will not worry about it now. I will enjoy our time together, for it is such a blissful time.

The Grand Duke and Duchess returned to Court in November, in the middle of winter. They had been gone for fourteen months. The Duchess wept when she saw her sons. "They are so grown and they do not recognise me!" In truth, the Princes kept near to the Empress and only approached their parents, most politely, when she instructed them to do so.

Later in her chambers, Maria said, "It has been a cold welcome from the Empress. I know the Grand Duke does not support the Empress's aims to build a Greek Empire but he is her son and she could show him more affection." She also added that they had been well received all over Europe and treated like royalty, which they were. Only at the Russian Court were they given no honours or respect.

Most of those who belonged to their circle at Court have been sent away, one of the Grand Duke's closest friends even accused of treason and banished for life. "I have rescued you from foolish friends and their intrigues," the Empress apparently said to her son. "The Empress is angry that we visited the King of Prussia, who accorded us all honours," Maria said, "but we could hardly have ignored him, could we?"

But politics is not the domain of court ladies, except for the Empress, of course, and so we turned to the boxes the Grand Duchess had brought with her from Paris. I was astonished at the number — about two hundred of all shapes and sizes — and impatient to see what was in them. There was a great quantity of elaborate dresses and materials and trinkets. The Grand Duchess had never been extravagant. "So many were eager for our patronage," she explained. "I could not refuse. And I'm sure the Empress will be interested in the new fashions." Word of the Empress's new dress code had obviously not reached Maria on her travels. We had opened only a few of the boxes when the Empress arrived unannounced. She hardly glanced over the piles of brocade and silk before saying, "They must be returned. You need not open the other boxes. Return them all. You may keep a few dresses for special occasions but otherwise at Court we now dress simply – in the Russian style. I will send the dressmaker to measure you for some sarafans this evening." The Empress then swept from the room leaving the Duchess in tears. "Do not weep," I said. "let us choose some that you might like to keep."

"I do not weep for the loss of my dresses," she said, "but for the loss of my sons. And now she may take my husband from me." I thought this a little dramatic and assured her the Empress was loyal to her family. "The Empress has resolved to be displeased with us," Maria said, "and there is nothing we can do to please her."

And so the Court of the Grand Duke and Duchess has become a dismal place where no one comes, for those who frequented it have been sent away and no one will risk the Empress's displeasure by befriending the Grand Duke or his wife. The little Princes continue to live in the Empress's wing. From being a calm oasis, the Grand Ducal Court has become a desert of loneliness. But I am very fond of Maria and will serve her as best I can. In the afternoons and most nights I have Uncle. And I need no more than that.

Tatiana
January 1783

In spring my life will change. The Empress has said that it is time for the Princes to have a tutor. Alexander will not be six until the end of this year and Constantine will only be four in April but the Empress says that their childhood has been long enough. They have learned a lot through play but now their lessons must be more structured.

They have started carpentry lessons with a German craftsman and will also learn other trade skills before beginning languages, history, philosophy, geography and many more subjects after summer. I will no longer be needed as a play companion.

The Empress is right, as she always is. I will be fourteen soon and I am to be appointed a lady-in-waiting. I do not think I will be sent to the Smolny Institute for Young Ladies after all. The Empress seems to have forgotten about it but I am not too disappointed. It was the Princes I liked more than the learning. As a lady at Court, I will still be near the Empress. And in any case, I must obey her in all things. This was her most important rule for the boys. "Obedience to your Empress is like a natural law," she explained to us one day. "Disobedience to her is as impossible as changing the weather."

I shall miss the Princes, whom I have been with for hours every day since their births. They are polite to everyone, even the servants, whom they may not command but only request. They never cry. The Empress says that children cry out of stubbornness or sensitivity and neither is to be encouraged. In fact, crying has always been forbidden.

They are both very lively boys, never still for a minute. The Empress does not allow idleness, and high spirits have to be channelled into play or exercise but the Princes have always been allowed to choose what they want to play. When they tire, they may read or converse. They often do tire because, on the Empress's orders, they have only seven or eight hours sleep every night. Baroness Dimsdale says this is not enough for growing children, who need, she says, at least twelve. "Well," the Empress said, "that may be the case in England but in Russia we know that God's blessings are given to those who rise early."

The Baroness also thinks that the boys eat too much fruit, that their rooms are kept too cold, that they are not clothed warmly enough, that they have too many cold footbaths and too many baths in general and that they drink water when they are thirsty (as long as they have eaten a piece of bread first).

The Baroness also says that sometimes children must be punished for their own good with a slap or a stick and she even quotes the Bible but the Empress has forbidden corporal punishment of any kind. In general, the Empress, while unfailingly polite, does not heed the Baroness's advice although her husband is the famous Dr Dimsdale who inoculates smallpox. The Empress has no time for doctors or medicines. She says they cause more damage than cure. When the children have a fever, their bodies must deal with it naturally, she says. It has sometimes been alarming to witness this "natural act of healing" but the Empress has never allowed the Princes to be bled.

No matter what Baroness Dimsdale says, I think the Princes are wonderful boys, thanks to the Empress, and I shall miss them dreadfully. I have written down all the Empress's rules of education and when I have children, I shall bring them up just as the Empress has the Princes.

Alexandra
January 1783

Dear Anna,

My confinement draws near and I must leave very soon for my husband's estates while the snow allows an easy journey by sleigh. I will do so as soon as Varvara and her family arrive. Uncle has had her recalled to Court on my advice. We cannot leave the Empress unattended, I argued, for those of her enemies who would seek intimacy and influence with her. Someone must be here to look after our interests. Tatiana is still too young to detect danger of a political kind and Nadezhda is easily dazzled by facts and figures. Katerina's husband will move to Naples as our Ambassador there and Katerina with him. Uncle leaves soon for the Crimea, which he has at last persuaded the Empress to annex to the Russian Empire. It was not an easy task to convince her and voices were often raised. "The Crimea is a weakness in our border, through which the Ottomans could reach the heart of our Empire," Uncle argued with passion. "The French took Corsica, the Austrians most of Moldavia, and there is no power in Europe which has not participated in the carving up of Africa, Asia and the Americas."

Catherine argued that annexation would lead to war. "Can we not just take a part of it?" she asked.

Uncle was frustrated. When we were alone, he paced restlessly, ranting dangerously against our sovereign. "What has become of the great woman who made the Russian Empire? It seems we have no Empress anymore. She is more interested in children, dogs, architects and gardeners than in the present safety of Russia and its future glory. She spends more time with her mad ex-lover than with me. Or Lanskoy. She has lost her senses." I urged caution. "You must return her to them gently," I said. "Do not badger her. That makes her stubborn."

In the end, he used her own vanity to persuade her. One night at dinner, where he had been most considerate to the Empress, entertaining her with his charming wit, he said, "It is good to see you smile and once we have annexed the Crimea, you will smile even more. You will bring greater glory than any other Russian Sovereign before you. Your immortality will be secured. You will achieve dominance over the Black Sea, just as Peter the Great achieved dominance over the Baltic Sea, for which he was much admired and envied. What a legacy he left us! What a combination of greatness it would be for you to emulate him. Imagine! An Empire stretching from the Baltic to the Black Sea." The Empress listened, enthralled. Her eyes shone. Uncle then added, "At present, the Crimea is a wart on your nose. You must get rid of it." The Empress involuntarily lifted a finger to her nose and then laughed heartily.

And thus was she persuaded. She wrote a secret letter to Uncle, which he showed me in triumph. ***We hereby declare our will***, the Empress wrote, ***for the annexation of the Crimea and the joining of it to the Russian Empire with full faith in you and being absolutely sure that you will not lose time and opportune ways to fulfil this.*** Uncle was jubilant. "Paradise will be ours!" he said, whirling me round, oblivious to my very expectant state.

Since then, Uncle has been very busy covering all eventualities before he sets off. Sweden and Prussia may rush to the Ottomans' aid, necessitating military plans to cover that. The army must be prepared to march south, as discreetly as possible. Most of the Baltic fleet must be sent back to the Mediterranean. It is a long list and there is a steady coming and going of uniformed men in Uncle's chambers.

Knowing the terrain his troops must expect, Uncle is introducing many practical reforms in the army. "Soldiers are not cannon fodder but they will be if they continue to dress as they do." High tight-fitting boots would be replaced by low loose boots, puttees by stockings, ceremonial swords by bayonets – no detail was too minor for him. "A soldier's garb must be fast, simple, up and ready for combat," he said. "This I learned from the Cossacks."

His most scathing criticism was reserved for how the troops were instructed to dress their hair. "What does a soldier need with a Prussian braid that takes hours to fix?" he asked. "Soldiers have no valets to prepare them for battle. No, hair must be short and need no more than a wash and a comb. The powder, fat, pins and all other hair aids must all be left at home!" He has had his own hair cut to encourage the men and he does look very handsome.

Uncle invited myself, Katerina and Tatiana to an intimate farewell family dinner. "Our paths must now go separate ways for the time coming," he said. "We have been loyal and loving to one another and I thank you for this. You are my family and will always be so. You may come to me whenever you wish, whenever you are in need. Alexandra will be leaving tomorrow with her husband, and Katerina, you too will follow your husband to Naples, as the wife of the Russian Ambassador." At this, Katerina burst into tears, throwing her arms round Uncle. "No, no, I will not leave you," she sobbed. "How can you cast me off so?"

"But I am going to the Crimea," he said, patting her head, "and that will be my home for the foreseeable future. It will be the land of my dreams, where classical heroes once lived, where the trees are lush with fruit and the breezes balmy." He seemed to fall into a reverie but was roused once more by Katarina's sobs. "There, there," he said, "Naples is nearer the Crimea than St Petersburg is. I can visit you and you may come to visit me once the war is over."

When I next write, dear Anna, it will be from Bila Tserkva. Please visit me there. It has been years since we have seen each other. If you let me know, I can ensure that our other sisters are there too.

With affection,
Your sister Alexandra

Varvara
April 1783

Dear Alexandra,

During the time at my husband's estate, I longed to be back at Court. I think you will find that life in the country is slow and measured and infinitely boring. Some would call it healthy and indeed there is good fresh air. But there is a lack of society, of happenings, of life.

The Court I have returned to, however, is disappointingly different from the one I left a few months ago. First, it does not look the same. Fashion is not allowed. How can one wear diamonds on a sarafan? And those ugly Russian headdresses! Secondly, everyone is so serious. Entertainment is forbidden, for the Empress has been saddened by the state of her mad ex-lover Count Orlov and we must all be sad with her.

And now he has died and we must be sadder still. She blames the doctors for not being able to cure him and has banished them all from her sight. We did not even celebrate her birthday because Orlov's death occurred just two days before. In any case, I am not sure a 54th birthday is cause for celebration. And while I am sympathetic to grief, surely she must have known for months that the Count was going to die?

Many say it was a release for him. Now he can be with his young wife, which is what he surely wanted all along. No doubt the Empress is jealous of that. Why is it that she must have every man adore her first? Why, she has even flirted with my own husband and, of course, he must return her compliments a hundredfold.

The Empress says, between her constant sobs, that she has lost the one person to whom she had the greatest obligation in the world. No one will explain what she means but rumour has it that Count Orlov made her Empress and then she refused to marry him, even after his brothers killed the rightful Emperor, her ugly husband, for her. What perfect drama! The drama now is less colourful. The Empress has made herself ill with weeping and has taken to bed with fever and delirium and has eaten nothing for days. Although she usually shuns doctors when she is ill, she even asked for a bloodletting.

Not even Alexander Lanskoy can console her. She holds his hand and tells him how wonderful Count Orlov was and how she should never have let anyone come between them. "I will never let anyone come between us, dear Alexander," she said. Lanskoy looks uncomfortable at such expressions of imperial devotion as well he should since everyone knows that the Empress's is not the only bed he shares. Time for a new favourite perhaps. That at least would be a proper happening.

It is all very tedious, Alexandra, and although I try my best to be helpful and compliant, there is nothing I can add to my life's story here. We all miss Uncle. He looked very handsome when he rode out at the head of his troops at the beginning of the month. His many lady admirers turned out in their dozens to wave their tearful farewells. I too shed a tear. There is not another man like him and I think very fondly of the time when I was his mistress. One cannot blame me for having fallen in love with him. He weaves a spell as no other man can, as Katerina has found out along with countless other women. I will always adore him although my husband, who is kind, has my loyalty.

I envy the few days Uncle spends with you for the christening of your son. He was pleased to be asked to be godfather. It was good of him to take Tatiana to you. She is rather lost now that she rarely sees the Princes, and the Empress has somewhat neglected her. Tatiana is at that age when one is neither girl nor woman. I am sure she will enjoy her visit with you. She has made Uncle promise that she may come to the Crimea when he has conquered it. I hope he does so soon since I would also visit him and I cannot wait for skies sunnier than here at this dismal court.

Here is some news of interest for you. The Empress will give Count Orlov's estate of Gatchina to the Grand Duke. It is, as you know, a very fine property with a sumptuous palace and twenty villages and is situated very well some thirty versts on the road to Moscow. The Empress was very fond of Gatchina and often visited Count Orlov there.

It is a strange gesture to give her lover's estate to her unloved son but it is conjectured at Court that she wishes to free herself of the Grand Duke's presence with a good conscience. She will indeed be happy to be rid of him and his wife, I think, for she has often referred to them unkindly as "my heavy baggage". Out at Gatchina the Grand Duke can march and parade his troops to his heart's content. The Grand Duchess is expecting another child soon. She hopes it is a girl and then she may keep her for the Empress has said she is only interested in boys. The Princes are to remain with their grandmother. My own three children are well looked after by their nurses. I visit them every day but shall wait till they can speak and behave with reason before beginning their education. I am sure they will turn out no worse, and perhaps even better, than the Princes, who have had the Empress's full attention since they were born.

Affectionately,
Your sister Varvara

Nadezhda
May 1783

The Empress has appointed a new Court architect. Giacomo Quarenghi is Italian and small and ugly but is brimful of ideas and drawings. He seems to distract the Empress from her present sadness. I think his styles are very mixed, although he calls them Palladian, but perhaps that is the attraction for the Empress. He will do what she wishes rather than trying to impose his own style. Mr Quarenghi praises the Empress for her wonderful and plentiful ideas but complains that he has so much work that he scarcely has time to eat or sleep. He has lent me his order book so that I may copy the projects as proof of the scope of the Empress's interests and of his own industriousness.

Three pavilions in the new garden at Peterhof; the Stock Market; a large building for the state bank; a very large two-storey block of shops for the fair in Irkutsk in Siberia; a church with a hospital attached for their imperial highnesses at Pavlovsk; a building to accommodate Raphael's murals; a façade for the colleges and church in Polotsk; the façade for the governor's residence in Smolensk; a palace and stables for General Zavadovsky in Ukraine; the Hermitage theatre modelled on the ancients; the façade of the new imperial palace in Moscow; a marble gallery for the Empress's palace which must be the richest in Europe; the façade of the College of Foreign Affairs; shops for silversmiths; five churches; a house for General Lanskoy in the new town of Sophia; professors' apartments at the Academy of Sciences; a great staircase at General Lanskoy's palace in Polotsk as well as three large gates in marble and bronze; two iron and bronze bridges for the place at Tsarskoye Selo; the renovation and expansion of the governor's residence at Voronezh as well as the archbishop's palace, the seminary, its bell tower and several public buildings; a pavilion with a large hall for music, two rooms and an open temple to Ceres, with a ruin nearby in the ancient style. The list is added to almost daily for the Empress is fond of planning. When I praised the numerous projects to my husband, he muttered that he hoped there were funds to pay for them and if so, he would wonder where they came from.

Mr Cameron is also working on many projects but particularly the new town of Sophia. He advertised for craftsmen in his native Scotland and seventy men with their families have just arrived by ship to build the town as the Empress wishes it. There are four master masons, eighteen plasterers, three of them masters, two master bricklayers with several apprentices, five smiths, two engineers, two architects and sundry others. The Empress has decreed that they should work till six in the evening, nine if necessary, but they may have a break for dinner at two in the afternoon. It is a hive of activity. The labour is done by Russian state serfs.

The town will provide such a magnificent view when it is complete. Mr Cameron has designed particularly pleasing façades for the houses facing the palace. The streets will radiate in a semi-circle towards the palace and the Empress has said that they must have a lighting system so that she may enjoy the view of the town at night. Mr Cameron has not decided whether to string lanterns across the streets or along them.

Varvara
August 1783

Dear Alexandra,

I have hardly the patience to write to you. The summer has been hot and tedious, the Court grows ever more dismal. The Empress's favourite composer has left; her great friend, my husband's uncle, the Governor General of the St Petersburg, has died; the philosopher Diderot is ill; or Alexander Lanskoy has fallen off his horse and damaged his chest ... almost daily the Empress declares some calamity. She often takes to her bed.

Another disappointment for the Empress was the birth of the Grand Duke's daughter at the end of July. She declared the little Alexandra "quite ugly". One wonders if a third grandson had been born, which Empire she would plan for him. Perhaps a northern one. The one outing the Empress did undertake was in June to Vyborg, which apparently was wrested from the Swedes by Peter the Great, to meet with King Gustav of Sweden. If I were a King, I would not meet on conquered territory. King Gustav's arm was in a sling since he had broken it while inspecting a parade. His horse threw him when a cannon went off. The Empress was very scoffing. "What King cannot keep his horse?" she said.

We were a small retinue of some fifty carriages but we had nearly 300 horses, which involved long changes at the posts. After crossing the water, we still had 120 versts to travel, which took us two hot and dusty days. We stayed but a few days in what was a rather desolate and windy place, the Empress informing the King of her intention to take the Crimea, "if we have not already done so". The King apparently considers Russia's imminent involvement with Turkey as an opportunity for Sweden to retake the Baltic Empire while our troops are deployed far from home. I garnered this information with a few well-placed bribes, as you instructed, but I am not as interested in political intrigue as you are and so you must not blame me if there was more to be found out.

We were all happy to return to St Petersburg and particularly to Tsarskoye Selo. The Empress is agitated by the lack of news from Uncle in the Crimea. She writes to him constantly. There is always a letter lying on her desk. I memorized some lines for you.

Not only do I often think of you, she writes, *but I also regret and often grieve over the fact that you are there and not here , for without you I feel as if I am missing a limb. I beg you in every way: do not delay the occupation of the Crimea. I'm now fearful of you catching the plague. Take every precaution.*

As you see, the Empress is still infatuated with Uncle. It is no wonder Lanskoy seeks affection elsewhere.

Her letters express her growing impatience.

I have had no word from you in five weeks. I expected the Crimea to be taken by mid-May and now it is the end of July and I know no more about it than the Pope of Rome. There are many rumours and much talk but I have nothing to refute them with. I beg you to write to me of the latest events. I am tormented by my own thoughts.

I must say it is very remiss of Uncle not to write to the Empress. Or indeed to take the Crimea.

Please return to Court, Alexandra. It is your duty to look after matters here, not mine. I am bored. I will go to the Crimea as soon as we have news of Uncle's victory there. I will go whether you come or not.

Your impatient sister,
Varvara

PART FOUR

Nadezhda
October 1783

Dear Alexandra,

Uncle has taken the Crimea – with hardly a drop of blood spilled, he writes. When he arrived in Kherson in May, he was greeted by chaos. "I worked without sleep for weeks to instil order and peace. Who would wish to swear allegiance to an Empire which cannot even govern a small town properly?" His tactic was to persuade the Crimean peoples to join the Russian Empire voluntarily. He treated them well and had hundreds of cattle and sheep slaughtered for great feasts. He promised to free them from the tyrannical yoke of the Ottomans.

One of these tyrants is, of course, Russia's own puppet Khan Shagin Giray, who refused to abdicate, citing Empress Catherine's personal promise of protection. This was Uncle's greatest difficulty, which was eventually solved by "an annual pension of 200,000 roubles and a convincing show of force". The Tatars and other tribes, Christian and Muslim, are now willing to pledge loyalty to the Empress. It will all be in place by spring. "Spring?" the Empress shouted while reading the letter out loud. "Why so long? What is Prince Potemkin doing?"

Plague has indeed arrived in the Crimea and Uncle has been busy putting the usual precautions in place: quarantine, hygiene, hospitals etc. He has fallen ill himself but not from plague, he assures us, but from exhaustion. "Despite this, I am still working for your greater good, my Empress. I am also in negotiation with the Kings of Georgia and with Persian Khans, who may wish to found their own state of Armenia under Your Majesty's protection. Tell your scribes to prepare much paper and ink for the list will be long when the Treaty is signed."

The Empress is not cheered by the news. She is anxious that something will go wrong before Uncle has arranged the formalities – France may intervene, the British may object to the annexation now that they have lost their colonies, the Ottomans may win allies like the Persian Aga, the Swedes may attack the Baltic – the Empress sees danger lurking in every corner.

She has ordered Uncle to return and report to her personally as soon as he is fit to travel. This would seem inadvisable. In his absence, something is bound to go wrong. Alexandra, we miss your cleverness.

You are always able to calm the Empress and guide Uncle. You really must come back to Court.

Your affectionate sister,
Nadezhda

Katerina
February 1784

Uncle has been here all winter, and so have I. My husband is happy in Naples surrounded by music. I do not care for the city although there is always something to do in the evenings and many charming people to do it with. But the days are long and empty and as soon as I heard Uncle was in St Petersburg, I rushed to join him. My husband did not prevent me. "If you are homesick and Prince Potemkin needs you, then you must go," he sang, out of tune as usual.

Although I have been with Uncle often and Alexandra is not here to scold me, it has been a joyless winter. The Empress greeted Uncle less than warmly on his return. People had been spreading rumours about him – how he lived in luxury, holding court like the Khan he had deposed, how the plague had been due to his negligence, how he was building his own fleet, how he intended to make himself Emperor in the South. He and the Empress quarrelled loudly on several occasions. Faithless, ungrateful, were the words Varvara overheard from the Empress. Uncle retired to his own house and refused to see the Empress. "I will stay here and let her find someone else to finish my work in the Crimea," he said like a stubborn child. I spent as much time as I could with him since few others did. Usually, there are carriages lined up outside his house with petitioners and well-wishers but now no one wishes to court someone out of the Empress's favour and the street is empty. Even his admiring women are rarer, which should please me but it makes me sad.

"The Empress is stubborn," he said, "but I am more so. She will lose the Crimea if she does not treat me with the honours I deserve." But for all his defiance, he was morose. "I have lost my paradise," he said. I was not sure whether he was referring to the Crimea or the Empress. Varvara and I did all we could to keep his spirits up, even burying

151

our own jealousy of each other. We wrote to Alexandra begging her to return. Only when we informed her that Uncle had disappeared into a monastery did she come. It is not Uncle's stays in the monastery which are worrying but his new resolutions when he emerges.

Alexandra did come and the Empress received her graciously, perhaps even gratefully. "Our little family is scattered," she said. "I so regret that." Alexandra made bold to say, "Indeed, Your Majesty. Your loyalty to your family, to us and to Prince Potemkin, has always surpassed rumours and envious opposition." This is not really true, as we know, but Alexandra says you sometimes have to give the Empress the words to make her own.

Alexandra also soothed Alexander Lanskoy, suspected of spreading the rumours about Uncle, assuring him that Uncle would be in the Crimea for years to come, building up the new Empire for the Empress. "He is like a father to you," she explained to him patiently, "and when the Empress praises him, it is as if your mother praises your father." Alexandra worked tirelessly to bring the Empress and Uncle closer. She would not see any foreign envoys although they petitioned her ceaselessly. "First, we must have order in our own house before inviting others in."

And order was indeed gradually restored. Alexandra told the Empress the truth, that it was Uncle who had conquered the Crimea peacefully, averting war, and that without him, she would lose it before the treaty was signed. But she also told her that Uncle would only go back if the Empress asked him personally.

At the end of January, I was just leaving Uncle's chambers one morning having failed yet again to lift his spirits, when Uncle's valet approached me with an envelope bearing the imperial seal. I rushed into Uncle's room with it, fearing some ill news. Uncle read it and shouted, "Her Majesty has promoted me to Field Marshal!" He was as happy as a child. Throwing on his fur dressing coat and wrapping his pink scarf round his neck, he marched off jubilantly. "I am going to prostrate myself at the feet of my Empress," he said.

Later we found out that the Empress has also made Uncle the Viceroyal of what she calls New Russia and the Crimea is to be known as Taurida, after the tribes who inhabited it in antiquity. I must attend to my wardrobe and perhaps order some new jewels, for I must not discredit Uncle in his new elevated position. On the contrary, I will make sure to enhance it. I wonder if I can go with Uncle straight away or if I must follow later. He has painted such pictures of life in his paradise, in what he calls his warm and lush Garden of Eden, with vineyards as fine as any in Italy and vistas of white cliffs and blue seas. I may, he said, lie on a divan all day but that I would not need a fur coat to wrap myself in. I am consumed with impatience to be gone from the dismal and cold Russian Court.

Varvara
June 1784

Dear Katerina,

No one knows where you are but I suspect it is not in Naples with your husband. I surmise that you have followed Uncle to the Crimea. He has been called back but I doubt you will come with him for he must make all haste.

We are in the midst of the most grievous time. Alexander Lanskoy is dead and the Empress is mad with grief. He was only twenty-six, just one year younger than myself.

It was on Wednesday 19th June as we were playing cards with the Empress that Alexander, dear gentle Sasha, complained to the Empress of a sore throat. She told him in her brisk way to go to bed and rest and not to think of it. The next day Sasha's throat was worse and he could hardly speak. He also had a fever. Dr Rogerson prescribed some powders but Sasha refused to take them. The Empress, by this time looking a little worried, sent for that German physician she sometimes consults to come from St Petersburg. Sasha was bled, his feet put in cold water and he was given many cups of warm herbal drinks. He slept most of Thursday but when we saw him on Friday, his face was very swollen and the tip of his nose had turned white.

Another doctor was summoned. This one gave him cold drinks and cooked figs. The fever became stronger. On Saturday he seemed somewhat better but by noon he was vomiting and that apparently continued all day. (I did not visit him after Friday for fear of contagion but the terrible sequence of events has been retold many times in Court.) A purple rash appeared on Saturday evening but the German physician was optimistic. "He will pull through if it doesn't go to his brain," he said. He did not say what "it" was.

On Sunday the Empress recommended that Sasha move to a room with more fresh air and a view of the gardens. You know how much she believes in fresh air. But that may have been his undoing although no one would say that out loud. He walked there himself, refusing to be carried, and fell into a delirium soon after. He was very angry that no one would bring his horses to his bed. I have never seen Sasha angry. The doctors hoped that the anger was a sign that he would soon vomit bile, which would apparently be a good sign. On Monday he grew quieter and weaker. By Tuesday morning he was dead and the Empress's cries could be heard through the whole palace. It was most heart-rending.

At first, she would not leave Sasha, clinging to his inert body most pitifully. We were only able to persuade her with the promise that she could return when he had been suitably prepared and dressed. But she did not return. She took to her bed and would not leave it. Alexandra and I sat with her. Her sobs were incessant and she would not let the doctors see to her needs. "How can one die of a quinsy? Why did you not save him? Be gone from me!" she screamed at them.

It has been ten days now since Sasha died but the Empress's condition is no better. We tend to her as best we can but she is most piteous. When she speaks, it is only of Sasha. "I brought him up, I formed him, he was to be my support in my old age. He was gentle and kind and honest."

Alexandra sent for Uncle immediately. But a courier takes at least twelve days and then Uncle, the fastest rider in Russia, needs at least ten to reach us. I do not see how we can manage even another week. Every day, although she knows not what is night or day because she has had her room darkened, the Empress asks, "Has Prince Potemkin arrived?" Her chambers are stifling and we sweat as we sit with her or try to change her bed linens. Where is the fresh air she so praises?

The stench from another quarter is overwhelming and permeates the whole palace. The Empress has refused to allow Alexander Lanskoy to be buried until Prince

Potemkin arrives to, as she says, verify the awful nightmare of his death. Our summer's supply of ice has been used up in trying to keep the body from decomposing in the summer heat. To make matters worse, the Empress has ordered that he be kept in the room where he died although a cooler cellar would have been better. "No!" she declares. "Sasha must have fresh air. I would not put my dog in a cellar." She talks of him as if he were still alive and perhaps she believes this, or hopes it.

I cannot stay here any longer. I shall go mad. We all grieve for the gentle Sasha but we should bury him and continue with life. But no, we are forced into what has become a tomb. I have begged my husband to take me away but he has said leaving the palace at this time would be a sign of great disrespect to the Empress. I know I have complained about the boredom of life at Court but I would willingly live without this drama. The Empress indeed may see herself as some tragic heroine from one of her operas but I cannot think which one. I cannot think at all.

I presume you are lain prone like a Persian princess, surrounded by piles of exotic fruit and sweets, devoted slaves fanning you with palm fronds. I envy you most bitterly. But you will be without Uncle. He will soon be with us. This is the only light in this very dark tunnel.

Affectionately,
Your sister Varvara

Nadezhda
September 1784

It has been a dreadful summer. I do not know what would have happened if Uncle had not arrived. The Empress may have died of grief. As it was, he arrived here little more than two weeks after the death of Alexander Lanskoy, having fortunately been found in the Ukraine where he was travelling with some English engineers. He covered the huge distance of more than one thousand versts in just seven days, such was his concern for the Empress. But it took him another two weeks to convince the Empress to allow dear Sasha to be buried.

Terrible rumours have accompanied the stench we must all live with. Some say Sasha died of taking too many aphrodisiacs to satisfy the Empress but the members of her close circle know that was not the real nature of their relationship. He was more like a son to her. She taught him and he learned. He never involved himself in politics, he never took bribes. His only weakness was precious gems, especially carved ones.

There have been awful descriptions of his stomach bursting after death. Proof of poisoning, the rumours cry, but as Dr Rogerson points out, it is a scientific fact that the gases in a corpse will find their way out. Some say his legs also fell off. It is an unsavoury topic but it is important to set rational explanations against scandalous rumours.

Poor Sasha was eventually buried at the end of July, more than a month after his death. The Empress could not attend. She had a sore throat and a fever and declared she would die like her beloved and be with him forever. Sasha's body, beautifully encasked at last, was first taken to the house which Mr Cameron had designed for him in Sophia. The jewelled panels are a wonder to behold and we cried to think that Sasha would never enjoy them. He was then buried in the new cathedral in Sophia.

Uncle has not left the Empress's side. She will see no one else except Alexandra and myself. Varvara left with her husband before Sasha's funeral. She said the fumes of contagion were not good for her unborn child. I am not sure whether she really is with child again.

By August, the Empress was attending to state business in her chambers, with Uncle's help. At the beginning of September, she suddenly made the decision to return to St Petersburg. On the 8th September she was present in the chapel of the Winter Palace for the Feast of the Nativity of the Virgin. It was the first time she had been seen in public since Alexander died. Everyone scrutinised her but she held herself well, with Uncle at her side.

But back in her room in the Hermitage – she refused to move into her chambers in the Palace because they reminded her to much of her grievous lost – she all but fainted. "I will do my duty as Empress," she said, "but my heart continues to bleed. I am in a most cruel situation and suffer like the damned." Uncle scolds her and cajoles her but he also holds her tenderly as she weeps and he weeps with her.

In her small stuffy room in the Hermitage she has immersed herself in a new project. She has been reading ancient Russian history and through a comparison of languages intends to show that the ancient Slavs were responsible for naming "most rivers, mountains, valleys and many other places in France, Spain, Scotland and other countries." Alexandra said it was a waste of time and that there was much to be attended to in present-day Russia but Uncle said it is a very good sign of healing that she is occupied. In the months since Sasha's death, she has not even wanted to see the little Princes but they are to come to the palace next week and we are of good hope that they will cheer the Empress.

I hope I have more good news to report in future. Uncle has said I may visit him in the Crimea to record many new and wondrous things. I hope that will be soon. My husband has given his permission.

Alexandra
January 1785

Dear Varvara,

Uncle has left at last. For months he played nursemaid to the Empress, neglecting all his responsibilities in the Crimea. She refused to let him out of her sight. I remonstrated with him that there was an Empire to govern and a new one to make and he must bring the Empress to her senses. "That is precisely what I am doing," he said, "but it is a slow process. I cannot leave her until she is strong enough. A weak Empress would be the end of the Empire. Her son would hand it over to Prussia."

"What she needs," I said, "is a new ... interest. Until she has one, she will cling to you. We must find her a handsome young adjutant."

"I am working on that too," he promised. And indeed there was always the usual line of young men hoping to catch the Empress's attention on her way to church. But she vowed that no-one would or could replace her beloved Sasha.

She stayed in her tiny room in the Hermitage and took to writing plays, of all things. The papers were piled everywhere and the desk and floors were covered in ink stains. She welcomed her grandsons again and they visited her often. They do well under their new tutor, Count Saltykov, and are charming, learned and very well-mannered. They are both handsome but Alexander's face is illuminated with an open kindness. It is easy to understand why he is the Empress's favourite. Her good humour was so much restored by December that she even declared her new granddaughter beautiful and said she must be named Helen after Helen of Troy.

The Empress started making up card parties again, with a small number of people, and she played billiards. But she would not let Uncle go.

"She will never be well until you leave," I told him. "You being here allows her to wallow in self-pity."

Eventually, he roused her interest by proposing a tour to her new Taurida. He talked of his projects: the building of a naval base at Sebastopol, which would harbour 100 ships; the construction of the fleet itself as well as merchant ships, for the Crimea would flourish on trade; the foundation of Kherson, which would be Russia's third greatest city and southern capital, after St Petersburg and Moscow; the cathedral there would be named St Catherine's Cathedral and he would commission an artist to paint life-size icons of St Catherine and St George; architects and engineers were being imported from the West, even gardeners; the transfer of thousands of soldier serfs had been organised for labour ... no detail was too small: the floating of wood from Chernobyl in Poland; plans for hospitals and breweries as well as normal dwellings ... the list was endless and Uncle was flushed with his own enthusiasm as he scribbled plans and lists as he talked.

But what caught the Empress's particular attention was Uncle's plan to build a "new Athens" in the middle of the steppes. It would be called Ekaterinoslav in Catherine's honour. It would be built in pure classical style with columned law courts, basilica-like public offices, an amphitheatre, a spacious forum, a cathedral larger than Rome's Vatican. There would be a musical conservatory – musical staff had already been hired from Italy, an Academy of Arts, schools and colleges, a university. Young people from Poland, Greece, Wallachai and Moldavia would study there and spread civilisation once more. Uncle, scribbling figures on yet another scrap of paper, calculated he would need 16,000 workmen for some nine or ten years for this one project alone. The Empress was caught by his enthusiasm and was soon busy asking questions and making suggestions. She made her own list of costs, the zeros swiftly increasing.

"It is a great and daring vision," she said, "and only you can make it a reality."

"Yes, but I do it only for your glory, my Empress," Uncle replied, "and you must come and bathe in that glory. The people must see who has rescued them from barbarity and despotism. They will fall at your feet."

The Empress listened, entranced. "Give me a list of all you need," she eventually said. "I will do all I can to accomplish our Greek Empire."

"And I shall go on ahead to further the work, for there is much of it, and to prepare everything for your visit," Uncle said. "Meanwhile, you can finish your legislation and perhaps promulgate it to mark your birthday in April. Your subjects will know that you have not neglected them, even in time of deepest personal grief." Before Lanskoy fell ill, the Empress had been working on a Charter to accord the nobility more personal rights as well as one to bestow self-government on the towns. She now promised, almost meekly, to finish this legislation. "Yes, my dear Prince, you do well to chastise me. None of my reforms will happen if the drafts remain scrolled up in a drawer." She immediately ordered her secretaries to retrieve the papers. And at the same time to bring her a map of New Russia.

Oh, it was good to see the Empress return to life! Uncle indeed knew how to sway her. They were like an old married couple and I sometimes wonder if there is not truth in the rumour that they were secretly married some ten years ago. There is at least strong loyalty to her on his side and need of him on her side.

Uncle left for the Crimea shortly after the New Year, with the Empress's blessing and copious tears. Soon after, she moved back into the Winter Palace but she still retires to her little room in the Hermitage, especially in the hour after dinner, which was normally the private time she spent with Alexander Lanskoy. A sign that her mourning was coming to an end can perhaps be seen in her desire to pore over the antique cameos and engraved gems which she and

Lanskoy had collected. They were kept in a cabinet of 125 drawers, which she ordered brought to her one afternoon. Four manservants were barely able to carry half the drawers in two large baskets. The Empress has commissioned a series of new cabinets for the stones, to be designed by Queen Marie Antoinette's cabinet-maker.

I have neglected my husband and children but now that the Empress is healthy, I think I can leave Court for a few months. I hesitate only because none of the family will be here. Katerina is in Naples, I think. She does not care to write. Nadezhda prepares to visit Uncle in the Crimea at his request. And Tatiana will go with her. Could you return to Court for some months? Has your child been born? I think you will find Court becoming quite gay again. There is to be a grand ball for the Empress's birthday in April. ***Tout le monde*** will be there.

With affection,
Your sister Alexandra

Nadezhda
May 1785

Dear Alexandra,

There is so much to record that I am sure I must spend every hour writing if I am to cover it all in my diary. But I know you are anxious for details of our stay here and so I shall try to write a concise letter.

I admire Uncle so much – how he manages scores of projects with tireless energy, often travelling hundreds of versts each day. He is so different from the way he is in St Petersburg. Here in the Crimea he is always busy, always cheerful, always enthusiastic and full of plans. One never finds him lazing in his chambers till late in the day half-dressed. He is up with the sun. He is much respected and instantly obeyed – like an Emperor, which in a way he is for he represents the Empress here in the building of her new empire. He has his own private Chancellery which employs some fifty clerks, who can also correspond in Greek.

We are very comfortably accommodated in a Moorish type palace with many cupolas and balconies. Uncle's grand palace is not yet finished. But Tatiana and I like it here. It is all that Uncle said – a land of warm sea breezes and abundant fruit. We sit on the terrace in loose kaftans, our hair unbound and free from the restrictions of the Russian Court. And its darkness. Here we do not need so many candles and often sit outside on the balmy evenings with the moon or stars for light.

When we have company, of which there is no lack, we dress in our best robes, thread our hair with pearls, and wear our finest jewels, for Uncle wishes us to soften what he calls his military air. There are other ladies present too of course and some of them have a fond affection for Uncle but I am not sure if he has a particular friend. He is gallant to all and divides compliments fairly. You instructed me to make sure no woman took an official place by his side and

I can assure you that that role is played by me. I am his hostess.

Tatiana and I have been paid court by several men of interest. They are mostly Englishmen devoted to Uncle and have worked at everything from building ships to bridges, planting vineyards and founding silk factories ... and they are handsomely hardened by it. They may don their fine clothes for dinner but when one glimpses them during the day riding hard on their horses, one is struck by their very manliness.

One such man is Uncle's close friend, the Englishman Samuel Bentham, whom you will remember for his ***amour fou*** with the Governor of St Petersburg's niece last year. He is but two years older than me but his experience in life has been a hundredfold. Oh, how I sometimes wish I had been born a man. Samuel Bentham has travelled throughout our empire with Uncle and has even been to Siberia. I must not complain because Uncle has been kind enough to have me visit the Crimea, which is indeed an exciting place, where much happens because Uncle makes it happen.

The Crimea, as Samuel has explained, is a region of great fertility but is worth nothing without settlers. Uncle had already encouraged retired and wounded soldiers, runaway serfs, noblemen who had lost land in the wars, Old Believers, Cossacks – a motley assortment. These early settlers, however, brought little expertise and that is what Uncle is seeking now. He has put advertisements in European newspapers, especially in Britain. Samuel has an elder brother Jeremy, and he searches England for all sorts of artisans to send to the Crimea: shoemakers, bricklayers, sailors, millwrights, windmill makers, botanists, milkmaids – the list which Samuel showed me is endless and varied but I shall save it for my diary for I wish to give you an impression rather than bore you with too many details, dear Alexandra.

Settlers are offered land, free cattle and farming equipment and have to pay no taxes for several years. Agents who find them receive five roubles per settler. Many have come. Over sixty Corsican families came together, many Mennonites from Danzig, settlers from Sweden – and Uncle even allows Jews from Poland as long as each brings five non-Jews with him. The population of the Crimea is perhaps 50,000 (counting only men and in any case there are few women, which will be a problem, Samuel says) but ten times that number are needed. Till now, some 30,000 settlers have come. "Your Uncle," Samuel said, "has the idea of importing British convicts, perhaps a thousand or two of them. The British cannot send them to the Colonies anymore since they have declared their independence." When I expressed my surprise that the area would be overrun by criminals, Samuel said, "Most are not hardened criminals. Many are in prison for stealing a kerchief or poaching small animals. And many have learned a trade." The only people Uncle has refused are Americans loyal to the British Crown, who asked to become settlers in the Crimea once the Colonies declared their independence from Britain. Uncle said they may be too political with ideas incompatible with Russian principles. "Yes," Samuel said with a laugh, "they may wish a democratic parliament and Prince Potemkin would not like that!"

Uncle has not only laid the foundations for wine-making (with 30,000 vines from Tokay in Hungary), mulberry plantations for his silk factories, one of which will manufacture silk stockings "so fine they will fit in a nutshell", sheep breeding for wool, cattle for cheese, forests of trees for timber – again there is a long list more suited to my diary than to a letter – but he has also begun a formidable navy. A war ship with sixty guns has just been launched at Kherson and is named ***Catherine's Glory***. It cost over 2 million roubles. I am no expert but Samuel says this is the most powerful battleship one can build. Uncle wishes a whole Black Sea fleet of battleships – perhaps some 25 of them – in the next two years. Samuel says Britain has 174 ships-of-the-line, as they are called, and we can never surpass that but I remind him of our Baltic Fleet which would add another 40 ships or so in total. "Then," he conceded, "you will have nearly as many as the Spanish or French."

We will be reluctant to leave Uncle and the Crimea. But we are mindful that you and Varvara and Katerina also look forward to coming and we cannot all be here together. In addition, my husband has been most patient. I hope your business ventures with him in the Urals have borne fruit. I would suggest leaving Tatiana here until one of you comes but I am not sure the ladies of Uncle's acquaintance would make suitable chaperones. At the moment, we have the beautiful and witty Lady Craven here, who lives and travels in scandalous liberty. She talks openly of her many lovers and recommends we try men from the "more normal walks of life for they are more vigorous than the hot-housed reared aristocrats of England or anywhere else." She has asked Uncle to introduce her to some Cossacks. She has also asked for two estates in the Crimea, where she says she would happily settle – although she is in romantic correspondence with Frederick the Great's brother-in-law, the Margrave of Anspach, who wishes to marry her. "And so he shall," she said, "but all in good time." You will see, dear Alexandra, that I cannot leave Tatiana alone here.

Your affectionate sister,
Nadezhda

Tatiana
June 1785

I still try to write only about good things in my diary. Samuel Bentham is a good thing and I think I am in love with him. He is at least ten years older than me and no doubt sees me as a child, which I am not. I adore his wild hair, streaked with the sun, his open face, weathered to a pleasant darkness, his energetic movements and his boundless enthusiasm for all he does and will do. He is much admired by the ladies here, married or not. Lady Craven is particularly open in her flirting. He has no doubt bedded all of them. I am glad he will leave soon, to return to Uncle's largest estate on the borders with Poland. I do not think there are so many women there. Samuel says Krichev is larger than any English county or German principality. It covers an area of some 100 square miles, very strategically placed between two great rivers which afford trade routes north and south, with 40,000 male serfs or vassals, over which he is "legislator, judge, jury and sheriff". I imagine myself at his side, supporting him in all his endeavours, of which there are many. I love to hear him talk about Krichev and think if I show interest, he might see me as a very good marriage possibility. Samuel has founded a brandy distillery, copper works, a tannery, a textile mill with nearly 200 looms for making sailcloth, twenty wheels for making rope for Uncle's shipyards, greenhouses, a shipyard and a mirror factory ... He is even thinking of cultivating potatoes on a large scale in anticipation of an increase in settlers. "Krichev," Samuel explained, "is your uncle's main supply centre – for his Black Sea fleet and for exports to Russia and Europe. It is his centre of economic power in the Crimea. But my main task at this time is to build ships – any kind, for war, pleasure or trade. I can spend what I like. The Prince has just commissioned me to build a luxury barge for the Empress when she comes to visit."

Mention of the Empress's visit gives me hope. Perhaps I may come too. I think I would make Samuel an excellent wife. I would be industrious and interested. I am loathe to return to the Russian Court, where everyone spends so much time and energy doing nothing.

I have been gathering interesting anecdotes for Prince Alexander and his brother, particularly about the Cossacks, who originally inhabited the Crimea but were defeated by our Russian forces led by Uncle. There are several tribes of Cossacks but one group will surely be of interest to the Princes. They comprised about 20,000 men and lived on an island in the middle of the River Dnieper, from where they controlled huge areas of barren territory. It was barren because the Cossacks did not farm. They considered farming to be work done by slaves and they were free men, which is apparently what the word Cossack means. These Cossacks were strong and cruel. Anyone of their own who betrayed them was sewn into a sack and tossed into the fast flowing river. Murderers were tied to their dead victims and buried alive. All Cossacks are very skilled on horseback but this group were equally skilled on boats. It is even said they could sail underwater with pipes to breathe through. Perhaps I should not relate that to the Princes – they may wish to try it.

Only men lived on the Cossack island. Women were considered a disruption to their strict military discipline. Uncle said that women are indeed a distraction, especially if they happen to be an Empress. Uncle has shown us drawings of these Cossacks and I consider them unattractive. They have moustaches which wing out, shaven heads but long hair tied at the back. They wear wide Turkish pantaloons with rich gold thread, satin kaftans, silk cummerbunds and turbans with ostrich feathers and jewels. Their profession is, or was, war. Uncle admires the Cossacks, particularly these ones, and has been trying to attract them into our army. I find them very frightening and am glad Uncle meets them elsewhere than in his house. Anyway, they would not wish to live in a house where there are women. I wonder where they do meet their women.

Gathering anecdotes for the Princes occupies me when I am sad that I soon have to return to St Petersburg. I imagine their rapt listening and enthusiastic acting of the scenes. But there is really no need for me to be sad since there will be little attraction here once Samuel leaves for Krichev in a few days. I asked Uncle if I may visit Krichev but he looked at me sharply and said, "Young Bentham is useful to me but not good enough for a beloved niece. He is too ... colourful." I think Uncle is more colourful than Samuel and he is good enough for the Empress.

Varvara
June 1785

Dear Katerina,

I will direct this to Naples although I harbour my suspicions that you are in the Crimea with Uncle. You might at least write to us – but then again, we know how little fond you are of any effort.

I was vexed that Alexandra and Uncle ordered me back to Court in spring. It was I who was supposed to go to the Crimea first but Nadezhda and Tatiana went before me and now I must wait my turn. Still, Alexandra was right. The dreadful cloud of grief at Court has dissipated and there is a light gaiety, even in the Empress. This may be due to the presence of a "new friend". He first appeared at the Empress's table at her birthday in April, for which I had not returned in time owing to the birth of my third child and second son. It was just as well since the grand ball Alexandra promised did not take place. The celebrations were quiet and much attention given instead to the new Charters which the Empress promulgated on her birthday. The details bore me, and I'm sure they do you too, but both the aristocracy and the burghers have been given significant new rights – a type of emancipation, my husband says. The Empress believes granting such personal freedom is the means to securing loyalty. My husband is well pleased. He talks about freedom from poll tax and compulsory service, more power over our serfs, the right to resources and manufactory on our estates, our own assembly, the liberty to travel, freedom from corporal punishment – I mean, who would flog a noble?

But to return to more interesting matters: the Empress's new friend is Alexander Yermolov. He is older than dear Sasha was but at thirty still young enough for the Empress. He is not particularly good-looking but a touch of something foreign in his features gives him an interesting look. He is fair-haired but has bronzed skin with dark almond-shaped eyes and a rather flat nose. Uncle, to whose retinue he belongs, calls him the White Negro. Uncle says he is limited in his interests but is honest and good and will serve the Empress well for the time being. Yermolov has been promoted to major-general and has been appointed the Empress's personal adjutant, moving into Alexander Lanskoy's chambers some eleven months after his death, which is a fitting enough time. He has, however, been in the Empress's close circle since her birthday some three months ago and has no doubt accounted for her very vibrant return to life, for which I am very grateful for we have had such marvellous fun at Court.

Another welcome addition to the Empress's inner circle is Comte Louis-Philippe de Ségur, the new French ambassador. The Empress is very taken with him, as we all are. He is about thirty years of age and has led a very full life, having just returned from fighting in the American War. He was friends with the philosopher Diderot and the Empress cannot hear enough about him. The Comte is also an intimate of Queen Marie Antoinette but on this topic he remains discreet despite our entreaties. The Comte has very pleasant features in a face perhaps a little too round, his lips always curved in smile, his eyebrows raised as if in constant surprise. He is extremely witty and his **bons mots**, songs, poems, a veritable flow of words, bubble forth like champagne overflowing – the image is the Empress's not my own. We sometimes laugh so much we have to beg him to stop.

At the end of May, the Empress decided to make an inspection of the canal system, which Peter the Great had begun and she has been expanding. The geography of it all, as you can imagine, is lost to me but its aim is to link the Volga River to the Baltic Sea for purposes of trade and later the Caspian to the Black Sea. The Empress illustrated all this on large maps but it escaped my interest and therefore my memory. We were a small group of less than twenty people, among them the Comte as well as the new envoys of Britain and Austria. Alleyne Fitzgerald, unlike his predecessor James Harris, is very reserved in the British manner and, although quietly witty, seems constantly puzzled by our antics. Uncle said it is important to keep Fitzgerald happy, for the new British prime minister, William Pitt, has declared, in what Uncle calls 'his youthful arrogance' – he is twenty-six – that he does not like Catherine of Russia and that no treaty will be signed with her under his government. He is also anti-Austrian but this does not bring bad blood between the two ambassadors. The Austrian ambassador is still the rather hideous Louis Cobenzl, who loves singing and women, especially if combined in his own person. He is very entertaining when lavishly dressed as one of the heroines of some opera. Uncle says more agreements will be reached between nations on our trip than at any diplomatic meeting and that we must be especially kind to the ambassadors even if they do sing in women's clothes.

Our canal trip took us away from St Petersburg for nearly four weeks. We travelled several days by carriage, I mostly in the Empress's, and she invited different members of the group to join her for different parts of the journey and so we were well entertained. But the Empress kept to a strict routine.

We started off in the mornings at the rather uncivilised hour of 8 o'clock after the Empress had worked for at least an hour and received the local dignitaries. We then travelled till 2 when we stopped for dinner at some village, where everything had been prepared to satisfaction. Before dinner, however, the Empress would visit the local church to pray and make a donation. She says it is important for the people to see her devotion. After a short rest, our journey resumed until 8 in the evening when we would relax with card games and entertainment, usually provided by the Comte.

The Empress was persuaded, surprisingly, to include Moscow on her tour, a city she is not fond of. But she declared it much improved and inspected some new palaces, none of which could rival her palaces in St Petersburg, Tsarskoye Selo or Peterhof.

From Moscow we travelled by water all the way along rivers, lakes and canals to Novgorod and then to Peterhof. The weather was warm and sunny and we lazed on deck lulled by the orchestra – each galley had its own. There was one special galley to prepare the mid-day meal and one for dinner in the evening, so we ate well and plentifully. It was a very pleasant journey. On the lake just before Novgorod, our galleys were surrounded by all sorts of craft, bearing boatmen and peasant girls colourfully dressed with flowers in their hair. They competed with each other in singing and playing their instruments. After dinner in the evening their melodies drifted out to us from the banks of the lakes.

Yes, Katerina, life at Court has been most pleasant, and it is a pity you have missed it. But then you may have been playing Turkish princess in Uncle's Moorish palace or holding court in Naples. Word has just come that Uncle is on his way here. What happiness! This means you are either with him or in Naples. I need not send this letter at all and you may read it when you arrive, which must surely be soon.

Affectionately,
Your sister Varvara

Alexandra
August 1785

Dear Katerina,

I am back at Court again and I was surprised not to find you here. Uncle has intimated that you had to return to your husband in Naples for reasons of health. As I understand it, you await a confinement. Uncle assures me your husband is very accepting, indeed grateful, for this child and will consider it an honour to bring it up as his own. Please do not make the matter complicated, Katerina. Uncle cannot be hampered by domestic matters.

You missed Uncle's Great Ball mid-summer. We have balls and masquerades every week but this was a grand affair, which took place in Uncle's Anichkov Palace. He still does not reside there but is always adding to it, most recently a third floor and a new façade of the Doric columns he so much likes. There were two thousand guests, dressed in a variety of colourful costumes, some very exotic. In the middle of the open hall, arranged on a huge pyramid, an orchestra and choir of more than 100 musicians played and sang. On top of the pyramid was a negro dressed in fine green silk playing a huge drum. It was a wonderful spectacle.

The dancing was lively, especially the quadrilles. The new finishing class of the Empress's Smolny Institute gave a very fine tableau, all of them looking young and sylph-like as woodland nymphs in sheer gowns. Princess Katerina Bariatinskaya, whom you may remember for her outstanding beauty, received particular praise and it is no secret to tell you of Uncle's interest in her. Well, you would not have him despondent. We must keep his spirits up. At the moment, he is very happy that the Empress is content with her White Negro, for he can now return to the Crimea and all the work that awaits him there. "You know, Alexandra," he said recently, "any power I have is greater when I am not in the vicinity of the Empress.

When I am in the Crimea, everything is in my hands and I must not seek the Empress's consent for every little, or even great, matter." The Empress, however, likes to have Uncle near her all the time. "Our two minds are better than one," she has remarked more than once. That may be the case but agreement or compromise comes only after long arguments and sulks between the two, which can last for days.

Uncle plans to leave as soon as possible now that the Empress, with Yermolov at her side, is happily settled into a calm routine – working, walking her dogs, playing with that white squirrel she tamed as well as her pet monkey, spending afternoons with Yermolov, planning excursions, teaching the Princes, writing plays – her scribes cannot keep up with her and must work late into the night. The architect Giacomo Quarenghi is designing a new theatre for the Hermitage especially for the Empress's plays, with seats, in a semi-circle, for 300 people. Nadezhda says it is a replica of an ancient Roman theatre and will have pink marble columns and classical statues.

And so all has returned to normal, the Empress content with a new favourite, busy with many plans and Uncle can concentrate on the new empire in the south. I think Uncle would wish to live permanently in the Crimea but the Empress wishes him here as often as possible. And he must comply, for she is the absolute ruler and can give or take as she pleases. In Uncle's absences, it is our duty to watch out for his interests and our own. We may be bolstered by our own marriages but we are still Uncle's family and may fall if he falls. Why, my own husband knows this danger and therefore is most tolerant of the time I have to spend at Court.

When you are back to health, Uncle has asked that you come to St Petersburg. I have to attend to matters on my husband's estates as well as my own business interests, and Prince Golitsyn wishes to return with Varvara to his own estates. Nadezhda might be very knowledgeable but she knows little of what is going on around her for she spends too much time in libraries. She also needs to be with her husband more. It is time she had a child. Tatiana is not yet wise to the ways of the world and we cannot expect her to take over the whole responsibility of our family's interests. And so you must take over. Uncle has asked most specifically that you do not go to the Crimea. I expect you here before winter begins.

With affection,
Your sister Alexandra

Katerina
August 1786

Dear Varvara,

It is some 10 months since I came to St Petersburg to do my family duty and I am vexed that I am still here. Surely you can take my place now? It is only fair that I may leave. Even Naples and my singing husband are preferable to the Empress's Court, where all must be done to please her without thought of anyone else's pleasure. Gone are the days when Uncle was here and the Empress was happy, and I lay on the sofa, or in Uncle's bed.

When I do manage to steal some time to myself, which is seldom, I dream of my time in the Crimea. I could not have stood the separation from Uncle had he not visited twice in these last 10 months. But he is different here. The sun does not shine from his eyes. He is morose and bad-tempered and his critics are proved right. In the Crimea, he is his true self – exuberant, witty, kind and generous, a whirl of activity and entertainment – and he laughs a lot. I think the Empress fell in love with the real Potemkin but turned him into something else.

The Crimea is his escape, his paradise, as he calls it. The air is gentle and the light is golden. There is always music. You know how he loves music – but the Empress is tone-deaf. "She cannot appreciate the complexity of music, only that which sounds easy to the ears, like those operettas she is so fond of and which I cannot bear," Uncle complained when he was last here. In the Crimea he keeps an orchestra, some sixty men, each with a different horn. It is truly wondrous to hear, like a huge organ. He also has choirs which even accompany him on his tours. He cannot be without music but here in St Petersburg he does not listen to any. He sits sullenly at dinner and very often does not pay attention, which angers the Empress. In the Crimea, he shines at table and eats heartily of the food, which is not as ornately presented as at the Empress's table but rich in delicacies all the same – caviar from the Caspian Sea, delicious dates stuffed with almonds, mounds of grapes, good wines and flowing champagne. He does not even wear his beloved jewels in St Petersburg. It is as if he extinguishes his own light when he is here. Or perhaps the Empress has that effect on him. At any rate, he is difficult and depressed and if I did not know him as he is, I too would shun his company as many do.

At least, I have been of some use to him. It was fortunate that I did not resume my duties with the Grand Duchess Maria since they now live in Pavlovsk, where I would have been far removed from the Empress's Court. Alexandra had arranged for me to take her place in the Empress's chambers. And so I learned early on of Yermolov's attempts to discredit Uncle. There were many rumours at Court, flowing from Uncle's enemies to Yermolov, who fed them to the Empress. It began fairly harmlessly. "I have heard that Prince Potemkin holds court like an Emperor in a very fine suit of clothes where every seam is embroidered with diamonds," Yermolov remarked. This I know to be true for I have often seen him dressed in that suit as well as others of great magnificence. He has a hat so heavy with jewels he cannot wear it and it must be carried by an adjutant. The Empress is used to Uncle's extravagances and has often encouraged him. Many of the diamonds he wears were gifts from her. ""I am sure he looks very fine," the Empress said mildly. "He represents us well."

But Yermolov's remarks became more insinuating and well calculated to rouse the Empress's jealousy. I was first seriously alarmed when Yermolov said Uncle had been accused of stealing Shagin Giray's pension. "Why should he do such a thing?" Yermolov asked the Empress with an innocent air. "Does the Prince not receive enough millions from yourself and from your enterprises in the Crimea? Shall we have the Treasury examine the accounts more closely?" At first, the Empress chided Yermolov for his mistrust but gradually her mood changed.

I wrote to Uncle to come to St Petersburg urgently. Soon after I was shocked to hear Yermolov say to the Empress, "I have heard that the Prince intends to marry and make his betrothed Queen of the South." This was perfidy and certainly untrue. The Empress turned to me. "Do you know anything of this?" she asked angrily. I assured her it must be no more than a very malicious rumour. "If the Prince has betrayed me in any way," she said, "I will replace him in my heart and as Governor of my provinces." Yermolov looked at me triumphantly with his narrow eyes. I hoped Uncle would arrive before it was too late.

I had no time to prepare him for he rushed in one evening as we sat playing cards with the Empress. He was dusty and dishevelled after thousands of versts of hard riding, but he had never looked more handsome. Yermolov in his fine silks was a milksop in comparison. "What is it you believe of me, Your Majesty?" Uncle shouted as he came through the door. The Empress rose from the card table, startled. "What should I not believe of you, Prince Potemkin?" she retorted. She then turned to the rest of us. "Leave us!" she said. Yermolov hovered by the Empress's side, looking smug. "You too, Yermolov!" Uncle shouted. There followed weeks of tension. Uncle was very bad-mooded and refused to attend the Empress. He even stayed away from the celebrations for the anniversary of her coronation. His behaviour was dangerous.

"Why can't you talk to her?" I pleaded. "Deny these rumours. Defend yourself."

"I will not demean myself," he said. "I will not grace such filthy slander with a denial."

Comte de Ségur also tried to persuade him to make peace with the Empress. "Otherwise, Yermolov will win. He will oust you, my friend," he said. "This is no time to be stubborn. You must use diplomatic strategy." The Comte knows Uncle well. He described him to me recently, as we were having a very pleasant tête-à-tête, as a man made fascinating by his contradictions. "He is a unique mixture of grandeur and pettiness, of laziness and activity, of ambition and indifference." I thought this very accurate.

"Don't worry," Uncle said scornfully, "no child is going to topple me. No one would dare to. I scorn my enemies too much to fear them."

He left Court, taking me with him, and we spent some time in Narva and then at several hunting lodges before returning to St Petersburg. There were many parties and we did not lack for pleasurable company. I was so concerned about Uncle that I also arranged for some of his most ardent admirers to spend a few hours with him. In any case, I could not keep up with his inexhaustible passions. Nothing could satisfy him.

Alexandra came at last. We needed her cool reasoning. She scolded Uncle. "You would forfeit all we have achieved, you would lose the Crimea, all for your pride? You must make your peace with the Empress!"

He was a stubborn as a child. "No, she must make her peace with me!"

"Then we must employ another strategy," Alexandra said. "We must present her with a new favourite."

Uncle was taken with the idea and suddenly his mood brightened. "Yes, and we must at the same time present her with an ultimatum. Me or Yermolov. She will choose me and fall into the arms of her new favourite. I think she tires of the White Negro, in any case, and will be happy to be rid of him."

And so it happened. Uncle introduced one of his young protégés, Alexander Mamonov, twenty-six years old, a very handsome and educated officer, cultivated and mannered, charming and courteous. Where Yermolov's features, especially his nose, are wide-spread, Mamonov's are very neat and tidy, almost pretty. Alexandra and Uncle spent hours telling him how to please the Empress. I felt sorry for the young man. The Empress is, after all, fifty-seven years old, has lost any figure she might have had under too much corpulence and suffers from indigestion problems. But Uncle was right. Having prepared Mamonov and introduced him to the Empress, he then told her bluntly a few days later, "If you keep the White Negro, I will never set foot in this Court again." Yermolov was formally dismissed the next day with 130,000 roubles, 4000 serfs, and orders to travel for five years at the Court's expense. Three days later Mamonov was appointed personal adjutant and moved into the favourite's chambers. The Empress's personal secretary reported to Uncle that they had slept till nine o'clock, some three hours later than the Empress's usual hour. Uncle was well pleased and guffawed loudly.

This was all last month. In the meantime, Uncle has left for the Crimea. I begged him to take me with him but he must ride hard and does not wish to be slowed by carriages. I intend to follow soon whether you come or not. I have done my duty, as you can see, and I yearn for a gentler life.

Your impatient sister,
Katerina

Nadezhda
September 1786

I have an important happening to record. Frederick the Great of Prussia has died. The Empress was never fond of him but his death left her thoughtful for a few days. "We were of the same era," she said. "We understood the etiquette of being enemies before we became uneasy allies."

Grand Duke Paul declares he will mourn his hero for six months. His faction at Court has been deprived of what they always saw as their powerful support.

Frederick is succeeded by his nephew, Frederick William, who bored us all when he visited our Court. "Goodness knows what we shall do with Prussia now that it is to be ruled by that fat, Prussian boor," the Empress said. "Austria is indeed more charming." She thinks, of course, of Emperor Joseph.

When the Empress heard that Frederick had left instructions to be buried with his favourite greyhounds, she said, "Ah, a kindred spirit!" The Empress, as everyone knows, is very attached to her own greyhounds. "One can forgive him much for that love, even supporting France against us. Or recognising those upstart colonies in America as a state. On that matter, age must have clouded his reason."

The King was seventy-four when he died. "If he managed it, then I will manage it too," the Empress declared. One could see that the death of this great sovereign, who had ruled for more than forty-five years, roused in the Empress thoughts of her own mortality. Fortunately, she has been distracted by her new favourite, Alexander Mamonov, who is fifty years younger than King Frederick the Great when he died. As she grows older, the Empress takes younger and younger lovers. It is as if she thinks they will be a source of youth for her.

Alexandra
December 1786

My esteemed Prince Potemkin, my dearest Uncle,

In one month we shall start our journey to the Crimea! The Empress has been most diligent in all the preparations and the mood at Court has been calm for the most part, marred by only one or two incidents. The first was the arrival of Diderot's books and manuscripts, which should have been an occasion of joy for the Empress. She had paid much and waited a long time for them, as you know. She seized upon his Observations of her Grand Instruction, eager to read the anticipated praise for her great work of legislation. But Diderot had written, "There is only a formal difference between despotism and pure monarchy. It is the spirit of pure monarchy which has dictated the spirit of Catherine II's Instruction. Pure monarchy remains as it is or reverts to despotism, according to the character of the monarch. It is therefore a bad sort of government." He went on to attack the meagre improvements to the lives of the serfs, on which he claimed our Russian Empire is founded. "There is only one way to avoid the abuses of serfdom: and that is to abolish it." The Empress was very upset. Mamonov was able to calm her, reminding her that words were not always true just because a philosopher had written them. In fact, a philosopher was far removed from the reality of government, which was the realm of a sovereign. The Empress rallied and declared Diderot's essay "utter drivel" and her own legislation excellent and beneficial to all in her empire. Mamonov has been a very good influence on the Empress. She calls him Redcoat for it is his favourite colour and he does look well in it. I must say you chose very well, Uncle. The Empress praises Redcoat at every public opportunity. She declares him as beautiful inside and out.

We also had a domestic crisis to deal with. As you know, the brother of the Grand Duchess has been the

Empress's Governor in Finland these past four years. He and his young wife, Princess Augusta, whom everyone for some reason calls Zelmira, still come to Court regularly to enjoy any festivities. After the last ball, Zelmira rushed into the Empress's chambers just as we were preparing her for bed and, weeping hysterically, demanded the Empress's protection from her husband, who, she claimed, regularly beat her to within an inch of her life. "It is because he prefers young men," she said. From what I know of the Princess, this statement is more likely to be true of her. In any case, the Empress relieved Prince Frederick of his position and ordered him to return to Prussia immediately. The Grand Duchess, as you can imagine, was distraught at this treatment of her brother and sent a piteous plea to the Empress saying her brother "did not deserve such public opprobrium, which throws me into despair and will be a dagger blow for those who gave me birth." The Empress showed me this letter as well as her answer. ""It is not I who cover the Prince with opprobrium. On the contrary, it is I who try to bury abominations in oblivion and it is my duty to suppress any further ones. I have done what I had to do and I have done well. The Princess will go to her parents and the Prince can go where he pleases."

As it transpired, the Princess's father would not take her, saying it was her duty to remain with her husband, and so the Empress has settled her far enough away, in one of her estates near Reval. I tell you all this, for the rift between the Empress and her son has been deepened by this incident and his allies and our enemies have been stirring discontent again. They now say the Empress is too old to reign and she must make way for her son.

The Grand Duke is also enraged that the Empress does not intend to take him and his wife on the tour to the Crimea next month but has declared she will take the Princes. The Grand Duke has said he will not allow it. His wife, he says, still suffers from the separation from her sons she was forced to undergo when they were little. She would not survive another separation. The Empress replied that the Grand Duchess has three daughters to console her and that the Princes are not hers solely but belong to the State and the Empress. The tone of their exchanges grows sharp.

For my part, I think it dangerous to leave a dissatisfied heir behind. Who knows what conspiracies his allies will devise in the absence of the Empress. Perhaps you can prevail upon her to leave the Princes at home. The journey will be strenuous. Prince Alexander has just turned nine. But I think the Empress wishes to keep him close to her for it is he she considers to be her heir, not his father. She would have no harm come to the child in her absence.

We are excited about the trip and very happy to escape Court life, which is becoming more and more confining. It is good to have our own families to escape to from time to time. We know that your position in the Crimea, permanent as it may seem, is dependent on the Empress's good will, which is easily swayed in your absence by those who are jealous of your good fortune. And thus out of gratitude for all you have done for us, we will continue to guard your interests at Court, no matter how tedious it is when you are not with us. We cannot wait to see you! We are so glad that we may all come.

By the way, the portrait that we all sat for during your last visit has been very well rendered. How handsome you look as we sit around you! Do not fear – Giambattisa Lampi has captured you most marvellously with your head a little tilted so that your eye cannot be seen. But if it were? Why, we love it. It is part of you. But I know you are shy about it and am pleased that the attention of the beholder will be drawn to your handsome features. We are all pleased with our own renditions, even Varvara, who is always vain about her appearance. How far we have come from the provincial girls we were ten years ago. I think we have acquired the sophistication we so envied at that time. And I hope we do you credit, dearest Uncle.

Your loving and respectful niece, Alexandra

Nadezhda
January 1787

We are now in Kiev, where we will be for the next few weeks while we wait for the River Dnieper to be free of ice before we continue our journey to the Crimea by boat. We have been on the road for some three weeks and I hope our stay here offers more interest than we have had thus far.

We left St Petersburg at the beginning of the month. It was bitterly cold, some 30 degrees below freezing, but we had bearskins and sable hats and wraps to keep us warm. It was a very festive atmosphere as our long procession left. All the church bells rang and the roads were lined with Her Majesty's subjects, taking farewell of their Empress for some months. Some of them wept openly.

We travelled with fourteen very large coaches, like houses on wheels, each pulled by thirty horses, for our party of twenty-two. The Empress's was the largest, with a sitting room, a library, a bedchamber and even a small dining room which held six comfortably. All the coaches were furnished and decorated with pieces from the palace rooms so that it felt very much like home. And this was perhaps part of the problem. As the British ambassador grumbled – he was often sulky because the Empress had not allowed him to bring his newly acquired Russian mistress – it was not like travelling. "It was," he said, "like having St Petersburg carried up and down the Empire. Same furniture, same food."

Comte de Ségur, Alleyne Fitzgerald and Count Cobenzl all travel with us since the Empress would have the ambassadors tell Europe of her achievements. She calls them her "pocket ministers". They are very well looked after. Here in Kiev, we have visited Comte de Ségur in the mansion allotted to him. He has an army of servants, valets, cooks, and footmen, a carriage with a stable of fine horses, beautiful furnishings, porcelain and linens, a full cellar of the best wines and champagne ...

"I had envisaged a different style of life on the road," he said. "I cannot see the foreign for the familiar."

When the Empress heard of this, she scolded him sharply. "I travel not to see places," she said, "but people. I know enough about places from maps, descriptions and much information that I could not acquire on a quick visit. I do my homework before I come. What I need to do is to give people the means to approach me, allow access to their complaints, and make those who abuse my authority fear that I will uncover their mistakes, their negligence and their injustice. That is what I gain from my travels. This is work, dear Count, not pleasure."

The Empress indeed works hard and her routine is disciplined. While travelling, she rose at six, worked on reports for three hours or received local dignitaries. She distributes what she calls "largesse to secure loyalty" in the form of jewellery, watches, rings and gold snuffboxes, which are much coveted. We normally resumed our journey about nine in the morning when the sky was lightening. Dinner was as near to two as the next town would allow. Church services were never omitted as the Empress said her subjects must see their sovereign as being directly linked to God. The bishop at Mstislav earned her particular admiration when he declared in his sermon, "Let us leave it to the astronomers to prove that the earth revolves around the sun: our Sun travels around us, and travels in order that we may have prosperity." Comte de Ségur declared it a very clumsy **bon mot** and has entertained us since with many Sun witticisms.

The daylight hours were short – it was dark by three in the afternoon but we travelled on for another few hours by the light of huge fires lit by the roadsides. The people flocked to watch our procession – in addition to the fourteen main coaches there were nearly 200 sleighs carrying hundreds of servants and all the luggage. The peasants threw themselves to the ground a quarter of an hour before our procession appeared and remained there for the same time after we had passed. How cold they must have been! At each post, 560 horses had to be changed. One would think that there would be chaos with so many animals and people to organise but everyone knew his or her duties and everything ran very smoothly. The Empress does not tolerate lack of discipline.

At most major towns on our route – Smolensk, Novgorod Severskiy, Chernigov, Nezhin – the Empress hosted a ball and although it was late afterwards, she generally worked another few hours on noting her comments of the day and marking Urgent Matters to Attend To as well as lists for the next day's visit. My sisters and I took turns in attending to her and even then we were so tired we drowsed in our own coach when we could.

When we left St Petersburg, Alexander Mamonov was feeling unwell. By the time we reached Smolensk one week later, he had a high fever and a sore throat. The Empress was distraught. "I cannot go through again what I went through with dear Sasha," she said. "To lose this best of men, he who brightens my days and nights, would be a blow I would not recover from." She determined to return to St Petersburg but Dr Rogerson said the best remedy would be to stay in Smolensk for some days of rest and warmth. We were all glad of the respite for although we travelled comfortably, our eyes were inflamed from the cold. Mamonov recovered and the Empress has treated him with great tenderness.

Kiev promises to be more interesting than the journey here. Some say it is Russia's oldest city and it certainly has many ruins of palaces and churches but its narrow streets are crowded with all sorts of people: Cossacks, Georgian princes, chiefs of the Kirghiz, wild-looking Kalmyks. It is hard to tell whether they throng here to see the Empress or whether they reside here. Comte de Ségur, who is always so apt, says it is like a "magical theatre that combines antiquity and modern times, barbarism and civilization."

Certainly, many visitors have come from Europe and from Poland to see the Empress. Prince de Ligne has arrived from Vienna and said there are reports in the foreign press that the Empress intends to stage a second coronation in what she calls New Russia in order to provoke the Turks and that many are flocking here to witness it. Uncle is expected very soon to be at the Empress's side when she first sees the empire he has created for her. "Ah," de Ligne says, "perhaps they will be crowned together!"

The Empress merely laughs at these rumours. "I have no need to crown what is already mine," she says. She is in very good spirits. She has a new little favourite to replace the little Princes, who could not come after all, much as she had wanted them to, since they took chickenpox just before we were to leave. Word has now reached us that they have scarlet fever. The Empress is very concerned but has been distracted by Alexandra's little son Alexander, who is now nearly five. Alexandra fetched him from their estate at Bila Tserkva, which is not far from Kiev. The Empress has declared him a clever and happy child. "It is as though," she says, "he has lived with us for a century." Varvara says that little Alexander is so like Uncle that the Empress can pretend it is their son – Uncle's and hers.

I note that there are few facts in my short account, which is disappointing, but the Ambassadors are right. There is little difference between life on the road and life at Court. When Tatiana and I travelled to the Crimea the year before last, we saw much more on the journey. But an Empress must travel differently.

Tatiana
February 1787

Samuel has promised to come and see me in Kiev. I await his arrival every day. He must come, for it is he who is building the galleys which will take the Empress to the Crimea. I was afraid Alexander Mamonov's illness would end our travels in Smolensk but all was well and we reached Krichev with only a few days delay.

It was so wonderful to see Samuel again! How handsome he looked in his uniform –green coat with scarlet lapels, a scarlet waistcoat with gold lace and white breeches. The Empress was well pleased with him.

"You are a trusted friend of our friend Prince Potemkin," she said in greeting. "And thus our friend too."

Samuel showed the Empress round all the works and factories, citing figures dizzying in their thousands – the brandy distillery made 25,000 roubles a year, the many looms another 25,000 roubles of cloth, the ropewalks 12,000 roubles worth of rope a week, canvas export worth 90,000 roubles. Samuel is not shy and talked much and with enthusiasm. He pointed out that the male serf population of Krichev had increased from 14,000 to 21,000 – in part thanks to the smallpox inoculation, inspired by Her Majesty. The Empress nodded gracefully as each achievement was listed and each compliment paid. Samuel talked of future plans for potatoes and English gardens, for steam engines and printing presses. "Everything can be imported from England," he said. "We already have many here who have come from England to offer improvements to Prince Potemkin's Governorate – and your Empire."

I had little time alone with Samuel apart from a few moments at dinner. I said I should like to come and work by his side, share his enthusiasm, and hoped he would take my meaning. He looked at me most kindly and said, "You must stay with your family and I will visit you all in Kiev."

Alexandra says he is charming and very clever but fond of adventure and women. She also thinks he will take an English wife were he to take one at all. But I will not give up. Varvara is of the opinion that his brother is much more suited to me. Samuel is the youngest of seven children but only he and his eldest brother survived into adulthood. Jeremy Bentham is much too old for me, he must be about forty. He is very quiet and scholarly and has a jutting lower lip, whereas Samuel's features are perfectly proportioned. But he is a philosopher and the Empress was soon deep in conversation with him after dinner.

From what I could understand of the conversation, Jeremy Bentham believes that the success of any ruler can only be measured by the ability to provide the greatest happiness to the greatest number. I thought this sounded very sensible. The Empress, however, said, "But one must ask what is meant by happiness, Mr Bentham," she said. "If you mean pleasure, that is not a sovereign's duty although she would hope for happy subjects. It is better to substitute security for happiness. Security is based on loyalty and duty to the sovereign who serves the people, as she sees fit." Mr Bentham looked as if he were going to object but Samuel burst in. "Let me tell you about my new invention for your trip to the Crimea, Your Majesty." And we all listened enthralled as Samuel described his "vermicular" – a series of floating boxes linked together and propelled by 120 oars. The Empress's would have six such compartments which she could use for different rooms. Samuel made notes of the Empress's comments and promised to incorporate them into the building of the boat, which would be brought to Kiev in time for the thaw, along with thirteen yachts and twelve more luxury vermiculars. I was so proud of Samuel! He is so inventive! He paid me little attention, nor did I expect any when in the presence of the Empress, but I made sure to sit by his side all evening. I pray that he will propose to me in Kiev.

Varvara
March 1787

I suppose I should record something in my journal from our stay in Kiev. I have little time for pen and paper, having been whirled off my feet with parties and festivities, which let up only slightly during Lent. Society is much more gay here than in St Petersburg. There seem to be few restrictions since everyone comes from a different background and in the absence of one set of rules, all have been abandoned. We do not live with the Empress, for whom a fine palace has been built, and so we do as we will – except in the Empress's presence, of course. The Empress maintains her dignified and rather strict manner – why, she even rebuked Comte de Ségur recently for a rather risqué witticism. It is good she is not witness to what is shared at table elsewhere.

Uncle has taken up residence in the huge Pechersky monastery, which looks more like a fortress. It is in truth a very spectral place. Uncle arranged for the Empress to visit its underground passageways and catacombs. There are seventy-five saints buried there – except they are not entombed but lying in open coffins dressed in silk robes. I did not stay to look too closely. A monk had guided us through the narrow passages – we had to stoop low and my back was aching. The smoke from the candles was suffocating. Several of our party turned back but the Empress moved on, surprisingly nimble, and we followed obediently although I feared we would be buried there too along with the dead saints.

But the wing that Uncle has taken over has been conjured into what Prince de Ligne calls "Asiatic luxury". He says it is "like being entertained by the vizier of Baghdad, Cairo or Constantinople" and since he has been to all these places, he must know. When Uncle attends the Empress, he dresses in his best uniform with medals and jewels but at the monastery he lounges on divans, a fur wrap draped over a long Moorish-styled silk shirt, his thick curls undressed. Everyone comes to him –Polish princes, Georgian princelings, Spanish counts. "Good Heavens!" Prince de Ligne exclaimed. "What a quantity of diamonds, gold stars, and orders! How many chains, ribbons, turbans, crownlets!"

There is a dearth of ladies so the company of myself and my sisters is much sought after. There are card games played for very high stakes, dinners and dances, with music and much laughter. When the Empress is present, the company is polite but when she leaves about 10 o'clock in the evening, the real entertainment begins. The few ladies present, some of them Catherine's ladies, some of them daughters of Uncle's generals, are prevailed upon to dance, which they do with an abandon they would not dare in St Petersburg. Uncle is very attracted to the young Naryshkina, whose dresses are extremely low cut, but we do not mind, for we are his family and here to stay while these butterflies are only passing fancies. Katerina is the only one who is put out by Uncle's little temptations. She considers herself sultana-in-chief. For the most part, however, the men seek their physical pleasures elsewhere – and must pay for them. There is much money to be made by these women of the night and it seems that they flock to the city under the guise of genteel widows with their daughters.

I do not mind an elegant adventure or two for myself but I choose carefully, for my advantage. It is also said that the Empress enjoys a discreet liaison from time to time but I think this is more rumoured by the gentlemen who would like to enhance their own images with an imperial conquest. She is still very fond of Mamonov although she does not show him public affection. Alexandra says she is very industrious in her work. She is completing a manifesto on duels, which she had previously prohibited but will now allow with lesser punishments. She has also brought all her notes on William Blackstone's legal works for she wishes to create new legislation. I would think she should be working on new laws for the Crimea, but perhaps that is Uncle's domain. He says he prefers her to spend time on duels rather than interfere too closely with what he is doing in the Crimea. "It is a different way of thinking," he said. "One cannot presume they are Russian. They are only that in name and it is a thin veneer."

The King of Poland, once Stanislav Poniatovsky and one of the Empress's first lovers when she was the young and married Princess Catherine, wishes to pay the Empress a visit while she is in Kiev. Uncle is working towards a treaty with Poland to support Russia against the Ottomans and to lessen the chances of Prussia gaining influence. It is all horribly complicated with talk of land acquisition, constitutions, and intrigues. The other day Alexandra was caught in the middle of a heated argument between Uncle and her husband Branicki, who is Grand Hetman of the Polish Crown, a position Uncle covets. Uncle has been buying up Polish land and boasts of a recent acquisition of 300,000 acres at a cost of two million roubles. Branicki accuses Uncle of a "private annexation" of Poland. They are all friends again now but it illustrates the heated complexities of the Polish issue. To my mind, the Poles are all charming tricksters, saying what they think you want to hear, especially to conquer a lady. Some, admittedly, are very handsome and can be excused. There are many **romans** in the making here. In fact, life has become a **roman**.

But pleasant as life is in this chaotic place, we all look longingly at the river, which is beginning to thaw. We should be on our way by the end of the month.

Katerina
May 1787

I am truly relieved to be gone from Kiev and have acquiesced to Alexandra's exhortation to sit quietly for a few hours at my much neglected journal. Oh, but how could I concentrate during those three months in Kiev, when Uncle was surrounded by beautiful women from all countries? Not all of them were ladies but all of them had charms to flaunt. Alexandra said I must not mind, that it is our duty to make Uncle's life comfortable. There is only a real threat if one of these temptations becomes permanent, of which, she says, there is no danger, for he has the Empress and all of us. It is true that we are always his official hostesses. And he treats us with great affection, showering us with gifts and jewels. But I am glad these women are not part of our journey by river. Life has returned to the Empress's rhythms and discipline, and our company comprises our trusted friends and the ambassadors, much as we were when we left St Petersburg, except for the welcome addition of Uncle and some of his retinue.

We did not leave Kiev until 22nd April, the day after the Empress's 58th birthday. (It is really an astounding age. I know few people so old.) Although the thaw had set in earlier, our departure had been delayed several times. It was rumoured that Uncle did not have everything as ready as he would wish but the Empress grew impatient and ordered the journey to continue.

Mr Bentham's galleys are wondrous. I share one with my sisters and Uncle, except for Alexandra, who travels with the Empress and Mamonov. Prince de Ligne and Comte de Ségur, have their own. Cobenzl and Fitzgerald share another. Each of us has a bedroom lined in Chinese red silk with gold trimmings. We also have a small study with a mahogany writing desk equipped with fine paper and inks, as well as a drawing room and a little music room (although each galley has its own orchestra on board which plays whenever and whatever we wish). We also have an ingenious water closet, with its own water supply from the river. The exteriors of the galleys are brightly painted in scarlet and gold, as are the oars, which dip in and out of the water with pleasing rhythm. I like to lie on a comfortable divan on the deck, lulled by the sounds of the splashes and of the birds.

When we near any habitation, the quiet is interrupted by the cheers of crowds along the banks and the booming of cannon in reply. Our galleys are followed by some 80 barges with 3000 soldiers and all our supplies. It must be a very fine spectacle for the onlookers, one they will see only once in a lifetime. The villages and houses we pass, even isolated huts, are abundantly decorated with flowers and arches. Our speed is slow enough to see everything at leisure although there are long stretches with no habitation. The Empress allows us much free time – which is why I am writing my journal, but in truth I do not mind for I feel content on the river, where life has slowed down. Our mornings are free to do as we please. We visit each other on our galleys and often take a walk along the riverbanks. At one o'clock a cannon announces the midday meal. Each day the Empress invites about ten guests to her galley but once a week she has the whole company, about 60 people, for dinner on the large dining galley.

A much anticipated event took place a few days after our departure from Kiev. The Empress was to meet with her former lover, the King of Poland, whom she had last seen thirty years ago. Uncle was sent to bring the King to the Empress's galley, where we all crowded to witness the meeting between the two sovereigns. Comte de Ségur stood beside me and whispered, "What will they say to each other, what will they feel, they who were united in love, separated by jealousy and pursued by hatred?" The Empress stood still and distant, hardly looking at the King. They exchanged a few stilted phrases of greeting, during which I had time to observe that the King was tall and carried himself well. He has a strong brow and a very finely shaped mouth, his face not yet ravaged by age. In truth, he looked much younger than the Empress.

The two sovereigns disappeared into the Empress's study, where they remained more than half an hour. When they emerged, the Empress seemed flushed and I fancy the King looked sad. We all then left for the festival barge for dinner. During the meal of many fine courses, the King hardly spoke and there were long silences, which even Prince de Ligne or Comte de Ségur did not dare fill. Uncle remained strangely quiet. The Empress then began talking without interruption, about her legislation, about what she had been reading, about her nephews, about her building projects. The King bowed his head in acknowledgment for time to time.

When she retired to her chambers for the afternoon rest, she expressed her anger. "Prince Potemkin did not say a word!" she said. "Why was he so maladroit? I had to talk all the time – why, my tongue dried up!" Uncle told me later that it was not his task to make political treaties. He had brought the King of Poland to the Empress of Russia and it was up to them to do the rest. It was also not his task to entertain the Empress's former lovers. I think he was jealous of the King, who, he said, was obviously still in love with the Empress. He had never married.

The King had arranged a ball in the evening followed by fireworks – truly magnificent – but the Empress did not attend. Perhaps she was too moved by meeting her former lover, perhaps she was disappointed in him, perhaps he was disappointed in her, perhaps she did not care to revisit the past.

A return visit had been planned by the King for the next day but the Empress ordered our boats made ready for departure. "Tell him, "she said to Uncle,"that I must keep to my itinerary. The Emperor of Austria awaits me. I cannot change my plans on a whim, as is often the case with Poland." I trust Uncle did not deliver the last part of the message, which sounded like a deliberate insult. Uncle said it was. It was a reminder that the King had not bowed to the Empress's will. He is intent on reform which will strengthen his country while she would wish to keep it weak under her influence. At least, this is what I understood but my grasp of politics is slight. Uncle was dejected. "She probably also reminded him – unwisely – that it was she who gave him Poland and that it is she who could take it away from him. They will now court Prussia," he said.

And so what we thought was a truly romantic love story has been no more than a political contretemps. Prince de Ligne pointed out that the King had been here for three months and spent three million roubles to see the Empress for three hours. Our sympathy was with the King, who has kept the Empress in his heart all these decades. One should never, Uncle said, destroy a dream by trying to make it come true. The King sent Uncle a note. *You know with what joyful anticipation I awaited the Empress. I was pleased when I saw her but I do not know her anymore. Although I am sad, I hope I may continue to count on your friendship.*

I am content with our journey. The water soothes me and even the weather is warmly clement. We are very much *en famille*.

Tatiana
May 1787

I should only write about good things but I now know that is childish. Life has many bad things too and they cannot be ignored. Samuel Bentham did not propose to me in Kiev. He hardly spoke to me. He was, admittedly, very occupied with the building of the boats for our continued journey but when I saw him at Uncle's, he was flirting with all those women who have nothing in their heads but themselves. He views me as the child I no longer am because my sisters treat my like one, not only because I am the youngest but because I am not yet married. But I am almost eighteen and I will tell Uncle I want to marry. The Empress is kind and while we were in Kiev, I preferred to spend time at her palace with my little nephew than at Uncle's wild parties. I told her about Samuel Bentham. She said, "He is a clever and most attractive man but he is not good husband material. He fears entrapment so prefers women who do not look for marriage. We will find you a husband and then you may be free." I had never thought about marriage as a way to freedom but I do see that my sisters may do as they wish and their husbands never complain.

On our river journey, I spend most of my day on the Empress's galley. It is peaceful there. Or was until most of the boats were grounded just a day's journey from where the Empress was to meet the Emperor of Austria. The Empress called the Austrian envoy. "You must get word to your Emperor that he must come to me." Cobenzl replied, "Your Majesty, I regret this may not be possible for we have arranged the place of rendezvous and His Majesty's whereabouts till then are unknown to me." Uncle said, "We must go by land. We cannot keep the Emperor waiting. He will see it as a slight. He has already condescended to travel here." There was much rushing around and shouting amongst the stranded galleys when suddenly what looked like a long series of boats came into view around the bend in the river. High on a platform on the first section of the boat was Samuel Bentham, shouting instructions through a trumpet. It was the vermicular. No one cheered, which I think Samuel was expecting. We were all too surprised by what seemed like a godsent apparition.

The Empress, Mamonov, Uncle, Prince de Ligne, Cobenzl and a few attendants, among them Alexandra, transferred to the vermicular the next morning and it wound its way leaving the rest of us to be rescued we knew not how. Samuel Bentham was the hero of the moment but I had hardened my heart against him.

Alexandra
May 1787

Dear sisters,

I am sorry you have not yet caught up with us but trust you will soon. The ambassadors have already joined us, as has my husband. But there is apparently a lack of horses for carriages. I will endeavour to describe what you have missed.

The meeting with Austria did not go much better than that with Poland. Sometimes dealing with sovereigns is worse than dealing with children. Uncle "found" the Emperor near the appointed meeting place. The Emperor then decided to "surprise" the Empress. Uncle immediately sent a courier to warn the Empress. Count Cobenzl sent a courier back to warn the Emperor that the Empress had been warned. What games! Sometimes I do not wonder that we often find ourselves in a political quandary.

We left the boat and continued by carriage, almost bumping into the Emperor's carriage in the middle of a field. Thus the "surprise" was effected to each side's satisfaction. The two sovereigns continued on in one carriage to a place called Kaidak, some 30 versts further. Only once we got there did we realise that all the supplies, or those we had for most were still in the stranded barges, were not with us. Uncle galloped off to fetch what victuals he could from the village and then insisted on cooking himself. The Emperor and Empress decided to help him and chaos ensued – but it was a merry chaos. "Why," the Emperor said as we sat down to the unidentifiable dishes, "the food is as bad as the company is good."

But that was the end of the good humour. The Emperor sulked. He criticised the inefficiency of our transport although Uncle assured him the main retinue would soon catch up with us. The Emperor also thinks the Crimea should be sufficient for Russia and has made it clear he is not prepared to go to war with the Ottomans for any more territorial gain. "Will the Ottomans come to my aid if Prussia makes war on Austria one day?" he asked petulantly.

We continued by carriage to Kherson, which we viewed with astonishment. Reports of Uncle's great achievements there, as you well know, had been met with scepticism in St Petersburg. Even I questioned that so much could be done in such a short time, and I am sure the Empress did too. We entered the city, for that is what it now is, through an arch on which had been carved ***This is the road to Byzantium***. There is a very large fortress, enough houses for 24,000 people, several very fine churches, 600 guns in the Arsenal, 200 merchant ships in the port as well as ships-of-line and frigates.

The Empress is very impressed – and perhaps relieved – to find such a flourishing town. But the Emperor continued to grumble. "Yes, a lot has been built very quickly in Kherson – and it shows." He also likes to criticize Uncle. "Why does he need 120 musicians with him?" And he passes judgment on everyone. "What I don't understand," he said one evening in the Empress's absence, "is how such a proud woman, and one so mindful of her glory, can show such a strange weakness for the caprices of her young Mamonov, who is really no more than a spoilt child." The Emperor is indeed not without his own weaknesses. Prince de Ligne caught him one morning trying to seduce a peasant girl against her will.

Uncle takes the Emperor's comments lightly. He says the Emperor is jealous. "But never fear," he said. "He will be even more impressed and in better mood when we cross into the Crimea."

And he was proved right. Our carriages were traversing a seemingly endless steppe with nothing in sight as far as the horizon. Comte de Ségur had just made a joke about the boredom of deserts and the Empress had snapped that he should go back to Paris when, seemingly out of nowhere, a horde of most splendidly dressed Cossacks, some 3000 of them, surrounded our carriages. They split into two perfect formations and simulated battle, whooping and whirling. It was a most exhilarating sight. "They can ride sixty versts a day, which no other cavalry can," Uncle said proudly.

Exhilaration of another kind awaited us at a small encampment further on, where we would spend the night. The tents were braided with silver and their floors sprinkled with many small jewels. The Ataman's wife wore a long robe of gold woven with many coins. On her head was a sable hat fringed with pearls which hung down over her face, like a sparkling waterfall. "It is like ***The Arabian Nights***," the Emperor said, happy once more.

We travelled on the next day and as we crossed into the Crimea, we suddenly found ourselves in a huge cloud of dust and thundering hooves. This was the Tartar cavalry, richly equipped with jewel-encrusted pistols and engraved daggers, their horses magnificently decorated with tassels. The Empress's carriage in which the Emperor, Prince de Ligne and myself travelled, received its own escort.

The road down to Bakhchisaray, the capital of the Crimea, is steep and our carriage seemed to go faster and faster, swaying from side to side, eventually careening off the path and threatening to topple. "The horses have bolted," the Empress said calmly. I feared our deaths. We could hear the Tartars shouting and glimpsed them through the dust crowding close to the carriage. "Perhaps we are being kidnapped," Prince de Ligne said. All of a sudden, we came to a shuddering halt and found ourselves at the tall forbidding walls of the Khan's palace.

Once inside, however, we were in a serene oasis of shady palms and scented blooms, of cooling ornate fountains and singing birds. It was enchanting. There are many buildings, all in different styles: Persian, Moorish, Turkish, Italian and even Chinese, for the Khan's aim was to better any palace in the world. The Empress is housed in the Khan's own apartments, which are very richly decorated in an oriental style. We have a lovely courtyard, surrounded by divans on all sides. The Emperor has been given the Khan's brother's apartment while Uncle and the ambassadors have been housed in the harem although we are assured its dwellers are not there, which is a pity. I would like to have met the inhabitants of a harem. Are they all slaves?

In the evening young women danced for us, Arabian style. I blush even now when I think how they moved their bodies so voluptuously to the Arabic music – although their faces were lightly veiled. The men were spell-bound. I was comforted to hear the calls to prayer, which are sung – most melodiously – from the mosque five times a day. "God rules here too," the Empress declared, "if in a different guise". We stayed only two nights before moving on to Sebastopol on the Black Sea, which was where the Emperor was finally convinced that Uncle's achievements were truly grand and worthy of praise – and no doubt envy.

Sebastopol is the navy base founded just three years ago but it now boasts a fleet of 150 ships. A salvo of guns from twenty frigates greeted us and it was as if the heavens had opened. After some moments of silence during which the noise still reverberated in our ears, Comte de Ségur said softly, "Magical. It is as if the Russian Empire has arrived in the south and her armies able to plant its flags on the walls of Constantinople in no more than thirty hours." Turning to the Empress, he said, "Your Majesty, you have finished in the south what Peter the Great began in the north." "It is to Prince Potemkin – to his efforts and zeal, his talents and labour, his loyalty and affection – that I owe everything," the Empress said. She then turned to Uncle and gave him her hand. He bent to kiss it and there were tears in is eyes.

And now Uncle, the great Prince Potemkin, the admired Serenissimus, has been proved the genius he is. It can no longer be denied. We are secure in our futures. The

Emperor of Austria is still jealous but admits that Russia has shown formidable strength. The ambassadors are now scrambling to be on our side. They may be unwilling to draw their countries into war but they send dispatches home warning of the danger of being left out of any victors' spoils. "But no one must think I need them," the Empress said. "I can go to war myself, if I wish." This is true – but not without the great Prince Potemkin.

Uncle has sent a courier to take our letters to Simferopol, where your carriages are expected daily. You will be with us soon!

With affection,
Your sister Alexandra

Nadezhda
June 1787

We were sorry to have missed a part of the trip with the Empress's entourage but on the other hand, we travelled with less spectacle which allowed not only for speed but also for more freedom. I have become quite a horsewoman, for sitting in the carriage became very stuffy and the views were hidden behind the dust on the windows. Tatiana and I rode often, relishing the fresh breezes and clear views. I am not sure the Empress would have allowed it since she does not like to see women on horses now that she herself, once a skilled rider, does not ride.

However, she did see some 200 women on horses! It was one of Uncle's many marvellous surprises for her. In St Petersburg the Empress had apparently once remarked that women in Classical Greece were probably of not much use, just like those in modern Greece. Uncle decided to prove her wrong and conjured up a regiment of Amazons! It is a marvel that he has time for such caprices when he is fighting a war, building towns and fleets – why, building a new empire.

The horsewomen were a most wondrous sight! They wore skirts of crimson velvet bordered in gold lace, matched with lace-edged green jackets, under shining copper breastplates. Over their hair, which hung down in long plaits, they wore white gauze turbans decorated with spangles and ostrich feathers. They had muskets, bayonets and lances. Their commander was a beautiful young girl, whom we later learned was Elena Sardovna, the wife of a captain, and but 19 years old. Tatiana and I begged the Empress to let us ride with them and she grudgingly gave her permission once Uncle had said she would not want Russian women to seem so useless. Elena organised uniforms for us, but not weapons as we would not have been able to ride one-handed as they did, and we rode as part of the escort of Tartars and Cossacks accompanying the Empress's retinue along the shores of the Black Sea, the water glittering one side, the mountains sweeping down on the other. As we rode, Elena told us that some of the "Amazons", as Uncle had named them, had come out to join their army husbands and had travelled as men for safety. Others had eagerly seized the opportunity to train in riding and shooting. "Most of us would rather gallop with the wind in our hair than be corseted at a ball," she said. "We enjoy much freedom here although the native women remain veiled when men are present." The Amazons had prepared a spectacle of their shooting skills for the Empress and were most disappointed when she declared there was regrettably not enough time for such entertainment.

Varvara said the Empress was put out by so much youth and beauty on horseback, reminding her of her own age. It was true that the men flocked round the Amazons whenever the retinue stopped. The Empress did give Elena a diamond ring worth 200 roubles and 10,000 roubles for her "troops". I was sorry to part with the girls. I would rather lead such a life than that at court. Or than that of a woman at court. Men have such freedom. Why, they may even buy women. Or even girls. Circassian girls are considered especially pretty and even the Emperor Joseph is said to have procured one to take home with him. Uncle is always offering them as gifts to his friends. I do not think the Empress approves.

I should note an incident here that occurred some days later. At dinner one evening, Prince de Ligne related an anecdote which did not please the Empress. "What's the use of going through an immense garden when one is forbidden to examine the flowers?" he said. "I was determined to see a Tartar woman without her veil before I left the Crimea and so persuaded the good Comte de Ségur to join me in my attempts." Comte de Ségur looked uncomfortable and tried to interrupt. "Come, come, de

Ligne! There is no story to tell!" But Prince de Ligne continued eagerly. "Yes, yes, it is most amusing. We rode into some woods near a stream and soon spied three damsels washing. Their veils lay on the ground. We crept closer but our expectations were dashed when we saw they were far from pretty. Indeed, very far! Mon Dieu! Their Prophet was right to order them to cover their faces!" He guffawed loudly, adding "There are some in our own society who would indeed benefit from a veil!" Some of the company had just begun to laugh when the Empress said, in a cold tone, "This is a joke in very bad taste, gentlemen. You are in the midst of a people I have conquered. They are under my protection. I wish the laws and customs of their religion to be respected. If any of my pages had behaved so disrespectfully, they would have been severely punished."

We rode up the steep hills to view Uncle's vineyards and gardens, his flocks of sheep and dairies as well as a very pretty pink Tartar-style palace. The Empress was delighted to find a fully grown English garden, with majestic trees and beautiful lawns. This was the work of Uncle's English gardener William Gould, who is as much of a magician as Uncle is. He travels where Uncle wishes with shrubs and trees, statues and ornaments in a cavalcade. He then sets up a garden in a matter of days. We were served English tea by two ladies, brought out from England by the Bentham brothers to set up a dairy. The butter and cream were delicious but the women were very forward in their manners and the Empress did not speak to them directly.

In the evening there was a banquet at the palace, followed by a most magnificent firework display. 20,000 rockets went off at once and the mountains were simultaneously illuminated with the Empress's initials – Uncle said 55,000 pots of fire were needed.

"The cost!" Emperor Joseph spluttered. "The labour of how many thousands! We would never undertake such a thing in Austria."

"No," the Empress remarked. "but that is why Russia is the greater Empire."

Our route has been taking us north, our return journey has started. But I am determined to ask my husband's permission to move to the Crimea. Katerina will stay with Uncle for the time being even although she has become only one of many favourites. "But I still want to be near him," she said. "He is my sun." We all love Uncle but I desire to live in the Crimea for there I see my freedom. I would be like Elena of the Amazons. Uncle said I may oversee the new library he is collecting for, which is to be the biggest and best in the world. Crimea is, as Uncle says, paradise.

PART FIVE

Tatiana
December 1787

Dear Katerina,

How fortunate you are to be in the gentle south! And Nadezhda will be joining you in the spring. Alexandra is at Bila Tserkva, only some 500 versts from Kherson so she is almost in the Crimea – but she must come to Court soon for all is not well.

But first, thank you for your congratulations on my marriage. I would like to have had you here. It was a quiet celebration and while I am happy to have pleased Uncle by acceding to his choice of his cousin for me, I confess that it would not have been my own choice. I still think of Samuel Bentham. Alexandra says I may have all the Samuel Benthams in the world now that I am a married woman but so far there is none that I would want. My husband, being 25 years older than me, is more like a father and while he resembles Uncle somewhat, he is nothing like him in character, being of a quiet nature and most accommodating. I understand why Uncle calls him The Saint. We pray before we retire and while I do my best to bring him comfort , as Uncle had wished, it is not a task I find very tasteful. I think he is more suited to the life of a monk.

My thoughts return often to our trip to the Crimea. How I wish I could have stayed, as you did. We reached St Petersburg during the third week of July, tired but happy after our magical journey of 6000 versts. The Empress had been gone for over six months. The Princes joined us south of Moscow and the Empress was delighted to see them well. My voice was hoarse from relating all our adventures, all of which they insisted on acting out.

The Empress was greeted warmly enough in St Petersburg but there is talk of food shortages throughout the country and the day after her arrival 400 peasant workers arrived at the palace to present a petition to her. She refused to see them and several were arrested, although released a few weeks later.

Perhaps more alarming than that is the tarnishing of Uncle's name. The Empress, ourselves, the ambassadors, everyone who went to Crimea are full of praise for Uncle's achievements, which we are happy to describe in detail at our gatherings. But there are those who will not believe it and I must concede that it is difficult to believe the palaces, the towns, the fleet, the entertainments, the wondrous spectacles, the cultivation ... if one has not seen it all with one's own eyes. "Ah, you have been reading ***Arabian Nights***," they scoff. The Grand Duke is particularly distrustful and the Prussian party feeds him his lines. "It is all a fraud, a mirage," the Saxon envoy Georg von Helbig has said. He even wrote an article on how the "magic" was effected. He said our cruise along the Dnieper was orchestrated like a play in the theatre, only on a grander scale. The villages did not exist, they were merely façades and the Empress saw the same villages five or six times. He called them Potemkin Villages. He even accused Uncle of forcing thousands of peasants from their villages in Russia to "populate" these false villages. Oh, there are so many lies in his article! He will not believe that those wonderful palaces we stayed in were more than a mirage, a fairy tale. Yes, they were as enchanting as in a fairy-tale but built – most beautifully – in stone. Uncle's enemies should travel there themselves but they prefer to make up lies which come from their jealousy.

The Empress defends Uncle but less vigorously than before for she cannot extol a paradise built on the toil of peasants who are now suffering bread shortages. The Grand Duke will not be persuaded of Uncle's achievements and has forbidden his sons, the Princes, to talk of the Crimea in his presence. Fortunately, they are not often with their father.

The Empress has been agitated about Uncle's health ever since he wrote that he had fallen into a fever, that he was exhausted and weak and – most alarming – that he wanted to give up his command. He wrote of Ottoman attacks on our ships, of their attempts to take Kherson. He wrote that a storm had destroyed our fleet at Sebastopol, which has destroyed him. "Almost dead," he wrote. Can any of this be true? You must write at once. The Empress must be reassured. I have written to Alexandra to come but perhaps it would be better for her to go to Uncle first. It is but a few days' journey from Bila Tserkva.

Your devoted sister,
Tatiana

Katerina
October 1788

Dear sisters,

You have all begged for news and I must tell you straight away that after a most wretched few months, when Uncle lay depressed and ill, he has much recovered. The turning point was to find out that the autumn storm had not destroyed his fleet after all – only one ship was lost. It has also helped that the Empress will send Prince Repnin, not only Uncle's trusted nephew but an experienced general, to aid Uncle and to take temporary command in case of future illness As the Empress has pointed out, illness is no reason to give up what has been conquered. "When you are sitting on a horse," she wrote in her letter to Uncle, "there is no point in getting off it to hold on to the tail."

Uncle has also summoned General Suvorov, who has fought at his side in many wars. He is a strange man. He is very small and has a face like a clown's. He is said to roll naked in the grass every morning and stand on one leg when taking parades. He asks his soldiers questions that cannot be answered and punishes those who answer "I don't know." One must hazard a guess, for example, to "How many fish are in the Black Sea?" He is extremely eccentric and unpredictable. He orders his men to use their sabres "as bloodily as they can" and not to trust the "fickle muskets". But Uncle says he is a brilliant general who has never lost a battle.

And indeed, without General Suvorov Kherson may have fallen. The Turks attacked the fortress which guards Kherson from the sea on 1st October. As Uncle was still recovering and not fit for military action, he gave command to Suvorov. The intrepid General led our troops in three attacks, one after the other, against the entrenched enemy and slaughterd most of the Turks. He himself was wounded twice but fought on, covered in his own blood and that of those he slew.

Uncle says we are now safe till the spring, by which time our fleet will be reinforced with ships from the Baltic. I have begged Uncle to rest at Kherson over the winter but he has insisted on setting up his headquarters near the Ottoman border in the garrison town of Elisabethgrad. I went with him, of course. What terrible weather! What roads! What mud! But Uncle set up his residence in a swiftly built wooden palace beside the old fortress and we soon became very comfortable.

We have many visitors flocking to be part of Uncle's entourage, especially French aristocrats who seek adventure and also haven from unrest in their own country. They are surprised to find Uncle's orchestra and choir here and are happy with our very busy card room and the huge billiard hall, where it is not unusual to see some thirty generals at play.

They are most surprised at the many young women who are here, some to be with their husbands, others to find lovers, many to gain Uncle's attention or affection. I am resigned to being his social hostess. His eyes are turned by the beautiful Katerina Bariatinskaya, now married to Prince Dolgoruky. She may be the acknowledged Aphrodite of the Russian Court, but she is outshone by Katerina Samoiova (so many Katerinas named in honour of the Empress!), the daughter of Prince Trubetskoy who married Uncle's nephew. Even although she is our relative, I must say her attractions to men lie in her willingness to please them, most boldly, rather than in any attributes of beauty – of soul or body. And she wears far too many jewels in a ridiculous turban. But men fall in love with her. She whom Uncle favours above all, however, is also our relative, Praskovya Potemkina, the wife of his cousin Pavel. She has a very unattractive figure, as you know, but her skin is dazzling white and her eyes dark and sparkling. Fortunately, she is not too intelligent and I can easily bend her to my will. Uncle said he cannot fight war without beautiful women around him. And so I manage his admirers and ensure that there are no sentimental upsets for him to deal with. Yes, imagine it! I who had tantrums when I could not have him to myself! The girls all know that it is only through me that they may have any access to Uncle and are willing to do my bidding. They know they can be sent home in a moment. I only have to invoke the Empress's displeasure at their behaviour and they beg my forgiveness. My only aim is to keep Uncle happy. He still comes to me for comfort. I am still his little kitten. And I can have anything I want here. I can lie in my furs all day if I like. And I sometimes do.

Uncle does not neglect his duties. He is amassing his army here and expects some 50,000 troops from the new levies. He is also strengthening the cavalry with Cossacks (and even Jews!) and is repairing the fleet. Samuel Bentham has been converting the imperial barges the Empress used on her tour of the Crimea into gun ships. Our navy has been enhanced by a very exciting arrival from America. You will have heard of the intrepid John Paul Jones, who, although Scottish, took on the might of the British navy most successfully for the colonies. For the Americans he is a hero, and for the English a lowly pirate. Uncle heard that Jones was at a loose end in Paris and invited him to come and help command the Russian navy in our fight against the Turks. "Fame attracts fame," he said. John Paul Jones, some forty years old, is quite handsome and bears himself proudly but there is something cold in his eyes and the curve of his mouth is a little cruel. He does not court the women in Uncle's circle but seeks his pleasures elsewhere. But Uncle is pleased with his new officer and has ordered the other naval commanders to work well with him. This does not go well with such as Samuel Bentham, who sees him as a revolutionary and a traitor, as do many others.

Rest assured, dear sisters, that Uncle is in better health and good spirits. He says we will defeat the Turks in spring.

Fondly,
Your sister Katerina

Alexandra
November 1788

Dearest Uncle, esteemed Prince Potemkin,

I would not add to your already onerous tasks but I beseech you to write to the Empress. You know that she has been unwell and a regular courier from you would ease her anxieties, calm her spirit and preserve her health. She has had to bear the Swedish threat of war all by herself and she cannot sleep for worry. King Gustav demanded the return of Karelia and Finland although Catherine herself had nothing to do with their acquisition, having not been on the throne at that time. He placed his ships at Reval and declared, most provocatively, that he would soon be lunching in St Petersburg. The Empress, her patience tried, had no choice but to declare war. "My people," she said, "will not complain for they know I never undertake an unjust war."

However, we eagerly awaited reports of your victories against the Turks, for to fight war on two fronts is a hazardous venture. Much of our Baltic fleet has been sent to the Crimea, as you requested, but a naval victory was crucial in preventing the Swedish army from invading Russian territory. King Gustav seized his chance to exploit what he sees as our weakness, our seas here unprotected as our ships fight in the Crimea. He has also had the audacity to call an end to our war with Turkey demanding that we give back all conquered territory in the Crimea to the Ottomans. The Empress has said he has turned mad, which may be true but does not make the threat any less.

While King Gustav is mad, the Empress is ill and has been since her birthday in April, which severe stomach colics forced her to spend in bed. None of the usual remedies helped, neither hot nor cold. In the end, Dr Rogerson persuaded her to take a tincture of opium. These are the most severe colics she has had and you know she has had many. She was very ill – I feared for her life. ***The***

Times in London even reported her death, which must have been an extreme shock for you if you read it, which I doubt, for you would surely have ridden back immediately. Alexander Mamonov has not helped much with his sulks. I overheard him saying that life with an invalid is tedious. The Empress tries to please him, even making him a Count of the Holy Roman Empire. He continued to sulk, of course, because he was not made a Prince.

Although we won the first battle against the Swedes, continued anxiety has caused the Empress pains in her chest and what she describes as a kind of rheumatism between her shoulders. It has been very hot – the thermometer shows 40 degrees – as if the weather has caught the Empress's fever. She has now been unwell for two weeks: colic, headaches, backaches, chest aches, fever. She does try to keep up with her work but it is mostly from a reclining position.

Please send a courier by return with news of what is happening. We have heard through the ambassadors that you will lay siege to Ochakov, which the Empress says must be taken (and wonders that it has not), if we are to secure the Crimea. Let the Empress know what progress you make, let her know that you are well. Let her know why you do not attack Ochakov, if the reports of thousands of her soldiers dying from dysentery and cold are true... Rumours must be dispelled by facts, and only you have those. I fear for her health. It has never been so bad.

Your respectful niece,
Alexandra

Katerina
December 1788

Dear sisters,

I write speedily that you will know the great news although Uncle has already sent his fastest courier. Ochakov has been taken! Uncle and General Suvorov led 30,000 of our troops against the well defended fortress. Uncle declared it a holy war against the infidel, in which no quarter was to be given. Our officers, and many others who fought for us, wrote farewell letters to their loved ones, which they entrusted to me. But most of the men, thankfully, returned – and have been well rewarded for their heroism, especially by the ladies here. We lost some 1000 of our men but 10,000 Turks were killed. The streets of the fort ran with blood, and the corpses piled up. It took only four hours for the Turks to surrender. "The bloodshed is due to your own obstinacy," Uncle told the Pasha, who apparently shrugged his shoulders and said, "Fate has turned against us."

It is impossible to bury all the dead and Uncle has ordered them taken out to be piled on the frozen river. I have been to see them. Some of the officers take the ladies out in sledges to view these human pyramids. It is a strange sight. They are frozen into death, some of them with scimitars still in their hands. It is a reminder of – and a monument to – the might of Russia.

The soldiers and officers brought wondrous jewels back from the city. What wealth had been stored there! There is so much that the soldiers who try to sell the plundered treasure receive little for it. I have received gifts of very fine pearls and diamonds from the officers. Uncle has an emerald the size of an egg for the Empress. But pray do not tell her of the surprise.

And so those who criticised Uncle for not taking Ochakov sooner, who did not see his tactics in laying siege and waiting for winter to give frozen access to the fort from the sea must now praise him for this most magnificent victory!

In haste and joy,
Your sister Katerina

Varvara
May 1789

Dear sisters,

It has been a most marvellous two months since Uncle returned to St Petersburg! I wonder, Katerina, that you did not accompany him. Uncle says that you are left in charge of his households but I am sure there are other attractions too. Nadezhda, he tells us, is very occupied supervising the collection of rare volumes for his new library, which he says will replace the legendary library destroyed in ancient times in Constantinople. In any case, you have both missed a most sparkling time at Court.

St Petersburg greeted Uncle as the hero he is. How wonderful he looked! Two hundred banners from the Ottoman Ochakov were marched by the Winter Palace. The banquet in the evening was one of the finest. Uncle received a diamond-studded baton, a gold medal and 100,000 roubles. The Empress was well pleased with him and seemed recovered from her ailments. But in the end she spoiled it for herself. She retired early, which I was not happy about for I wished to enjoy the festivities. She had quarrelled with Mamonov, which was nothing new. She will not see that he deceives her with Princess Sherbatova, her own maid-of-honour. But what should he do? She is nearly 60 and he not yet even half her age. But I think she was crying more about Uncle. He has been unfailingly polite to her, but he has not treated her as a woman likes to be treated. He reserves those graces for plump Praskovya, whom he has brought with him. And for the many other young and beautiful women who surround him. The Empress must know she is old and unattractive – well, it must be said. Even an Empress cannot hold back age, although she has made a valiant attempt and few women even reach her age, let alone expect to have a lover. Why, her legs are so swollen they have lost their shape. Her voice is hoarse and she has lost some teeth so she rarely smiles. Her teeth had always been so good. Oh, how awful old age is. I hope I escape it. Why, Ivan Chernyshev is decomposing before our very eyes. Wherever he appears, there is a terrible stench. The footmen follow behind him, sprinkling lavender water.

But to return to the Empress – after the celebration banquet she cried and cried. And the next day too. It was most tedious. I eventually sent for Uncle, for that is whom she really wanted. Her quarrels with Mamonov were only a pretext for her tears. Uncle came and spoke to her sternly and perhaps somewhat impatiently. "Spit on the pup!" he said. "Get rid of him!" This is not what she wanted to hear. She wanted Uncle to speak soft words to her, but one could see he was eager to get back to the happy life of Court – as I was. How energetic Uncle is! How handsome, even more so than before! A man of fifty, with power, fame and a fine figure is irresistible.

While all is gloom in the Empress's chambers, the Court whirls from one entertainment to the next. I have had many new dresses made and my husband says he cannot keep up with my need for jewels. But one cannot wear the same necklace twice! The latest fashion here is to wear a cameo of Uncle or a belt with ***Potemkin Victor*** emblazoned on it. I am having one made with small diamonds like stars studded round his name.

We had prepared such splendid celebrations for the Empress's 60th birthday but again, she spent the day crying in bed. Alexandra talked to her as a nurse would to a child. "You must tell me what is wrong, Your Majesty, for only then can we remedy it."

"There is no one thing," the Empress said mournfully. "Alexander Mamonov is so aloof. Prince Potemkin is so busy. The Emperor Joseph is very ill and may die, the Swedes prepare for a new campaign, the Turks are amassing troops again, the Poles are plotting with the Prussians against us and England encourages them – I think there is plenty to cry about but none of it has a remedy. I cannot fight everyone."

We report everything to Uncle, of course, and eventually he saw that he could not leave to tackle the new Turkish threats without putting the Empress's house in order. While the Court danced on, and I with it, Uncle spent more time with the Empress. They quarrelled, Alexandra said, over how to proceed with Prussia. "Prussia must be appeased by allowing it to take what it will in Poland," Uncle argued. "I cannot battle the Prussians while there is no peace with the Turks." I think this a most rational approach and my husband voiced the same opinion. But the Empress insists there are other ways but does not say what. Exasperated, Uncle has written her a plan of possibilities and asked her to adhere to it while he secures the Crimea – yet again. It is a real danger with 100, 000 Turkish troops said to be amassing against us. But the Empress would not let him go. "I need you near me," she said, sounding like a lovesick girl. Uncle changed his tactics. He complimented the Empress, flattered her in the old way, wrote her little notes, gave her presents and slowly her tears dried. He instructed Alexandra to find a likely replacement for Mamonov to distract the Empress, someone loyal to our family. This is no easy task since few are willing to take it on.

Uncle now leaves in two weeks. How eager he is to be gone! "Constantinople has never been nearer our grasp than now! Would you forfeit this great prize?" he asked the Empress. And thus she was persuaded. The Court will grind to a halt without him and the retinue he attracts. I wish to come to the Crimea but my husband wishes me to spend time with him and our children at our family estate. But once Constantinople is taken and Uncle is established there, I will take my place at his Court. He has promised.

Affectionately,

Your sister Varvara

Alexandra
July 1789

Dear Katerina,

I send this with the imperial courier to Uncle and must write speedily. The Empress has written to him of her latest tragedy but you must not let her tears persuade him to return.

It is not really a tragedy at all. Before he left, Uncle tasked us with finding the Empress a new adjutant to replace Mamonov. Our diligence yielded few results. Her eye had wandered where we had not directed it. But I will relate that in due course. Suffice to say, this attraction moved her to release the sulky and ungrateful Mamonov, so she wrote him a letter offering to arrange a marriage for him with the only child of Count Bruce. Although barely 13 years old, she is already well-formed and mature. And one of the richest heiresses in Russia. A truly generous offer.

On receipt of the letter, Mamonov rushed into the Empress's chamber and threw himself at her feet.

"Thank you for your generosity," he stammered. "It overwhelms me but I cannot marry Katerina Bruce."

"But what is wrong with her?" The Empress was startled.

"I do not love her!" the fool burst out. "I love Princess Daria Sherbatova and have done for a year and a half. I have already promised myself to her. I beg your permission to marry her!"

The Empress would have fallen had we not supported her. Mamonov kept talking excitedly, giving the Empress all the details of the intrigues and secret assignations, the love letters and deceptions. He seemed proud of his dealings. I shouted at him to leave. I all but pushed him out the door and he was still shouting, "But I love her!" at the top of his voice.

225

I rushed back to the Empress and tried to persuade her to rise from the floor. "I am most cruelly deceived yet again," she sobbed "Why did no one tell me?"

I said one could not accuse without proof, which we did not have, which was of course a lie, but that Prince Potemkin had tried to warn her.

"You are better off without him, Your Majesty," I reassured her.

In the end, she acted most nobly. Two weeks later Mamonov and Sherbatova were married and the Empress wept at the wedding. She placed a diamond circlet on Sherbatova's head and blessed her with an icon. She bestowed 2500 peasants and 100,000 roubles on them and sent them off to Moscow, where Mamonov will be bored.

Thus the Empress was catapulted into the arms of a new lover – just a few days after the revelations – but one not chosen by ourselves. He is a protégé of Count Saltykov, who heads the Grand Duke's Court. As such, he cannot be considered a friend of the Potemkin family.

Platon Zubov is undoubtedly handsome in a very swarthy way – in fact, the Empress calls him Little Blackie. To bestow a nickname, as you know, is a sure sign of her affection. He is only twenty-two years old and indeed small in stature but strong of figure. The only life he knows is Court life and his education is sadly lacking, which has aroused the Empress's educational ambitions. "I'm doing quite well for the State by educating its young men," she said with a return to her old humour. Zubov is something of a hypochondriac – perhaps they discuss their illnesses together. I fail to see what else they do. Uncle has pointed out that the Empress often just wants to look at these young men, a feast for her eyes. Like his supporters, Zubov is greedy, ambitious and shallow and fortunately not too intelligent. He spends hours in front of a mirror having his hair curled. He has pet monkeys. That is perhaps what he is, the Empress's pet monkey. So please tell Uncle not to worry. Let him congratulate the Empress on her new found love. He will probably not last but at least he has stopped the Empress's tears for the time being. I will be vigilant and alert Uncle to any changes contrary to our interests.

The events in France are alarming. We have read of the storming of the Bastille prison and the violent demands of the people. The Empress says that's what comes of promising constitutions. "It will never happen in Russia," she said, "for we know that all power must be kept in the sovereign's hands. Besides which, our people are loyal to me for I care for them as a mother does." I trust she is right but there are those who fear that recent unrest amongst the serfs may be fed by ideas from the French populace.

We eagerly await news of victories against the Turks. Uncle must remain where he is. I will deal with the Empress and all matters at Court until victory is secure.

With affection,
Your sister Alexandra

Nadezhda
December 1789

Dear Alexandra, dear Varvara,

I write to you to in the hope that one of you will come. Indeed one of you must come.

Uncle's armies, with great help from General Suvorov, move from victory to victory against the Turks: Focşani in July, Rymnik in September where the Turks lost 15,000 men, Akkerman's surrender in October, the surrender of Fort Bender with its 20,000 men in November ... Uncle is rightly declared a great hero and the Te Deums sung in his honour in St Petersburg are well justified. General Suvorov has been made a Count and received a whole wagon of diamonds from the Empress. The Empress writes to Uncle with each new victory. ***I love you very, very much***, she writes, ***with all my heart.***

Uncle has set up Court in Jassy, the Moldavian capital, to spend the winter recovering from the many campaigns. And to negotiate peace with the Sublime Porte. Meanwhile he lives like a Turkish sultan. He is surrounded by princes and ambassadors from countries I had never heard of – and I have been diligent in my learning. Jassy is home to a mélange of peoples as can be expected from a city surrounded by the Russian, the Ottoman and the Hapsburg empires. It is a veritable Tower of Babel on the streets: Greek, Turkish, French, Arabic and many languages I cannot identify. There is much familiar alongside the exotic. In the bazaars French couture can be found a few steps from colourful and aromatic spices.

The rulers of this area, known by the old Slavic name of Hospodar, are Greek-Turkish and have paid exorbitant sums to the Ottoman Sultans for the privilege of their position. The present Hospodar is grateful to Uncle for removing the financial onus imposed by Ottoman dominion. The aristocracy are mostly boyars from Rumania and live in grand palaces built in the classical style. They are immensely rich and wear an abundance of diamonds and rare jewels. When I was first invited into one of their palaces, I was shocked at their women (some of whom may be their wives – it was difficult to tell). They wear short transparent shifts with gauze shawls round their necks and arms into which are sewn pearls and gold coins, with necklaces of coral and lapis lazuli around their necks. They are soft and gentle in their manner, lying on their divans, sipping sherbet. One even showed me a volume of Voltaire she was reading. They are beautiful but have very prominent bellies, which they do not try to hide but rather it is the part of the anatomy they leave uncovered, for it is a sign of beauty. The ladies who flock here from Russia and France are dismayed to find their own charms are ignored for the divan ladies. For the princes here consider it a mark of hospitality for the guests to enjoy their women .. and they do. The only restriction is that they must be checked by a doctor beforehand.

And this is the paradise Uncle has always longed for. He hopes the Moldavians will accept him as their benevolent overlord. He moves from palace to palace in the region with – according to my last list – twelve carriages of books (chosen by myself from our growing library collection), twenty jewellers, 23 carpet weavers (all women), 100 needlewomen, a troupe of actors, his orchestra of 200 hornplayers, his choir of 300, a corps de ballet, his gardener Gould with his numerous workers, his architect and stonemasons ... Towns appear out of nowhere, gardens are laid overnight, concerts are given. He is like a magician. Although always on the move, he lives well, ordering hampers of food from all corners of the globe. A recent consignment contained smoked salmon, dried salmon, marinated salmon, Dutch herrings, Livonian anchovies, smoked eels, mussels, two barrels of apples, as well as bottles of Lacrima Christi from Naples, champagne from Reims, red and white wine from Burgundy, rum from Jamaica ... I check the lists and they are long.

There is an endless succession of parties, feasts, theatres and ballets and although none would dispute the fact that Uncle is a connoisseur of music, the emphasis at these gatherings is more hedonistic than cultural.

Praskovya is still his chief sultana and her ambitions know no bounds. Uncle is besotted with her. He calls her "soul of my soul" and showers her with gifts and jewels, even naming two ships after her. She only has to mention a certain perfume and Uncle sends a messenger off to Paris to obtain it for her. The last shopping list I had to compile for her included the usual ballgowns of every hue and material, seventy-two pairs of shoes, six dozen pairs of silk stockings as well as corsets, rubies and fresh flowers. I have also had to listen patiently as Uncle describes the palace he is going to build for them, their love nest as he calls it. I may be interested in architecture as Uncle rightly surmises but I do not need to hear the intimate details. I can comment on fountains and on paintings of Hero, Leander, Apollo and Daphne, even on the most ardent poems of Sappho which are to be inscribed on tiles. But I lose patience with him when he tells me of the erotic painting of Praskovya he plans to have done – she in "a white short dress, girded by a delicate lilac belt, open at the breast, hair loose and unpowdered, the chemise held by a single ruby." The bed would be surrounded by curtains as "thin as smoke" in a room made of aquamarine glass. The most luxurious place would be the bath, which would be surrounded by mirrors, and the waters would be scented with rose, lilac, jasmine and orange. Oh, I feel like shaking him. He is like a lovesick boy. And for whom? Why, he did not even sink to such sentimental depths when he was in love with Varvara or Katerina, who are so much more beautiful than plump Praskovya.

Of course, he cannot help but be caught up in the hedonistic atmosphere in which he now lives, especially since, as we all know, it always seemed to be his natural leaning, but I think we must worry about his obsession with this one person. He already calls her his Queen. It is not a far step to Empress. Katerina is of no use. She herself has moved to join the household of the Hospodar and there she lies with his ladies all day. "It is the life I always yearned for," she told me from the divan where she lay with the other ladies, as lightly clad in Turkish costume as they were.

Sutherland, Uncle's Scottish banker who has seen to his finances for many years, came to me recently. "You are as sensible person," he said. "You must know that Prince Potemkin now owes me 500,000 roubles, which I have financed by other loans. If he can spend so extravagantly, he can pay me, and I my own creditors." I tried to bring up the subject with Uncle. "I do all this for the Empress's glory and it is she who pays for it all. I have nothing of my own." He has promised to try and procure 200,000 roubles for Sutherland. Meanwhile, his last Paris bill for Praskovya was 50,000 livres.

I will leave soon to return to my husband and home even though I have not finished Uncle's library. While it is a noble undertaking and will benefit scholars to come, I cannot remain where sensual pleasure is the only goal. Uncle has always been extravagant in his tastes but he has now added capriciousness and voluptuousness. I no longer recognise him. He seems driven by some demon … or drunk on his own victories. He swears his love and loyalty to the Empress but his greatest wish is to establish his own empire here in the south, and for this he will cling to the Crimea. I will leave it to you as to how much the Empress must learn of this but either one of you must come to bring some order into his life or the Empress must recall him on some pretext to remind him of who he is. If not, she may have an Emperor – and Empress – within her own Empire.

Your affectionate sister,
Nadezhda

Alexandra
February 1790

Dear Nadezhda,

I hope this letter reaches you before you leave. I hope it can persuade you to stay until I can come, which I do intend to do having taken your warnings most earnestly. But it is not a good time to leave the Empress. She has lost Austria, so important in the fight with the Ottomans. She did, however, take the news of Emperor Joseph's death very well. "My poor ally," she said, "died hated by everyone." It is said that he suggested his own epitaph: ***Here lies a prince whose intentions were pure but who had the misfortune to see all his plans collapse***. "That," Catherine said, "is the problem. Intentions must never be confused with plans. I will not founder by the same mistake."

In truth she needs many plans. Uncle's lack of progress on the peace front with Turkey has led to uncertainty which allows time for others to redraw territorial maps and ambitions. We are surrounded by enemies. The Swedes, backed by British money, continue to attack us at sea. More recently, the Ottomans have offered to pay Sweden one million piasters a year to prolong the war against. Prussia is prowling around Poland and has been negotiating secretly with both the Ottomans and the Swedes. Wherever one looks, there are enemies of Russia, jealous of the jewel she has won in the Crimea. The Empress's faith in Uncle does not waver but she grows impatient. She must tread the boards of diplomacy with her enemies while waiting for Uncle to deliver formal cession of the Crimea. I do my best but our old allies have all gone and I have spent huge sums of money on information. The Empress has also taken practical measures. Her new levy of men, five in every 500, has yielded over 90,000 new recruits. But that is what they are – recruits. We need experienced soldiers and officers. We cannot fight war on all fronts. Uncle must resolve the Crimean issue swiftly, then attend to the Swedes before St Petersburg falls.

And please tell Katerina that she must get off her divan and see to curbing Praskovya's power over Uncle. She must be discredited. Perhaps there is another young beauty to entice him away? Katerina must see to it. She understands these things. Tell her I will have the Empress recall her and send her back to her singing husband if she does not make some effort.

In haste,
Alexandra

Varvara
June 1790

Dear Alexandra,

Nadezhda did not exaggerate. I am not easily shocked but what I find here at Uncle's headquarters makes the ***Arabian Nights*** seem like a book for children.

I caught up with Uncle in Bender, which is where he has now set up his headquarters – you will remember that is the strategic fortress which, despite its 20,000 defenders, yielded to Uncle without a fight. It is huge and forbidding, built high above the river. Uncle does not reside there but in a nearby palace.

Katerina led me through a maze of corridors and anterooms to his private chambers. There we found him reclining on a divan, dressed in a huge sable coat with little or nothing on underneath as is his wont. I did not look too closely as my attention was drawn to the six women who lay sprawled on the divan with him. They were clad in Turkish costume, which, as you will know, means in very little. The silk of the divan shone silver in the candlelight, the carpet was threaded with gold, fresh flowers and glittering rubies were strewn around, heady incense wafted from little burners, attendants stood around with carafes of wine and silver platters of dainties.

Katerina had told me that she had succeeded in separating Uncle from Praskovya by dangling the beautiful Princess Katerina Dolgorukaya before him, which was a good choice. She has always been acclaimed the prettiest girl in all of Russia. At twenty-one she is still young enough to seem innocent, which she is not. She is married and her husband dares to express his dislike of her proximity to Uncle, but Uncle has apparently boxed his ears and threatened to send him to Siberia. I immediately knew which one of the ladies on the divan was Dolgorukaya. Not only did she stand out for her most enviable figure, slim but curved where men like it, her skin as smooth and unblemished as ivory, her unusual light grey eyes, her long abundant tresses covering her barely clad shoulders, but it was she who lay closest to Uncle. He caressed her most familiarly, as if they were alone. He greeted me warmly but then said, "Have you come to scold me? Has Little Mother sent you?" He has always referred to the Empress as such but it now seemed more derogatory than affectionate. I am only a few years past thirty but I felt old and wise and wished to leave what seemed like Uncle's private dream as quickly as I could. I asked Katerina to show me round the palace.

Uncle had apparently decided to build underground passages to facilitate visiting his mistresses – Princess Dolgorukaya must share him as every woman in his life has done – in the different parts of the palace but in the end the project turned into a vast subterranean palace decorated with Greek columns, splashing fountains, velvet sofas, galleries for orchestras, banyas of great luxury ... I felt as if I was being drawn further and further into his dream. I cannot write of some of the things I have been told and seen. If I tell you that he orchestrates his ... pleasure with drummers and grenadiers, you will ask me to desist. The drummers must drum and at a sign from Uncle, the grenadiers must fire their 100 cannons. The sound of the drums is enough to drive the men into a frenzy and the girls run screaming through the corridors, but slowly enough to be caught. Princess Dolgorukaya's husband apparently remarked caustically, "What a lot of noise about nothing."

I have told Uncle how we are beleaguered by the Swedes, how Prussia is ready to pounce, how the Empress's health is suffering from the weight of all the concerns she has. He knows all this. "I will write to Little Mother. She must know that I do not neglect my duties. The Crimea will be ours. But she is right. I have had enough of Turkish fairy-tales. I will have them know that if they want peace, they must do it more quickly or I'll defeat them again in war."

Our ships are indeed in good shape and ready to sail. The soldiers are adequately housed in their tents and Uncle sees that they are well provisioned. They drill every day, their uniforms clean and their weapons shining. It is such a contradictory mixture: Uncle's decadence on the one hand and his discipline on the other.

As you requested, I have also given Uncle a copy of that seditious manuscript and have told him it is probably the work of that ungrateful wretch Alexander Radischev. What impertinence! Brought up at Court, sent to Leipzig University at the Empress's expense and then to publish a book against her and Uncle! I read it myself on the long journey here and am appalled at the accusations within it. The author calls his ramblings ***Journey from St Petersburg to Moscow*** but he must have travelled in another country for I have crossed our Empire many times and I have not encountered the oppressed slaves he talks about. Our peasants are loyal and well looked after subjects of Her Majesty, whom Radischev calls a tyrant − tsar, shah, khan, king, bey, nabob, sultan ... He hurls the insults in profusion. Uncle guffawed, however, when I showed him the passage which referred undoubtedly to him. I quote it here for you:

As soon as he began to climb up the ladder of ranks, the number of oysters at his table began to increase. And when he became Viceroy and had a lot of his own money and government funds at his disposal, he craved oysters like a pregnant woman. Asleep or awake, he thought only of eating oysters. While they were in season nobody had any rest. All his subordinates became martyrs. No matter what happened, he had to have oysters. He would send an order to the office to furnish him a courier at once, to dispatch with important reports to Petersburg. Everybody knew that the courier was sent to fetch

oysters, but he had his traveling expenses granted anyhow.

"Well," Uncle said, "he has that right! I do love oysters and will do anything to get them. Especially," he added with a wink, "because they are a powerful aphrodisiac!"

He does not seem to take seriously that the work contains many ideas of the French Revolution. "That is no danger in Russia," he scoffs. "Our very souls are loyal to the Empress, who rules by God's will. No serf would rise against her."

I trust he is right.

I have done my duty – reported to you the state of affairs here, reported to Uncle the need for speedy action if Russia is not to be vanquished by its many enemies. I will now return to my husband's estate and to my children. I once wanted my life to be a ***roman***, with adventures, admirers, affairs. But I now see I prefer my safe fairy-tale, where we all live happily ever after in the serenity of our country estate.

Affectionately,
Your sister Varvara

Nadezhda
April 1791

Alexandra has tasked me with an account of important events in this past year. She herself is too busy to record them. And indeed she works tirelessly to keep an even balance at Court.

When I look back to last year, our fortunes did not seem favourable. The Swedes inflicted a terrible defeat on our fleet in June. We lost 64 ships and 7300 men. And there was still no word of peace or victory on the Ottoman front. The Crimea was not secure after all. We doubted that we had indeed conquered it. Unrest was growing within the Empire, with more peasant uprisings inspired by the treasonous Radischev's writings. He was arrested and admitted to being the author of that seditious book but declared his loyalty to the Empress. The Empress, however, said the French poison had to be stamped out as one would stamp on a cockroach and Radischev was sentenced to death. But others, including Uncle, warned her against such a reaction. "Do not make a martyr of him," he wrote. "Let your deeds speak louder than his words." Catherine then commuted his sentence to exile in Siberia where he went meekly and gratefully.

In the end, Gustav of Sweden was generous in victory – or perhaps just as exhausted from war as we were. Besides, he realised that he was really fighting for the British against Russia and once their subsidies dried up, his will to fight died too and he sued for peace, which was signed last year in August.

Of graver import was our continued war against the Ottomans. Uncle's new offensive, begun in June, was halted at the fortress of Ismail, a garrison of 35,000 Turks. It seemed impregnable. The walls were four miles in circumference and protected by moats fifty feet wide and twenty feet deep. Russia, under General Suvorov, offered the Turks the chance to surrender so that innocent blood might be saved. Their commander answered with a defiant show of banners on the ramparts, "The Danube will stop its course, the heavens will fall to earth before Ismail surrenders." The Danube did not stop its course but it ran red with blood. Fighting went on for twelve hours, 60,000 men locked in battle at close quarters. Despite the odds, it was our troops who triumphed, but in a rampage of carnage. Ismail was taken with the loss of 20,000 Turks and another 11, 000 taken prisoner. Even a last attempt by 4000 Tartar horsemen who burst out from the underground stables in a surprise attack, trampling over the dead and injured, splattering blood and bone in all directions, were brought down by Russian swords. The streets ran with blood, corpses were piled high and still our soldiers did not desist. They took the clothes from the dead, pillaged houses and shops and continued to kill even when it was no longer necessary. It was a great victory but not Russia's finest hour. The news was brought to the Empress by Platon Zubov's brother Valerian, who serves with Uncle. It is from him I have the details, both strategic and gory, although he himself was not at the battle. And neither was Uncle. He stayed at Bender and continued life as if there were no battle to be fought. He later said he had to keep the attack a secret from the enemy who, he said, must be taken by surprise and therefore not even his own staff could not know of it. "The slaughterer must never show his knife," he apparently said. "Secrecy is the soul of war." He sent General Suvorov to do the work while he lingered with his favourites.

Princess Dolgorukaya has been replaced by Sophie de Witte, a Greek despite her name and said to be the most beautiful woman in Europe. She was sold at the age of twelve by her mother, a poor vegetable seller, to the Polish Ambassador who procured girls for King Stanislav. Other men coveted her and she was bartered on for profit until a Major de Witte bought her for 1000 ducats when she was fourteen, and, more importantly, married her. He then sent her to Paris to learn manners and French, and the capital fell at her feet. Her sister was sold as a child to an Ottoman pasha and it is said that Sophie was able to barter much information she received clandestinely from her. In this way, she came to Uncle's attention. What more intriguing – a beautiful spy with golden hair and violet eyes. Valerian says that after she appeared at Bender, Uncle lost his head to her. "She is an intriguer, a Venus with Oriental charm and the only woman who can still surprise me, " he said. Her husband declared publicly she was not Uncle's mistress but his friend. No one believed him. In any case, as the streets of Ismail ran with blood, Uncle was playing cards with Sophie de Witte and the rest of his harem. I do not like this story for it puts Uncle in a poor light but it is most probably true since it was in keeping with the Prince Potemkin I had experienced in Jassy. I do not think the Empress has been told. I would hope not.

Valerian also brought a request from Uncle to be allowed to come to St Petersburg. "Since I belong to you, all my wonderful successes belong to you too," he wrote to the Empress. "And I would share them with you as I look upon your face." The Empress hesitated. She wrote that her health was not good, which was true. She had been afflicted by many ailments in addition to her usual stomach complaints. She was convinced a gout had reached her stomach and bowels but she was sure a daily glass of malaga with pepper would cure it in a matter of weeks. She would then welcome Uncle in glowing health, as befits a hero. It was rumoured that she feared Uncle would remove Platon Zubov although he had never met him.

Meanwhile, the fall of Ismail had once more roused the jealousy of others, particularly Britain, which had effected an alliance with Prussia and Poland. If Russia did not return to a ***status quo ante bellum*** i.e. give up the Crimea, William Pitt, the Prime Minister, said Britain would attack Russia by sea and Prussia by land. His threats were made real with Frederick William of Prussia amassing 88,000 men in east Prussia while the British lined up over 50 ships of war. And Uncle did come to St Petersburg – with his new mistress to host a great ball.

The roads to the city were brightly lit with torches for a week before his arrival. And when he arrived, all of St Petersburg fell at his feet. There were balls and concerts, banquets and feasts. The women wore medallions and belts with his portrait. The men bowed to him. And he moved among them like a god. He wore his white uniform of Grand Admiral of the Black Sea Fleet, covered in diamonds and medals. The nobles tried to outdo each other in the magnificence of their invitations and some bankrupted themselves in the attempt.

The Empress was overjoyed by Uncle's presence. "Your Uncle," she told us in her ante-chamber as we were adorning her with her favourite diamonds for yet another festivity in Uncle's honour, "has returned to us much embellished by his victories. He is as handsome as the day, as gay as a lark, as brilliant as a star but more spiritual than ever. And," she added, "he no longer bites his nails." And indeed Uncle did shine most magnificently and we basked in his light. We were all eager to see the infamous Sophie de Witte while Princess Dolgorukaya sulked at home.

He unveiled his new beauty, so to speak, at the great ball given by Prince Nassau. Uncle wore his famous hetman uniform which is said to be worth almost a million roubles in the jewels which adorn it. Sophie de Witte appeared in a very diaphanous Greek style dress, which left modesty and imagination behind. Her eyes are truly beautiful, large and deep violet in colour, which contrast well with her golden hair, which she wears loose. It is even more golden than Varvara's. Her pose is dramatic rather than natural, like a marble statue. Her eyes may be beautiful but they reflect a cold heart. The Empress was very graceful and presented her with a pair of diamond earrings.

It was difficult to direct Uncle's attention to the many diplomatic problems facing us. The Empress had asked him to negotiate a sum of money to entice Gustav III into an alliance with Russia instead of with Britain, which was offering Gustav subsidies for the use of his ports in a war against us. Instead, Uncle invited the Swedish envoy to attend the rehearsals for the great ball he was planning. Alexandra was present and reported that the emissary had left complaining that Uncle had dazzled him with diamonds, walked him through fifty apartments in his palace, subjected him to long monologues about his campaigns in the Crimea, and made him watch quadrilles being rehearsed for six hours. In the end, the envoy left telling Alexandra that he would inform Gustav that Russia was ruled by an entertainer. It is true that Uncle is easily bored. One sees his face suddenly cloud over and then he claps his hands for a new idea. My husband says it is the plight of a man who has all his desires satisfied and there is nothing left to want so he tries to create more desires in himself.

When his mind can be turned to political matters, Uncle wishes to pacify Prussia but Catherine will not hear of it. They argue as in old times, Catherine in tears, Uncle marching off in a sulk. Platon Zubov is of the Prussian party, along with the Grand Duke, and Uncle does not like this. "How can I fight Sweden, England, Poland, Prussia and the Turks?" he roars. "All at the same time? Let me at least deal with them one after the other."

In the end diplomacy won. Pitt was attacked in his parliament for wishing to defend a "horde of barbaric Asiatics". Horatio Nelson of the navy said there was no way to get at Russia's fleet with narrow seas and no friendly ports. Soon the cry in England was "No war with Russia!" Alexandra said our bribes had borne fruit.

Now all attention is directed to Uncle's Grand Ball, which will take place very soon – on 28th April in honour of the Empress's birthday. I am sure I will have much to report after that.

Nadezhda
May 1791

I take up my pen again, somewhat reluctantly, for I do not think I am the right person to record the excesses of Uncle's ball. Extravagance rarely impresses me unless it also has a practical end. Alexandra says it is for this reason I am the best person. Katerina would enthuse too much, Varvara would get caught up in sharp comments about the women, Tatiana would talk only of the Princes. I, she said, would be like an artist, sketching accurately what I saw. Sketches would indeed be an excellent idea but for the fact there would be far too many needed.

The masquerade began at 6 p.m. and the Empress arrived an hour later. Uncle stood waiting to greet her at the very imposing entrance to his new palace. Its Doric columns bestow on it a pleasingly classical look, which belies the almost baroque exuberance of its interior. Uncle looked very handsome in a red coat with a gold and black diamond-studded cloak over his shoulders. In truth, he wore too many diamonds – on his shoe buckles, the seams of his stockings, his belt, his sword – why, he even had some plaited into his hair. He could not wear his hat for it is weighed down with diamonds and as usual an attendant followed him carrying it on a velvet cushion. How absurd to have a hat so embellished one cannot wear it.

The Empress was much more modest in her attire. She wore a long-sleeved Russian-style dress, almost a sarafan, in a fine purple silk adorned with only one diamond brooch and a very beautiful diadem on her head. Uncle took her hand and guided her along the path formed by two lines of footmen in fine livery of yellow, blue and silver. Each of them held a candelabrum of some fifteen candles.

There was a moment of panic when the crowds suddenly surged forward with a great shout. About 5000 people had turned up for the feast Uncle had gifted to the inhabitants of the city. They had waited in the heavy rain all day and as soon as the Empress's carriage was seen, they took this to mean that the feast could begin. Catherine looked startled. She later said she had thought it was a French-type revolt but once she saw the people filling their pockets with food, she laughed and said, "I hope they leave enough for us!"

The lines of footmen continued under the columns, illuminated by hundreds of torches, into the Cupola Hall, where 3000 guests, in colourful costumes, waited to greet the Empress. The Hall is the largest in Europe and can hold 5000 people. The ceiling is over 20 metres high and hung with massive many-tiered chandeliers of black crystal. The whole is supported by two rows of 36 Ionic columns − Ivan Starov, the architect, called it a "poetry of pillars", and indeed their slender symmetry is very aesthetic. The floors are inlaid in intricate designs with precious woods. The Hall was ablaze with light for the ball, not only from the chandeliers but also from the thousands of torches burning around the periphery. Music was heard but its source not seen for the organ, the orchestra and choir were hidden on two upper galleries. "Celestial harmony," the Empress declared as she looked up.

From the Hall one's gaze − and the Empress's that evening too − is drawn towards the Winter Garden, which is the largest in Europe and almost the same size as the rest of the extensively spacious Palace. The huge glass hall is supported by columns in the form of palm trees which cleverly contain warm water pipes, creating a climate where flowers, shrubs and trees grow in profusion. Parts of the walls are lined with mirrors, behind which are immense stoves. Of course, the guests were unaware of these devices but I had pored over all the architect's plans. Lamps are hidden in artificial bunches of grapes and pineapples studded with twinkling diamonds. Silver and scarlet fish swim in enormous glass globes. The cupola is painted like a blue sky with white clouds, form which hangs a yellow sphere, on which the Empress's initials are emblazoned in gold it. The symbolism is somewhat obvious. Below on earth, so to speak, Uncle has had a temple built on a pyramid of diamonds in which there is a statue of Catherine, her robes flowing in smoothest marble. The inscription reads ***From Potemkin to the Mother of the Motherland and my benefactress.*** Later the Empress remarked to Alexandra that it was a very fine sentiment but not a very romantic one.

The first entertainment took place in the Winter Garden. Uncle led the Empress to a dais covered in Persian carpets and once they were settled on the divans, two quadrilles, each of twenty-four children, emerged from the tropical gardens. The most beautiful children in St Petersburg had been chosen, including, of course, the young Princes. It was indeed a lovely spectacle. The boys were dressed in Spanish costume of sky blue and the girls in pink Greek dresses. Both were adorned with many jewels, which sparkled in the candlelight as they danced, which they did most elegantly and with great precision. Prince Alexander danced a complicated solo in one quadrille while Prince Constantine danced in the other quadrille, more simply but just as perfectly. It was indeed a most accomplished performance for the boys although I suppose Alexander, already fourteen, must be described as a young man.

Tatiana seems to think so. She cannot hide her affection for him and Varvara and Katerina tease her mercilessly about it. There is no reason why she could not soon become his mistress. The age difference of eight years is of no import but unfortunately Tatiana does not have the attractions of a mistress, or perhaps the aspirations, and since her marriage she has been most listless. A new Samuel Bentham is not in sight, not to mention the real one, whom Uncle has sent off to pursue further adventures on his behalf in far Asia. I would gladly have gone with him had I been born a man. He is to command troops at the Chinese-Mongolian border, form new alliances, find new lands, open trade with Japan and Alaska ... He and Uncle also devised a plan to conquer China with 100,000 men. But that must wait until the Crimea is secure. But I digress – to subjects which interest me more than extravagant balls in St Petersburg – and so I will resume.

After the quadrilles, Uncle led the Empress to the Gobelins Room, where colourfully woven tapestries featured women from the Bible, such as Esther, Rachel, Ruth, all most beautifully rendered. Many guests later examined them more closely, searching for the face which was most similar to the Empress's. In the middle of the room stood one of Uncle's magical surprises – a huge life-size golden elephant covered in emeralds and rubies. It was ridden by a blackamoor mahout in Persian robes, who gave a signal and curtains were raised to reveal a stage and amphitheatre. Two French comedies and a ballet were presented, followed by a procession of all the peoples of the Empire, including captured Ottoman pashas from Ismail, in their national dress. It was a very long procession.

After that, the ball began. The whole palace was a blaze of light. Uncle had detailed a plan for hundreds of servants to light the 20,000 candles and 140,000 lamps with military precision so that they all burned at the same time with the same brightness. The disadvantage of turning night into day was that the illuminations exuded great heat and soon our wrists tired from fanning ourselves. The Empress played cards more than she danced and then retired for a short rest. Uncle had given the Empress her own suite of rooms in his palace just as he has apartments in her palaces. I know from the architect's drawings that in the Empress's bedchamber there is a secret door behind a tapestry which connects to Uncle's rooms.

About midnight the Empress returned for supper. Her table was richly set with gold and crystal and Uncle's famous Sèvres dinner service. Uncle stood behind the Empress and served her until she asked him to sit beside her. After a supper of delicacies presented like works of art, the ball began again, with concerts in different rooms for those who were too fatigued to dance, especially if they had eaten too much. The Empress stayed until 2 a.m., which is four hours longer than she normally stays, which was a great compliment to Uncle. Of course, everyone watched to see if she would really leave in her carriage or whether she would retire to her rooms in Uncle's palace. Uncle, of course, hoped for the latter as he wished to be restored to her full favour. He had arranged for the orchestra to play one of two melodies, depending on her choice. When he realised she had indeed called for her carriage, he fell to his knees in front of her with his hand on his breast, which was the sign for the musicians to play the farewell song. It was that lover's lament, which everyone knows, the one with the chorus, "The only thing that matters in the world is you."

After the Empress had left, Uncle's spirits darkened. My sisters and I went to give him solace just in time to overhear Countess Zakrevskaya, an old favourite of his, say to him, "I don't know what will become of you, Prince Potemkin. You are younger than the Empress and will outlive her. You will not be first man of the empire anymore and you will never be content to be second." Uncle answered in a sad voice, "I am not sure that I am first man anymore. And in any case, I will die before the Empress. In fact, I will die soon." Katerina rushed off to find Sophie de Witte, who had been ordered to stay in the background so as not to upset the Empress with her beauty, to come and cheer Uncle. Alexandra fussed around him most maternally. "You have done too much, Uncle. You have over-exerted yourself."

"But have I done enough?" he asked morosely. "Does she still love me or is she rushing back to Zubov?"

I omitted to mention that Uncle had not invited Platon Zubov to the ball, which the Empress will certainly not have taken kindly. He is, after all, her chosen lover. I fear Uncle has spent half a million roubles in vain.

Alexandra
August 1791

Dear Uncle, esteemed Prince, Serenissimus,

How I wish I could add King of Poland! Are our dreams to come to nothing? Has the so-called Polish Constitution robbed my children of their future? The Empress rightly calls events in Warsaw a revolutionary sickness, spread from France. The Constitutionalists now boast of having a limited monarchy based on the model of parliamentary England, whose rebellious colonies dare to call themselves the United States of America.

This was your plan for Poland – a federal union of independent states. What will happen to the quarter million serfs you have amassed on your Polish estates, the basis for your principality and from which you could be elected King? Will you not invade with your Cossacks as you once planned? The Empress insists on you settling the Turks once and for all but I do not think she is aware of the danger in Poland. A hereditary monarchy instead of an elected sovereign! The crown would go to Saxony. We must reverse this revolution. My husband works on your behalf in Warsaw. He too deserves to reap the rewards of his efforts on Russia's behalf these last years. He too wishes to see our son succeed you as King of Poland. This was our plan. You must conquer all Turkish resistance and turn your troops to Poland before it is too late! The Empress has given you permission to do so. Make haste. Once the Empress no longer rules – and she is often ill – we have no future in Russia. Grand Duke Paul will rid himself of all the Potemkins as soon as he can. And now our future in Poland, our safeguard, is being snatched from us. Already my husband is being called a traitor for supporting Russia.

I knew after the ball that our favour was falling. Platon Zubov is efficient in spreading rumours against you. He unsettled the Empress while she was weakened by her ailments by telling her you want to take her place. He complains that he would be twice as rich if it were not for you. He threatens to leave her if she prefers you. Oh, why did she not allow you to go to Poland and deal with these Constitutionalists! Why did she order you to the Crimea when your generals could have taken care of the Turks, as they have been doing in your absence. Oh, why must you always obey her?

    Respectfully,
    Alexandra

Alexandra
October 1791

Your Majesty, my Empress,

You have instructed me to write, sparing no detail, however upsetting. I shall endeavour to suppress my own tears as I do this for I am aware that Your Majesty requires a clear account and not one coloured by my own emotions, painful as they are.

On your instructions, I hastened to Prince Potemkin after we received the news of the death of the Grand Duchess's brother from fever while in Uncle's service. Your Majesty's fears of contagion were well founded. As I have now learned, the Prince collapsed at the funeral of his adjutant. He followed the cortège on foot in the heat for miles and then drank two glasses of water at the burial place, throwing his normal caution to the wind. He seemed to be already in the grip of a fever, mistaking the funeral hearse for his carriage and trying to climb into it. He was persuaded to rest and his physicians treated him with cinchona bark, successfully it seems, for after a few days, he was able to return to Jassy, which is where I found him, still lightly feverish but active.

Although the fever did return at intervals, laying him low with terrible headaches and delirium, he would rise again as soon as he was able. He did not neglect his duties although I confess I begged him to. He supervised the peace talks, regrouped the army in case war broke out again, deployed the fleet to Sebastopol. He could not possibly have done more. He even summoned his Polish allies to discuss future plans. He enjoyed his music and was writing hymns. He was particularly fond of one and had it played or sung to him almost daily. "And now my soul, fearing and hoping in the abyss of its wickedness, seeks help but cannot find it." I remonstrated with him that it was over-melancholic. He eagerly awaited the arrival of a talented composer called Mozart from Vienna, recommended by our envoy there and who had agreed to come to serve Prince Potemkin for an indefinite period. Since the Prince was enthusiastic about this composer, I hoped his arrival would lift his spirits.

Many of the Prince's close entourage also fell sick with fever but recovered in a few days. Although the Prince always rallied, he was afflicted again and again and it seemed that each attack left him weaker. The doctors recommended moving him to the fresh air of a country house and Sophia de Witte and myself accompanied him. He was to eat little – Your Majesty knows of his gargantuan appetite and the physicians opined that this burdened his constitution too much. We devised a sparing but healthy diet of fresh vegetables and juices, which seemed to have a positive effect on his health. He was less agitated but continued to worry about many things, including yourself, Your Majesty. He began to talk about leaving this life, which alarmed me and I urged him to look forward as his Empress had ordered. I read him your letters, which he kept with him at all times, tied in a bundle, "near to his heart" as he said. "I love her and I hope she loves me. I have told her a thousand times but please tell her again although it is now too late," he would often urge me.

Just as we thought he was recovering, his fever suddenly became worse and he groaned in pain, complaining of pains like daggers in his ears and chest. He said the only way to vanquish these pains was to distract the body's attention to other pursuits. He ordered a ham, salted goose and several cooked chickens, which he devoured ravenously and washed down with beer and wines. His favourite sterlet was brought by fast courier. The pains did seem to ease. He sweated profusely, which the doctors said was a good sign. He called for bottles of eau-de-Cologne and emptied them over his head. After several days, he asked for his confessor. "Let all stay and hear what the meaning of my life has been," he called as myself and the doctors prepared to leave his chamber. He talked quietly to Bishop Ambrosius and then said, very calmly and lucidly, "Let it be known that I have never wished evil to anyone. All I wanted was to make everyone happy." We all tried to hide our tears.

He seemed better the next day and was much cheered by the arrival of a letter from Your Majesty as well as your gifts of a fur coat and silk quilted dressing robe. He wept then and wrote in a shaky hand, "Dear Little Mother, life is hard at the moment but even harder for I cannot see you." On his birthday, 30th September, he wept most of the day. "I will see no more than these 52 years," he said between his tears, "and I will never see my Empress again." He refused to take the cinchona bark infusion prepared for him by the physicians. He wanted to ride into the steppe, to "wide open spaces" but he was too weak to even raise his hand. He gradually slipped into unconsciousness and we were sure his end was near. I never left his side, holding his ice-cold hand. After nine hours, however, he suddenly woke and insisted on the excursion to the steppe. Since our gentle refusals agitated him, we eventually acquiesced and transported him, wrapped in furs, to the carriage in an armchair. Before leaving, he dictated a letter to Your Majesty.

Dear Little Mother, most Merciful,

I have no energy left to suffer my torments. The only escape is to leave this town and I have ordered them to carry me forth. I do not know what will become of me.

Your most faithful and grateful subject

Your Majesty will have noticed on receipt of this letter that he was too weak to sign his name.

We rode several hours and the Prince seemed to worsen. "Are we there yet?" he asked often. Since we did not know his destination, we said, "We can stop now." "No, no drive on!" he gasped. Finally, he said, "There is no point. It is enough. Stop and let me out."

253

The Cossacks accompanying us carried him out. I held his hand and wiped his sweating brow. He was barefoot but wearing the fur-lined silk dressing gown Your Majesty had sent him for we had carried him straight from his bed to the carriage. We had fortuitously stopped at a spot which gave most wonderful views of green valleys and hills. I was relieved. "This," I thought, will refresh Uncle. This is what he wanted to see, not his sickroom." There were several carriages of people but I was too distracted to notice more than the bishops and generals, some Moldavians in their tall hats and several Cossacks.

I ordered a Persian rug placed on the grass for the Prince to be laid on. "I want to die in the field," he said. "You will not die," I reassured him, "but only rest a while." He asked his Cossacks to build him a tent of their lances covered with blankets and furs. He repeatedly patted the inside pocket of his robe, which bulged with packets of Your Majesty's letters.

He deteriorated rapidly, shaking, sweating, moaning. "I am on fire," he called. He then said the light grew dark in his eyes and he could only hear voices. Bishop Ambrosius put an icon in his hand, saying, "We can only trust in God now." Uncle moved the icon to his lips. Removimg the icon gently, I took his hands in mine and embraced him for I now accepted that his time had come. "Forgive me merciful Mother Sovereign," he said. Those were his last words.

Everyone fell to weeping and I fainted but it must have been only briefly since I woke to hear someone asking for coins to place on the Prince's eyes, as our custom dictates, and because of his high station, gold coins were called for. But no one had any coins, whether gold or silver At last, one of the Cossacks produced a five-kopeck copper coin and we had to make do with that for the Prince's good eye. As the Cossack stepped back, I heard him mutter, "Lived on gold, died on grass." There were no stones to mark the spot so one of the Cossacks thrust his lance into the earth so that we could later erect a fitting memorial.

Unrest followed while we awaited Your Majesty's instructions. It took seven days for you to receive the news and seven more for your answer. In the meantime, who was in command? What about the peace talks? Where should the Prince be buried? Those were dark days.

A post mortem was conducted by the doctors since there had been rumours of poisoning. They declared it was a "bilious" attack. Our dear Prince was then embalmed and dressed in his uniform, his heart being placed in a golden urn, perhaps to be returned to Your Majesty. He was laid in state on a dais covered in rich gold brocade. His open coffin was lined in pink velvet, covered with a canopy of rose and black velvet supported by ten pillars and surmounted with ostrich feathers. His orders and batons were laid out on white cushions. His sword and hat lay on the coffin lid nearby. Six officers stood on guard.

His funeral procession was fittingly ceremonial but sombre. The streets were lined with soldiers standing to attention, the coffin was carried by his generals to the hearse, which was harnessed to eight black horses. 120 soldiers in long black cloaks followed bearing torches. After that came Turks, Moldavians, princes from the Caucasus, all in colourful costumes since black is not in their tradition, but there were many Europeans in funeral dress. As the coffin was carried into the Church of the Ascension in Jassy, the bells tolled and cannons were fired.

We are destitute without our great Serenissimus. Our hearts are broken. But your grief, Your Majesty, must surpass all others. Know that in us, his nieces, who loved him like a father, the great Prince's love and loyalty to Your Majesty will live on. In trust, we throw ourselves on your Mercy.

Your faithful servant,
Countess Alexandra Branicka

Nadezhda
October 1794

My journal has long lain neglected. It has not been a time for recording life, which has been difficult enough to live. Not only were we numbed by the loss of our beloved Uncle but our future at Court, or indeed in Russia, became less and less secure. We watched the Empress lurch from one health crisis to the next, willing her to live on as we knew that should Grand Duke Paul become Emperor, he would be less than merciful to us. He would wipe out all trace of Prince Potemkin from the Court of Russia and we, his orphaned nieces, would be foremost on his list. This has not happened although the Empress's health does not improve. But let me endeavour an ordered account of events.

When news of Uncle's death reached us at our various homes, where we had taken refuge from the vagaries of court life, my sisters and I set off immediately to join Alexandra in Jassy. For this reason we were not with the Empress and when she herself was confronted by the terrible tidings. We only heard that she had collapsed in loud sobs before closeting herself in her chamber for days. We returned from the Crimea after Uncle's funeral and it was a long, cold and joyless journey. By the time we reached St Petersburg, it was November and preparations were underway for the Empress's name day. It was our intention, and that of many others, to use the occasion to bring some light into the darkness of her mourning, but in the end she refused to attend the dinner or the ball, saying she could not tolerate the noise. She did not even attend the church service in her honour.

Instead, the Empress summoned us to her and said she wished to hear everything we could tell her about Uncle's death and funeral. Alexandra had already written to the Empress at length on these matters but it was as if she wished to torture herself again and again. "How can I live without him?" she asked tearfully once we had exhausted our tellings. "Everyone is sticking their heads out like snails, trying to replace him. But that is impossible because someone like him would have to already be born and the end of this century announces no geniuses." She read to us words she had penned to describe Uncle, praising his breadth of spirit and magnanimity, his military talents, his wise counsel as a statesman, his courage of heart and his passionate affection for herself. It was like a private memorial service. In the end, she became angry, crying out, "Oh, he did me a cruel turn by dying. I must bear the whole burden alone." My sisters and I remained silent. "I have decided," the Empress continued a little more calmly, "that the Zubov brothers are men of spirit and understanding and the elder one already possesses infinite knowledge due to my own efforts." This is what we had feared. The Empress's favourite, Platon Zubov, had moved swiftly after Uncle's death, reassuring the Empress in her despair that he and his younger brother could take over all of Prince Potemkin's offices and duties. What upstarts! Their combined ages – twenty and twenty-four – do not add up to Uncle's years.

But there was nothing we could do. The Zubov family gradually increased their favour and influence with the Empress. A year after Uncle's death, the Empress made the Zubov brothers and their father Counts of the Holy Roman Empire. Some months later Platon Zubov was made Governor General of the Crimea. All Uncle's work stood to be undone.

The year following Uncle's death threatened the unity of our own family just when we should have been standing together against the threat of the Zubovs. The complexity of Uncle's possessions did not allow for a swift settling of his estate. There were talks of debts and more debts. His enemies at Court, led by Platon Zubov, listed all the monies he owed the Treasury and demanded payment. In a strange coincidence, Uncle's Scottish banker Sutherland had died the day before him. He was said to have embezzled two million roubles. Most of the Court were indebted to him, including the Grand Duke Paul and, of course, Uncle but it was to Uncle's estate that the Treasury turned. There was talk of us, his nieces, being responsible for Uncle's debts, that Alexandra and Varvara, who both have very rich husbands, must pay. Alexandra said these were just attempts by Uncle's enemies to ruin us.

The Empress stood by us, declaring that although Prince Potemkin had often used state money for personal reasons, as his enemies pointed out, he also used his own money for state business without sending in accounts. In truth, he acted much like the Empress in this respect. In the end, the Empress paid many of Uncle's debts and bought most of his possessions for over two and half million roubles, including the Tauride Place and all his art collections. The Empress entrusted the inventory lists to me. Uncle had paintings by da Vinci, Raphael, Rubens, van Dyck, Watteau, Murillo ... over a thousand rare books including 150 Greek works from the early 16th century ... jewels worth more than a million roubles ... many unique artefacts like a bronze oak tree covered with mechanical birds. I listed everything meticulously for the Empress but when I saw his 73 diamond and pearl-encrusted kaftans, I broke down and wept.

The Empress seemed to view Alexandra as Uncle's heiress, which threw Varvara and Katerina into rages of jealousy. "Why, she is not even the eldest of us," Varvara rightly declared. The Empress gave Alexandra Uncle's apartments in all her palaces, including the servants and an allowance to run them. She is constantly making her gifts of money, houses and jewels – as if she is still showering her affection on Prince Potemkin. Alexandra's husband administers Uncle's estates in Poland, which is tantamount to owning them.

Still, we have all received largesse thanks to the Empress's purchase of Uncle's possessions although it is far below the share we expected from the total sum. Alexandra says there are other relatives to consider, private debts to settle, rewards to be given to his loyal subjects, especially in the Crimea, estates to be run ... Her list is long. We are all aware that when Grand Duke Paul succeeds the Empress – as he must since he has refused to renounce his claim in favour of his eldest son Alexander – it may all be taken from us. And then Alexandra will have the most to lose.

The Empress cannot live forever, nor for much longer. She is now over sixty and has ruled for thirty years. Her health is precarious. Her colic and gout attacks are more frequent, her legs are very swollen and covered with open sores, which she bathes in sea water for relief. Recently she fell down the stairs, injuring her knee and now she limps. She says herself she has outlived everyone, pointing out that there are few still alive who witnessed her arrival in Russia fifty years ago. It is not only people who are disappearing – the world as she knew it and perhaps helped to form, she says, is also vanishing. "They are killing Kings and Queens," she said. King Gustav of Sweden was shot at a masked ball and died later of his wounds.

As an erstwhile supporter of enlightened philosophers, the Empress now finds her old friend Voltaire being blamed for such terrible events. When the news of Louis XVI's execution reached her in January 1793, the Empress took to her bed. She ordered six weeks of mourning for "the death of the King of France cruelly murdered by his rebellious subjects". She severed all ties with France and banished all French citizens from Russia. French goods were publicly burned and French wines and spirits emptied into the Neva. Towards the end of the year Marie Antoinette was executed.

"Ideas on paper have been turned into horror, murder and mayhem," she said. "I no longer claim affinity with the ***philosophes*** for their only objective is destruction as experience has now shown. I have been deceived." Even Shakespeare's Julius Caesar has been banned, for its subject is regicide. The Empress has ordered the closing of many private presses to hinder the spread of "French" ideas.

The Empress still rises early to work in her study but it is doubtful that she is working on reforms for her empire. She deals with petitions, mostly from nobles squabbling over lands. A portion of her time is devoted to dispensing largesse to secure loyalty. Many of the recipients are suggested by Zubov. She buys houses and palaces from those in debt and gives them to her favourites. Alexandra is often on the list. The Empress calls me to assist her for although she has her secretaries, she likes my hand and efficiency with lists. She devises unusual gifts for foreign dignitaries and rulers. Recently she sent a snuffbox with her portrait on it worth over 10,000 roubles to Prime Minister Pitt in England. She completes all these tasks with enthusiasm but one is left wondering who is ruling the country. And who will rule it when she is no longer Empress. These are unsettling thoughts.

I read over what I have written and am dissatisfied with the lack of proper facts. Perhaps, however, facts will come more quickly than I would want and I may not like them. The death of the Empress would be one such fact. Emperor Paul would be a second one. It is perhaps better to continue in conjecture and uncertainty.

Tatiana
March 1796

Dear Varvara,

You write that you would like to hear news from Court. How clever you are not to be here! One must tread carefully for there are many pitfalls. Platon Zubov and his family amass wealth and influence while the reins of power seem to be slipping from the Empress's grasp. I too would rather be elsewhere but until I find a second husband, I am safer with Alexandra, who navigates the complexities of court life with her usual cleverness. I was not much saddened by the passing of my ailing husband. I married him for Uncle's sake and now they are both gone. I hope to find a young and handsome husband for I am weary of old flesh. And one who can give me children, which my husband seemed unable to do despite his desperate attempts, which wearied me, and I think him too.

You, dear Varvara, have been blessed with many children and have recently given birth to another son, just like Alexandra who now has a fifth child. Some women bear children most easily. Although Grand Duke Paul cannot be considered a specimen of manliness, being more on the puny side despite his constant military parades, his wife has borne him eight children. Her last confinement ended in a most difficult birth, which almost took her life. We were sure the child, another daughter, would be the last. The Empress declared the baby Olga huge. "Why," she said, "her shoulders are almost as wide as my own. It is little wonder she almost took her mother's life." The Empress is not pleased that the Grand Duchess has borne only girls since Alexander and Constantine. "They are a drain on our resources," she declared. The Empress seems to forget that she was born a girl. Early in January of 1795, the Grand Duchess was delivered of yet another girl. Olga, still not much more than a baby, was very sick and died the day after the new child's baptism. The Grand Duchess is inconsolable but the Empress says she has more than enough children and should not grieve too deeply.

But you wish to know about more happy events, which due to your own confinements you have missed. I suspect, however, that you do not wish to return to Court and are happy with your husband and children on your estate. How I envy you! And who would have thought that you, our great beauty, much sought after at Court, who whirled from one party to the next, would be the one to settle into conjugal happiness? Perhaps there is such a thing as true love – I imagine it as constant and peaceful. You have been fortunate that it found you. But let me continue with another story that might also lead to true love.

The Empress, wishing to marry her grandson Alexander as soon as possible after his fourteenth birthday, had the two Princesses of Baden-Durlach brought to St Petersburg. It was the talk of the Court that the Empress favours only marriages with Germans for her heirs. It is in this that her own nationality comes through, much as she declares she is Russian. She justifies her choice by claiming marriage with Russian nobility would open the way for jealousies and feuds. There was no rancour at Court, however, when the Princesses arrived for one could not but be enchanted by them. Despite their young years Louise, then aged thirteen, and her sister Frederica, only eleven, bore themselves very well. Their mother is the sister of the Grand Duke's first wife Natalya – again these intricate webs of relations of which the Empress is very fond. I was appointed as lady-in-waiting to the Princesses and was delighted with my new duties. We spent the entire day after their arrival preparing them for their presentation to the imperial family. Their hair had to be dressed in a style more fitting to the Russian Court, for they wore it very long and loose. They laughed at the paniers they had to wear under their dresses, never having worn hooped underskirts before.

They were given a warm welcome, especially by the Grand Duchess Maria. Prince Alexander was less than polite, not even approaching the Princesses. Indeed, his stare was quite hostile. I felt ashamed for him for I know what a charming young man he is. Princess Louise confided later that she did not consider him as handsome as she had been told he was. I did not agree with her, of course, but refrained from giving my opinion. The Empress was unperturbed by her grandson's lack of enthusiasm. "Of course, he has no thought of girls in his innocent head," she said with a smile. "But I am preparing him, leading him into temptation as it were." And that is what happened. There was no opportunity lost to bring Princess Louise, whom the Empress declared perfect for her grandson, and Prince Alexander together – seated beside the Empress at table, partnered for dances, little soirées with games and music just for the Princes and Princesses. I envied Princess Louise her proximity to the Prince but we are born into the lives we have and must accept them.

One evening some six weeks after her arrival, and shortly before the Prince's fifteenth birthday, Princess Louise rushed into her chambers waving a letter which Alexander had slipped to her. In it he said he was authorised by his parents to tell her he loved her and to ask if she could find happiness in marrying him. She was overjoyed. "I have achieved that for which my parents sent me here!" The Princess immediately began lessons in Russian and religion. Six months later, on a beautiful day in May, she was baptised in the Orthodox faith, receiving the name Elisabeth, and immediately afterwards she was officially betrothed to Prince Alexander. Everyone agreed that although still little more than children, they did look as if they were in love with one another. In September 1793 they were married in a very emotional ceremony in the Winter Palace. The young couple looked like angels and moved the hearts of all who saw them, even my own which had long been consumed with fervent admiration of the Prince. The Empress shed tears as she blessed them, even the Grand Duke Paul had to wipe his eyes while the Grand Duchess Maria and all her children sobbed loudly. There was not a dry eye in the chapel. The wedding of the innocents was a release for the Court to enjoy something beautiful and wholesome after all the upsets of wars and deaths. The newlyweds seem happy together. Princess Louise, or Grand Duchess Elisabeth as she is now known, gazes at her husband (I cannot get used to this word, I who have known the Prince since his infancy, which does not seem so long ago) with adoration. I am no longer a lady-in-waiting – I think the Empress still sees me as some kind of governess for unmarried ladies – and Princess Frederica was sent back to Germany immediately after the wedding although I think it would comfort the new bride to have her sister with her here. The Empress, however, said, "We are her family now. She is Russian and will become used to it, as I did when I was her age and alone here in Russia."

The Empress soon turned her attention to a match for Prince Constantine. He is fiery and unpredictable but the Empress is very fond of him despite his pranks and mischief. Once again, princesses were brought from Germany, this time from Saxe-Coburg. There were three – Sophie, Antoinette and Julie – so close in age that one could barely tell which was the eldest. It is actually Sophie, who is the same age as Prince Constantine. All three are very pretty with fine features and slim figures. The Empress even remarked that it was a very difficult choice and it was a pity her grandson could not keep all three. But Prince Constantine was swift in picking out the youngest, Princess Julie, and indeed she matches his temperament well, being mischievous and lively. I am once more appointed lady-in-waiting and I can only say she is a handful. But Constantine declared immediately in his outspoken way that he would have her and no other although the Empress tried to persuade him that it would be the eldest daughter who would inherit Saxe-Coburg. "What need have I of such a small state when I will be Emperor of New Greece?" he retorted. The Empress was charmed into agreement and just ten days after their arrival, the matter was settled. Princess Julie's mother and sisters left.

Constantine and Julie are like two imps running around the palace – their high spirits cannot be quelled. They are in such contrast to the harmonious togetherness of Alexander and Elisabeth. Constantine offers his betrothed his attention through wild games. He makes her play military marches on the harpsichord, for example, while he marches round with trumpet and drums making the most awful din. Recently, I had occasion to question her about marks on her person, knowing that Constantine twists her arm and I have known him to bite her but she says only that he had been a little rough in their game of Blind Man's Buff, which, being a favourite of the Empress's, I cannot forbid them to play. The Empress says once they are married, Constantine will be able to show his affection for the Princess in a more fitting way. At the moment, she claims, he is frustrated by his own innocence.

The Princess, however, began to lose her brightness, becoming pale and agitated. She said she missed her sisters and mother. I think it was very hasty of the Empress to send her sisters away – at least one could have been allowed to stay, but in this matter the Empress is adamant. Brides of Russian princes must become Russian and sever all emotional ties to their families, just as she did fifty years ago. The baptism – in which Julie was given the name Anna – and betrothal took place in February, when winter still hung coldly over us, with the marriage following soon after. I am sorry not to be with the Princess anymore. She is unformed and needs guidance and has many romantic notions in her head, which cannot be filled by Constantine. I trust her sister-in-law, the Grand Duchess Elisabeth, will be kind to her and be the anchor she needs. I cannot forget little Julie's shock when she came across her betrothed using rats as live ammunition in his gun practice.

I think in the end she did not wish to marry him. The wedding had to be postponed because the bride was suffering from fever brought on by a toothache. The Empress went to visit her and two days later the little Princess appeared at the altar, somewhat pale. But it is done now. And she must make the best of it as we all have to do. Marriage is a lottery in which one hopes to find happiness, as you have done, dear Varvara. I hope I do too.

Your sister,
Tatiana

Alexandra
January 1797

Dear Anna,

A new year begins and a new era. As I look back on the five years since Uncle's death, I see that his going was the beginning of the end. He was the Empress's anchor and therefore the mainstay of the Empire, of the Empress. Without him, favourites ruled, battles were lost. Russia was a rudderless ship. The Empress haunted Uncle's palace like a ghost, or as if she was looking for his. She often stayed there, claiming it was easier for her to manage since there were no stairs to climb. And indeed as her years advanced, her health deteriorated. She once said she did not want to outlive any glory she may have. But the sun was already setting.

Some will say the Empress continued to rule well, pointing to the peace with Turkey ratified a year after Uncle's death, reaffirming Russia's territorial gains in the Crimea. Others will point out that the great Catherine subdued Poland, quite bloodily, and carved it up with her new allies, Austria and Prussia. She took the lion's share, some 120,000 square kilometres, with her partners receiving not even a half of that each. "My part," she boasted, "is sung. It is an example of how it is not impossible to attain an end and to succeed if one really wills." Partition had never been Uncle's aim and he would have fought against it. The dreams of our own family on the throne of Poland, by legitimate means, are now gone. I think the Empress had always been afraid of Uncle's extensive territories in Poland, seeing them as a base of rival power. She used the new land gains as a source of rewards, gifting over tens of thousands of Polish serfs to her friends. My husband has also been rewarded but he will no longer meddle in the affairs of Poland on Russia's behalf. What he did, he did for Uncle and for our family.

In the end, the Empress was undone by her own weaknesses, the first of which was Platon Zubov, who attempted to replace Uncle in all things. The Empress made him Prince of the Holy Roman Emperor and showered estates, money and jewels on him. Some said his power was even greater than Uncle's had been but this I doubt. Uncle was a genius and Zubov was a nothing who preyed on an ageing Empress. She praised him as the greatest genius Russia had ever known, which was an insult to Peter the Great, to herself and to Uncle. No matter how often she repeated it, it would never be true.

But the conceited Zubov believed it, acting as if he were the Emperor. There were more attendants in his chambers for his daily ***lever*** than in the Empress's. The street outside was blocked with carriages. My husband attended once and recounted that Zubov imitated Uncle in appearing in a dressing gown gaping open to show he wore nothing underneath. Everyone had to remain standing while his valets placed his wig and dressed him carefully. He ignored everyone who attended no matter how high their station. No one was allowed to speak. The petitioners and sycophants fixed smiles on their faces and tried to catch Zubov's eye. I rage even now when I think about it. He was no better than the pet monkey he pandered to.

And he acted like a monkey, not a man. It was an open secret that he had developed a passion for Alexander's wife Elisabeth. He followed her everywhere, mistakenly believing he was not noticed. One of her ladies told me that she had to pin the curtains of the Grand Duchess's chambers together since Zubov used a telescope to spy on her. Poor Elisabeth was often reduced to tears but knew she could not complain to the Empress about her favourite, against whom no criticism was tolerated. When the Empress did allow his obsession to come to her attention, for she wilfully ignored it for several months, she did no more than gently reprimand Zubov, forbidding him to direct glances and sighs to any but herself.

Platon Zubov may have been the Empress's greatest weakness but her greatest mistake was in not disinheriting her son, which Uncle had urged her to do many times. It seems she did not have the will although she made a few half-hearted attempts through the Grand Duchess Maria, hoping she would persuade her husband to renounce the throne in favour of their son. The Empress argued that Paul was already past forty and Alexander's youth would provide more continuity. But everyone knew that the Empress did not like her son and the Grand Duke certainly scorned his mother and all she stood for. What did she think he was training his 2000 troops at Gatchina for? It was not the harmless game she took it for. And this we have learned to our cost – and hers.

But my thoughts leap ahead of my narrative. Order brings clarity and it is clear that the betrothal of Alexandra, daughter of Grand Duke Paul, was a key happening. In the choice of husband for her granddaughter, the Empress had followed Uncle's advice. He had always recommended a marriage alliance with the son of King Gustav of Sweden, at that time just a boy. He had now taken the throne after his father was assassinated, but at the time I write of, he was not yet crowned as he had not yet come of age. The Empress was in very good spirits since Grand Duchess Maria had at long last borne another son at the beginning of summer 1796. The Empress had eagerly taken over the supervision of his upbringing. In her relief at the child not being another girl, she turned her attention generously to her eldest granddaughter Alexandra, who had just turned thirteen. Alexandra would be a perfect match, she said, for the seventeen year old Gustav IV of Sweden. The young King was invited to Court and arrived with his regent and a retinue of some 150 people. The Empress was very taken with the uncrowned King and indeed he presented himself as a handsome, intelligent, cultivated young man. He wore a long black coat in the Swedish style and his long hair reached his shoulders. The

Empress was not pleased with Alexandra, who had arrived to meet him with her eyes red from crying for she had lost her little dog. But the two young people seemed to find pleasure in one another's company. There was only one obstacle (as we thought at the time) – the King was betrothed to the Princess of Mecklenburg. He promised to break off this betrothal but begged that his intention be kept secret until it was done. Three weeks passed with the King and his attendants enjoying many festivities at Court while talks of the most delicate nature took place to draw up a secret marriage proposal. Alexandra was allowed to dance with the King – he danced extremely well – and her 13 year old innocence was most touching.

The unexpected second obstacle should never have been one and if Uncle had been here, he would have steered the Empress in the right direction. The Empress insisted that, after marriage, Alexandra be allowed to remain in the religion in which she was born and brought up. While Protestant princesses must convert to the Orthodox faith if they marry into the Russian imperial family, conversion the other way is not allowed. The King was not inclined to agree, saying a Queen of Sweden belonged to the faith of the people she ruled. He pointed out that Catherine had changed her religion when she married the heir to the Russian throne. The Empress, although very fond of the charming King, said condescendingly. "You must listen to the advice of your elders, especially one who has experience in ruling on the throne for thirty years. You, on the other hand, have not yet even ascended yours." And this was her mistake, treating the King as a child.

In the end, King Gustav promised that Alexandra would never be compromised in her conscience as regards her religion. The Empress arranged for a betrothal, which would remain secret, that is unofficial, until the King came of age in a few months when it would be declared publicly. All parties – courtiers and clergy, both Swedish and

Russian, an excited Alexandra and her ladies, the young King looking very handsome – met at the appointed time. As the treaty was passed over for signing, it was noticed that the conversion clause had been left out. The King explained that he had given the Empress his promise and that should be enough. Messengers were sent to the Empress, who did not attend due to the unofficial nature of the ceremony. She requested that the King's word be put in writing. The King said, "A sovereign's word should never be doubted." The Empress said that it was agreements between sovereigns above all that demanded a written document. Courtiers ran back and forth all evening, while we all stood in our finery. The poor child Alexandra burst into tears, believing she had done something wrong.

In the end, four hours later, about ten o'clock in the evening, the Empress sent her apologies saying the ceremony was postponed. I rushed to her chambers and found her marching up and down, limping but with some of her old vigour. "How dare such a young man contradict me! What an embarrassment he has caused me!" She thrust into my hand a paper he had written, saying, "And he thinks this will suffice?" I quickly read the King's words.

Having already given my word of honour to her Imperial Majesty that the Grand Duchess will never be embarrassed in her conscience as regards her religion, and Her Majesty having appeared to me to be content with that I am sure that She can have no doubt that I know well enough the sacred laws which this engagement imposes on me for every other piece of writing to be entirely superfluous.

I personally thought it did suffice. Political advantage often involves compromise, but compromise was one thing the Empress never entertained. It was Uncle who always knew how to temper her obstinacy. I begged Her Majesty to rest for she was becoming more and more agitated but she would not desist. "Have King Gustav summoned to me in the morning." I nearly pointed out that one did not summon sovereigns, no matter how young.

I was present when the young King arrived the next day with his uncle. He looked pale and tense. The Empress, holding out his paper, said that she respected his solemn promise that Alexandra may keep her own religion and that he now must add it in writing to what he had already written. The King barely glanced at the paper in her hand. "What I have written," he said, "I have written. I will not change it. I will not have my word doubted." His regent whispered to him frantically in Swedish but the King stood stiffly and would not be moved.

The celebration ball in the evening took place all the same but there was no joy in it. The King did not approach Alexandra. Another week went by with meetings and talks. But neither the King nor the Empress would yield. Oh, how we all longed for Uncle's wisdom. He would have found a way for the Empress to agree without losing face. In the end, it was agreed to postpone the betrothal until the King had reached his majority in a few months. But everyone knew it was the end of the proposed match.

The matter had taken its toll on the Empress. As soon as the Swedish delegation had left, she became more agitated, giving vent to the anger she had endeavoured to keep under control while the Swedes were at Court. "I have never been so insulted in all my life!" she shouted. "The King fails to understand that the first effect of his unconsidered action would be that Alexandra would lose all respect in Russia. Neither I nor her father nor her mother nor her brothers and sisters would ever be able to see her again and she would never dare set foot in Russia. This would mean she would also lose respect in Sweden and her very considerable dowry would be at the mercy of that poor and greedy country. It would deprive her bit by bit of her money and anything else of value." Her face was flushed red, the veins in her forehead pulsing. I had rarely seen her so angry. "A Princess of Russia does not change her religion," she declared. But it was really more that an Empress of Russia had been bested by an uncrowned King of Sweden that upset her.

She fed her anger daily and would not let the matter rest. Instead of trying to calm or distract her as Uncle would have done, Zubov added to the flames of her ire. "Let me take a fleet and show them who are masters of the Baltic," he said. Her agitation continued for some weeks and so it came as it must.

On a cold winter's morning early in November, we found the Empress collapsed in her water closet, her eyes closed, her face purple. I had been called by her personal maid who was alarmed that the Empress had been inside for over half an hour. The poor woman did not have the courage to open the door, which she would have been unable to do in any case since the Empress was partially blocking it. We called for valets, and with much unworthy manoeuvring, we freed her from the water closet. Six strong men managed to carry her back into her chamber and lay her on a mattress of Moroccan leather. It would have been impossible to raise the weight of her body onto her high bed. The Empress remained in an unconscious state although I chafed her hands and wiped her brow with moist cloths. When Dr Rogerson arrived, he said it was a stroke and that there was no help. He bled her and applied Spanish fly to her feet but I think only to disguise his helplessness. The Grand Duke Paul arrived and forbade anyone, including his son Alexander, to enter the chamber. I think he feared the Empress would regain her wits long enough to name her grandson her successor – as she should have done long ago. But it was too late. By evening it was certain the Empress would never wake again and her family was let in to see her. Blood seeped continuously from her mouth. "Her brain disintegrates," Dr Rogerson said. Grand Duke Paul settled with his papers in the little study behind the main chamber. Anyone wishing to speak to him had to walk past the Empress on her mattress on the floor. On the next day, Paul ordered the last rites for his mother. The palace was soon full of his Gatchina guards in their Prussian uniforms, running backwards and forwards carrying out who knows what orders. Paul ordered all his mother's papers to be brought to him as well as all papers of the state. In the evening, the imperial family gathered round the Empress as she took her last breath.

I requested some privacy that I and her other ladies might wash and dress the body appropriately, for the Empress was still in her night robe. We dressed her in a simple gown of blue velvet with silk trimmings and arranged her hair. After kissing her hand, the members of the imperial family left for the chapel where Paul and his wife awaited their oaths of allegiance.

Emperor Paul, as he now was, ordered six weeks of mourning during which time his mother's body, after embalming, would lie in state, with her closest ladies and courtiers keeping watch in relays of two hours. We dressed the Empress in silver silk brocade, although it was more a front than a full dress but it looked very well with all her orders pinned to it. We placed a gold crown on her head. The Gospel was read out continuously by the priests taking turn. It was a time of great darkness and uncertainty. In our helplessness, we were strangely grateful for the new Emperor's decisiveness although we knew it could not bode well for most of us.

The Emperor Paul first took terrible revenge on his mother. He had the tomb of his murdered father opened and its coffin brought to the Nevsky monastery, where he had a solemn requiem sung and an imperial crown placed on the coffin. Almost four weeks after the Empress's death, Paul brought his father's coffin in solemn procession to the Winter Palace and placed it beside that of his mother. We were horrified. The Empress was being reunited with a husband she had despised and overthrown and, some say, murdered. "This was and is her rightful spouse," Paul said. "No other had claim to this honour."

The Empress's subjects were now allowed to file past the coffins in two rows and this they did continuously for three days. It would have continued for another three but the Emperor ordered the coffins to be transported over the frozen Neva to the Cathedral of St Peter and Paul, where all Russia's monarchs are buried. There both coffins lay open to the public for two weeks before they were buried side by side in marble tombs. Paul had cleverly inscribed the date of their births and burials, not their deaths, thus rewriting history to make it seem as if Catherine and Peter had never been separated. How abominable we found it! How Catherine would have turned in her grave, returning to wreak revenge on this desecration of her life and her loves, above all Uncle. Catherine is said to have kept a certificate of her secret marriage with Uncle and no doubt this has been consigned to the flames by Grand Duke Paul along with all else he burned.

The new Emperor then set about obliterating all traces of our dear Prince Potemkin, Serenissimus. He began with the insult of turning Uncle's beautiful Tauride Palace into barracks for the Horse Guards. He has banished or imprisoned Uncle's allies and rewarded or recalled his enemies. The Emperor has even ordered Uncle's body be disinterred in Jassy and buried in an anonymous grave. Not an hour passes but the Emperor issues some edict of change, on his own authority, consulting no one. There are rumours he will even disband the Senate.

Platon Zubov, who hid away at his sister's house in fear of the Emperor, who as Grand Duke treated him with open scorn, has had of his all his estates and offices taken from him and ordered to return the bulk of jewels and treasures, which the Emperor said rightfully belong to the State. Zubov obeyed every order meekly and loudly swore his loyalty to the new Emperor at every opportunity.

Oh, I was so tired of it all. I politely requested that I be allowed to return to my husband's estate and devote the rest of my life to my children. The Emperor, to my surprise, granted my wish so not only have I escaped with my reputation and person intact but I have also kept my estates and my wealth.

Twenty years have passed since we first arrived at the Russian Court, innocent and naïve girls from the province. How eventful our lives became! But my aim was always to secure a good future for myself and my sisters. I think I have succeeded in this to some degree. I am still well regarded at Court and my influence reaches beyond our own borders. I have not counted my wealth but I should say I have about twenty-eight million roubles. I have a good husband and a healthy family. I am content. Much as I tried to do the same for our younger sisters, their paths were not as disciplined, often strewn with passion. Varvara did remove herself from the web of Court affairs in which she was caught up and is happy with her Prince Golitsyn, who is a good man, and her still growing family. It is perhaps true that a good marriage makes a good life.

Katerina lives happily in love with her Italian Count Giulio Litta, whom she married after the death of her mad singing husband. She wants for nothing and may lead the life of languor and luxury she desires. Tatiana, who sought a young second husband, has now married a much older one. Prince Yusupov is said to be a descendant of a Tartar Khan and I think he reminds her of Uncle. She has begun collecting jewels, just as Uncle did, and Prince Yusupov indulges her new passion, even securing for her a pair of Marie Antoinette's earrings. Nadezhda lives quietly, in harmony with her husband and her books.

We owe it all to our Uncle, Prince Potemkin, may God rest his soul, and to the love and favour the Empress Catherine bore him. Their story may have been one of power and passion but I ask myself what is left of it all now that their bones are turning to dust under the ground.

Even after death, happiness and peace elude them. Catherine is buried together with the husband she hated and Uncle's bones are to be disinterred and buried anonymously. I have designed a monument for him on our estate and will do all I can to preserve his memory in the minds of people as long as I live. As for Catherine, history will judge her as it does all sovereigns while we lesser, perhaps more fortunate mortals, are easily forgotten.

With affection,
Your sister Alexandra

THE END

Author's Note

Potemkin's nieces did exist and did indeed belong to Catherine the Great's intimate circle. They were not only Potemkin's protégées but, apart from Tatiana and Nadezhda, at various times his mistresses.

Their mother, Potemkin's sister Elena, married a member of the Baltic-German Engelhardt family and bore him six daughters – and one son. I have dispensed with this son, who was a trusted aide-de-camp at Catherine's Court, mainly because his sisters lent themselves better to the writing of letters, diaries and journals.

The oldest sister Anna, who serves only as a convenient recipient of Alexandra's letters in the book, also existed but was married before her mother died and so did not need Potemkin's protection. Her husband, Mikhail Zhukov, served as Governor of Astrakhan from 1781 to 1785.

Nadezhda, the plainest of the nieces, actually married in 1779 before her sisters, possibly because Potemkin was not attracted to her. This first husband, Colonel Ismailov, who died two years after the marriage, was superfluous to the narrative and so when Nadezhda marries in this fictional account, it is for the first time.

Most other details about the nieces are based on historical evidence: Alexandra was a very successful business woman, Varvara was a great beauty who wrote sensual love letters to her uncle, Katerina was languorous and passive ... Their own daughters inherited their charms and flirtatiousness: Alexandra's daughter Lise, having married the son of one of Potemkin's enemies, was involved in a secret affair with her cousin when Alexander Pushkin fell in love with her. She became his muse and is said to have been the inspiration for Tatiana in ***Eugene Onegin***. Katerina's daughter, also named Katerina, was known throughout Europe as the Naked Angel because of her transparent dresses, also as the White Pussycat for her sensuality. She became Metternich's mistress and bore him a daughter. She was also a close intimate of Alexander I (Catherine's favourite grandson). She later married Lord Howden, an English diplomat, and wore her transparent dresses into old age.

While Potemkin had his nieces and many, many other women, Catherine had her official lovers – her personal adjutants – who shared her bed and a place at her side in Court. They were pawns in the political life of the Court as rivalling factions sought influence with the Empress through their own candidates. Catherine certainly had other unofficial lovers, some of them documented, but in the thirty-four years of her reign, ten official ones are acknowledged, most of whom appear in the book. (Her twelve-year affair with Grigory Orlov at the beginning of her reign, however, is dealt with fully in the first two books in the series: ***A Princess at the Court of Russia*** and ***An Empress on the Throne of Russia.***) Catherine's last lover, Platon Zubov, was one of her son's assassins four years after he took the throne as Emperor Paul I.

Eighteenth century Russia is peopled with eccentric characters, from charlatan magicians to transvestite ambassadors, from intrepid women adventurers to cruel sultans, from pirate heroes to decadent hedonists. Many of them appear on these pages as they were indeed part of Catherine's canvas. I have also sketched in the broader political strokes to give an idea of the world as it was developing then, from the American War of Independence to the French Revolution.

There is no scarcity of material for it was a century where the literate were devoted to the pen: detailed correspondence (Catherine herself was a prolific letter-writer), diaries and journals, ambassadors' dispatches, memoirs ... there is no need to invent. In joining the various mosaic pieces together, however, I have used the occasional fictional stitch – moved time a little, stolen words from one to give to another – but with the aim of authentic and accurate historicity to render not only the flavour and reality of the world in which Catherine ruled but also a portrait of Catherine herself as Empress and woman.

In one area I have deserted accuracy. With the reader in mind, I have taken the liberty of simplifying names. Each Russian name generally consists of three parts, used in different combinations depending on who is speaking or being spoken to. Thus one character may appear under three or four names. I have dispensed with this, as with the widespread use of diminutives, for ease of comprehension. I have also used both Russian and English forms of names for ease of identification amongst same-named characters: for example, Catherine and Katerina, Paul and Pavel. I have also not adhered to rules of transliteration in Russian names (persons or places), often choosing the version more familiar in the non-Cyrillic form.

The following biographies, to which I am also indebted, particularly to Simon Sebag Montefiore's work, can be recommended for further reading:

John T. Alexander, **Catherine the Great. Life and Legend** (Oxford University Press, 1989)

Simon Dixon, **Catherine the Great** (Profile Books, 2010)

Isabel de Madariaga, **Russia in the Age of Catherine the Great** (Yale University Press, 1981)

Virginia Rounding, **Catherine the Great: Love, Sex and Power** (Hutchison, 2007)

Simon Sebag Montefiore, **Catherine the Great and Potemkin: The Imperial Love Affair** (W&N 2011)

The following recently published book is an excellent account of Catherine's great love affair with the arts:

Susan Jaques, **The Empress of Art** (Pegasus, 2016)

I would like to thank all my readers, past, present and future, and especially Teresa, my invaluable First Reader.

Printed in Poland
by Amazon Fulfillment
Poland Sp. z o.o., Wrocław